Dedication

To my father Jay
– my own "Finn MacCool" and all that implies

Also to the Lilly clan of Southwest Virginia, specifically the best grandparents, uncles and aunts, and parents to raise our generation:

Glen & Bessie

Beatrice & Cecil

Guye & Pat

Gene & Helen

Bobby & Shirley

Jay & Billie Jean

Acknowledgements

This book developed over generations.

For me, the first notes of the story formed as I realized that everything I knew about my father consisted of discordant opinions, including my own. My first-hand experiences with him created a very different tone than the ones played out with my grandfather or my uncles. Family dynamics created the main melody of the tale. Listening to each individual note and chord then assembling them back together became an enlightening but painful process.

Composing these thoughts into a story took years and many dedicated critique partners, including Sally Stiles, John Conlee, M. Lee Alexander. Thank you for the drinks, the encouragement, and the deadlines. My editor, Lisa Kline, made sure the journey through the ages connected and that I didn't repeat myself too often. I'm grateful for her guidance. My proofreader, Dawnna Barnes Hale, has supported me in my creative endeavors since we were both in sixth grade.

Brad, you gave me the time to finish this book. Thank you. Kathy and the nieces and nephews bringing up the next generation: please remember your actions speak louder than words. The more diverse the voices, the richer the chorus.

Greg Lilly

Cherokee McGhee
Abingdon, Virginia

Cover Design by Braxton McGhee
Floor Cloth in Title Letters: Lilly Family Heirloom
Wolf Prints © Chinch/Shutterstock.com
Title Font "Another Name For" © junkohanhero/dafont

ISBN 978-1-937556-14-3

First Paperback Edition 2021

Published by:
Cherokee McGhee, L.L.C.
Abingdon, Virginia

Find us on the World Wide Web at:
www.CherokeeMcGhee.com

Printed in the United States of America

Chapter One

Taliesin's tongue felt dry and thick. The bed sheets puffed and fell over his knee as the breeze from the table fan fluffed a corner and tickled his foot with each rotation. A tune hovered in his head in rhythm to the fan's creak. The June sunrise had not attempted the day yet; darkness clung to the bedroom like the humid air from the open window. He was not alone in the bed, but he couldn't quite place the face or the body. He needed to urinate – now. His bedroom, yes, he knew how to find the bathroom down the hall. Where the hell is my guitar? No memory came to him as he stood over the toilet trying to aim with half-closed eyes.

The gig had finished, and as usual, Taliesin had ended the night at the bar. Now, a stranger slept in his bed. Or was it? This was his hometown. He knew just about everyone. He decided not to flush because it could wake his guest.

When he entered the bedroom again, with eyes adjusted for the darkness, he modified his thought: not guest, but guests.

The Cullop twins slept sound and safe. One in the bed, one on the floor next to the window. He would be hounded by the other guys in the band. This wasn't the Twin Fantasy his band mates talked about, although this was apparently his since the evening had worked out this way. Stephanie curled on the side of the bed like a tawny panther, while Paul sprawled out on the floor. Those Cullops had always been a rowdy family.

He searched for his Fender electric guitar and found it leaning against the far corner, next to the chest of drawers. He grabbed it and went into the den to quietly strum and think. A lyric floated in his mind that he tried to net and pull onto paper. Images filled his mind, dark and hovering shapes, a full moon casting a dry light on a meadow of tall grass swaying in the night breeze—capture the sound, he told himself. The rhythm, the percussion of the cool wind, the thirsty grass, an ocean wave, the lonely crickets, the calm light – slapping, squeaking. The earlier hours re-formed in his memory. The bed had squeaked to a rhythm. Stephanie. Paul. And him.

"Geez," he said. "I gotta get out of this fucked up little town." The memory formed tighter, more vivid, and brought a smile to his lips. He realized how thirsty he was. A beer sat on the coffee table in front of him. He shook the warm can. It was about half full, and no cigarette butts floated in it. He turned up the can, sucking down the sharp tang of stale beer.

"Hell, just get another out of the Fridge," Paul said, standing at the bedroom door, not bothering to cover himself. Taliesin held up the warm beer as Paul walked behind the couch on his way to the kitchen. He grabbed the can, took a swig as if to confirm its sorry taste, and dropped it in the trash. "Tal, that shit is awful."

"Why'd you try it? You think I had something you might miss out on?"

Back from the refrigerator, Paul handed Tal a cold beer and popped one open for himself. "What you working on?" he asked, sliding down on the couch next to Tal and grabbing an embroidered pillow from the floor. He placed the pillow, stitched with musical notes, over his crotch and rested his beer on it.

The streetlight's silver beam through the broken blind gave Paul a halo on his thick hair the golden color of a Sam Adams pilsner. In that light, at that moment, Taliesin remembered Paul thirty years earlier when they were in elementary school together: The little tow-haired kid who could hit a baseball over the fence. A few years later, the youth who first bedded a girl and told the other boys what it was like. The high school quarterback who lobbed the long pass down the field to win the homecoming game...and win the homecoming queen's virginity. Now, here they sat, in the dark, drinking beer, after a three-way: Paul, Tal, and Stephanie.

Stephanie honed the twin role as if she and Paul had been born identical. The fair hair, handsome features, and athletic body graced her as well as her brother. She'd played volleyball, ran track, and led the cheerleaders. She'd dated Taliesin during the football season and switched to the basketball team's captain during the winter months.

Not that Taliesin felt betrayed by her wandering affections. He had his own fan club and didn't like to stay with one girl too long. Dating for more than a couple of months tended to make parents and teachers think wedding plans would surface after graduation. Like his father before him, a wife did not fit into young Taliesin's plans.

Plans that had not panned out as he'd navigated through his twenties. The music had always come to him, the notes played with emotion, with precision, with intelligence – and yet he hadn't made the Nashville scene.

The day after high school graduation, he'd hugged his mother, grabbed his third-hand Martin guitar, and steered his Chevy Camaro toward Nashville – a pick-up truck would have been more classic, but he hated trash-bagging his belongings in case of rain. Freedom – smooth and liquid – caressed away the childhood haunting memories and young-man perceived responsibilities. Time to focus on himself and to realize his dreams. He paid his dues, as the industry liked to phrase the department store clerking, telemarketing, and bartending jobs that sustained the hopeful. A few contacts he made brought in some studio work, but no big breaks, no discovery, no record contracts. "Not commercial, too lofty," agents and producers had labeled his songs. "What the hell is an archetypal tale? Sing about trucks and drinking and hurting," one executive advised.

The Camaro found its way back to the interstate, and before Taliesin could think about it, he passed through Knoxville and headed back to Bristol.

"Sixteen years," he said and took a swig of the beer.

"What?" Paul asked, his head leaning back on the couch, eyes closed.

"Sixteen years since I came back from Nashville."

"That place is full of crap. Man, you got the talent. Who'd you have to sleep with to get a contract?" He slapped Taliesin's head with his free hand; a grin brightened his face as he rolled his head to the side and opened his eyes. "You're my horse if you never win a race."

"Thanks, buddy. Don't you think you should go home to your wife?"

"I'm married?" Paul faked a horrified, wide-eyed expression.

"Yep, and take little sister too." Tal sighed. He wanted to be alone. The Cullop Twins could find their way home. With the guitar as a crutch, he pushed himself off the couch and stepped over Paul's knees. Between the blinds, he saw Stephanie's minivan. "I'm guessing Nate has Stephanie's kids this weekend."

"Took them to Dollywood," Paul said and set the beer and embroidered pillow on the coffee table. "That's why she wanted to hit the bar tonight."

Taliesin knew that sensation, the ache that something better might be around the corner, the fear of settling, the excitement that the next strike would be the big one. Songs, bands, lovers, husbands and wives, none of them satisfied the urge. The same urge that had sent Paul away from his wife, that drew Stephanie from her empty home, that tempted him to hang at the bar after the gig—the prospect of something better and brighter.

"Shit," Taliesin said when he noticed the clock on the cable box under the television. "I got to help Grandmaw Roane tomorrow, today I mean. Haul Steph's ass out of my bed and ya'll go home. I need some rest."

"Want me to help?" Paul asked. "I haven't seen your grandma in months."

"Do you really want to muck out her goldfish pond?"

"Naw," Paul said, finding his pants behind the couch and pulling them on. "Have fun with that. Hey Steph," he yelled into the bedroom. "Let's go. Bristol's own Keith Urban needs his beauty sleep."

The Cullop twins stumbled around and found the rest of their clothes, each hugging Taliesin goodbye before heading out the door and climbing into the minivan. The headlights swept across the room as Tal strummed his guitar in the dark.

Taliesin scooped up the goldfish in a long-handled net and dumped them into a bucket. The remaining fish splashed around in the excitement of being grabbed at, stirred up the water and grime into a murky, dark soup that Taliesin couldn't see into. His hands searched under the water's surface to drive out the delinquent fish as the last of the water siphoned through a hose.

"Grandmaw Roane, how many fish did you have?"

"Did?" she asked. "Boy, I better still have them."

"Count in that bucket," he said and pointed at a roiling container of goldfish and muddy water.

"I can't count them. As the water goes down, you'll see anything left flopping. Want a Coke?" she asked.

She turned and headed back to the house without waiting for his answer. Of course he wanted one. He knew she would bring two even if he had said no. Cokes and a slice of pound cake, that was her energy boost for her grandkids. Her gray head bobbed as she walked slowly toward the old stone house – made from river rock that her husband's father and mother had brought to the farm in the late 1800s. Grandmaw Roane seemed to be slowing down, her steps more unsure, her hair and skin looked thinner, her frame smaller. But with her physical appearance showing the years, her mind still operated at double-time – a quick-step mind trapped in a waltz body.

The hose slurped its last bit of water and one goldfish dawdled in the muddy pond bottom, flipping its tail in the muck, slinging it in Taliesin's eyes when he bent down to grab the fish and throw it in the bucket with the others. "You little bitch," Tal muttered and pulled off his t-shirt to wipe the mud from his face. Not that it really mattered since he was covered with the rotting smell of decaying leaves, uneaten fish pellets, and fish shit. He sat on the edge of the pond, adjusting the rocks so he had a comfortable seat and savored the cool breeze drifting under the oak and across his sweating skin.

"You look like your father sitting there," Grandmaw Roane

said, as she walked up with her garden basket containing two Cokes and two waxpaper-wrapped slices of cake. "He was a good boy just like you."

"Thirty-nine ain't no boy," Taliesin said with his mother's incrimination of his cheating father ringing in his head. "Do you know I'm older than Dad ever got?"

"Yes, I know," she said in a voice he could barely hear.

Maybe talking about her long dead son wasn't the thing to do because he had heard how elderly people began to live in the past, sitting around alone with only their memories to keep them company. Maybe not remembering accurately, but how they wanted the memories to be. He wasn't sure if amended memories led to withdrawal, or if it was a product of being withdrawn – either way, he wanted to keep the day fun and light for her. "Let's go skinny dip in the creek," he said, and to his delight, she giggled like a little girl.

"That would put you off women for good, seeing this old wrinkled body by the creek side. But when you were a baby, I'd take you and your cousins down there and we'd spend the afternoon swimming like those goldfish."

He couldn't remember swimming in the creek with her, but it sounded like something they would have done. He gulped down the Coke she had handed him and wiped his hands on his khaki shorts to clean them off just enough to hold his slice of pound cake. The taste of the cake, light and springy, held only a trace of the fish essence.

"I want you to do something for me," Grandmaw Roane said, more serious than Taliesin expected.

"Of course. Anything."

"You need to go on a quest, a treasure quest," she said, as she sat down on a flipped over five-gallon bucket.

"Like for pirate's gold?" He sounded a bit more flippant than he had intended.

"It's all gold when you get old," she answered. "There is treasure if you make it back."

Odd, he thought, she's never been a drama queen, why the

vague answers? "Grandmaw, what are you talking about?"

"You're special Taliesin. Some of the other cousins are too."

"Some?" he asked and had to laugh because he had a bushel of cousins on this side of his family. But then he remembered that he was different, that he had other cousins who didn't fit in, more insurgents like him, not always on purpose, but when he didn't seem appropriate or suitable, he would usually revolt, cause a scene to overshadow that feeling of innate strangeness. A roar would distract people from his peculiarities. He had seen the same trait in a few of his cousins, mainly Brigid, the hell-raiser girl who was too smart for the local high school and turned the University of Virginia upside-down with her rebellion.

"It doubled in your generation," Grandmaw Roane said.

"What? Being special?" he asked.

She only smiled.

"So, this task you say I should do," Taliesin began.

"Not a task, a quest. There's a big difference." She nibbled on her own piece of pound cake. "We've lost our way, been diluted by a thick wave of conformity, thick as molasses and as dark."

"Conformity," he said and thought about the word and how he somehow bucked the concept of compliance most of his life. "Nashville. Thinking about that last night. Sometimes it's easier to go with the flow – as they say."

"Bullshit," Grandmaw Roane spat the word. "That's the lazy way. I taught my boys – at least I tried to teach them – to be their own man. Some took it too well, while others hid from their nature like hiding from a wolf. Your daddy was the wolf that scared his brothers."

"You mean he was the non-conformist?"

She just smiled and took another bite of her pound cake. The wind ruffled her short gray hair. She looked up to the trees and grinned.

"Sometimes it gets awful hard swimming upstream." Taliesin finished his cake and drained the last of his Coke. He stuffed the waxpaper into the Coke can and set it back in the garden basket at the feet of his grandmother. "Thanks, Grandmaw. I'm going to get this stuff out of the bottom of the pond. Where you want me to dump it?"

"I'm not finished talking to you," she said. "You need to find your father."

The statement rattled him because his father had been gone – likely dead – for almost thirty years. Taliesin's mother had rarely talked of her husband Finn because he had walked away from them when Taliesin was still in fourth grade. The uncles had stepped in to help raise Talie and usually cursed the name of their youngest brother for abandoning his family and responsibilities. "Good ol' Finn 'MacCool' MacGuire," he said with a tinge of bitterness. "Uncle Brendan would have loved to have caught up with him."

"Don't hold any poor feelings toward your daddy. He's my baby boy, was then and always will be. Brendan was a hothead. Those boys fought like dogs all their lives, but Finn felt different from his brothers – seventh son of a seventh son."

"Shapeshifter." Taliesin knew the legend; his cousins would needle him about his father racing across the hills, transformed by the light of the moon into a mangy wolf. "Scared his brothers?" he asked.

"Lots of things scared those boys," Grandmaw Roane said. She finished her pound cake and folded the waxed paper into ever decreasing squares until it fit into the opening of the Coke can. She set it beside Taliesin's in her basket – his crammed in, hers neatly folded. "Some had more balls than the others," she said with a slight laugh.

"Don't take a lot of balls to walk off and leave your family," he said. Heat flared to his cheeks and neck.

"I knew it would come out," she said, as if happy to have provoked his anger at his father. "I tell you I was mad at him for the longest time, too. But I raised him. I knew him. I knew that look in his eye. He wasn't going to be a father in the way that Brendan was, or Oscar, or Lionel, or even his own daddy was to him."

Confusion shrouded Taliesin's mind. "Are you saying he's alive?"

"Don't know," she said. "Your momma was the one who said he was dead. Got her divorce and never looked back."

"Now Grandmaw Roane, you can't put no blame on Momma for moving on with her life. Hell, she waited for him for seven years. Virginia law only requires twelve months." His grandmother's words cut through the haze. "You are saying he's not dead?"

"Never saw a death certificate," she said, grabbing the basket and standing up from her bucket seat. "I want to know before I go."

"This won't bring him back," Tal said. His father had deserted him when he needed him the most. Taliesin felt that story should stay buried.

"I need this settled in my mind. Something kept him from coming back to you and me. If he's around, I want to lay my eyes on him one last time, hug my boy. If not, I get relief in the knowledge he's in a better place, and when this old body gives out, I will be with him again."

The thought that his father might still be alive hadn't occurred to him in years, but as he looked into his grandmother's pale blue eyes, he knew she yearned for closure that her youngest son could not come back to her, that his absence wasn't something that he could control. She needed to know he was dead. Taliesin needed to know that too. He had to determine that Finn 'MacCool' – the woman-chasing wolf of Washington County – had found what he was hunting for, and it had kept him from returning to his family.

Chapter Two

Cliodhna watched her co-worker, Jessie, in the chair as the doctor's assistant pierced the skin with a needle, injecting bacterium into her facial muscles. Clio squirmed in her seat. She was next.

Jessie flexed her face as if to help the Botox settle in. "Much better," she said to no one in particular. The straight-backed metal chair's vinyl seat squeaked as she waddled her butt a few degrees to look in a wall mirror by her shoulder. "See? Not so bad," she said to Cliodhna.

Jessie's dark brown hair, walnut-colored, usually hung to her shoulders, but for the procedure, she had gathered it into a ponytail, casual and flirty. Not quite thirty-six years old, she was a bit younger than Clio, but had taken to the cosmetic procedure two years ago. "Better to catch those wrinkles early," she had said when confessing her secret to Clio one morning. "No different than coloring your hair," she had added.

Now, as Clio pulled her own hair back in preparation for her turn, she doubted if she could allow that needle to stab her in the face. Yes, she did cover the early gray that slipped into her raven black hair, but that was only because with her hair so dark, the gray hair seemed to fly up to the surface and wave in the wind, attracting unwanted attention. It had to be tamed and color seemed to do it, or at least made the gray strands blend in with the rest.

The assistant asked Clio to trade places with Jessie and began scrutinizing Clio's face. "Frown, please." The woman's breath smelled of chicken salad, the type with Vidalia onions and sour pickles. "Now, relax your face, please," she instructed.

Relax? Cliodhna couldn't relax with a needle poised with poison.

"Cliodhna," the doctor's assistant said. "That's an unusual

name. Family name?"

"In a way," Clio said, trying not to move her face with the needle hovering above, selecting targets. "Irish. Distant ancestors from Ireland."

"We call her Clio," Jessie offered to the assistant as if they were all girlfriends at a martini party. "It's easier than KLEE-uh-na," she sounded it out, apparently because the assistant had pronounced it differently each time she said it. "Clio is a software representative like me."

The woman didn't seem impressed with their career choices, but kept inspecting Cliodhna's face. "Software," she said slowly as if musing the concept, "never could understand the stuff."

White-hot pain stabbed into Clio's forehead. She felt the needle pull out.

Bright-colored posters with illustrations of female faces and their common wrinkle areas lined the wall, and Cliodhna re-read them, hoping to distract her mind from the sharp point poised to jab again.

"Amazing," Jessie continued talking and freed her hair from the ponytail, "that so much can be written into a computer program. Computer software doesn't care if we have wrinkles, but our customers do."

The needle stung Clio two times near her right eye, then once by her left. "Not really," she said in a voice that held a slight tremble. "I tend to think the customer would like a more experienced rep. Someone who looks like they have survived several implementations and version upgrades."

"Dream on," Jessie said and laughed. "And just wait until Devin sees you. He'll flip."

Her forehead became a target once more. "Flip? Hope in a good way," Cliodhna said, then closed her eyes as the needle neared her brows.

Cliodhna had met Devin several years before when a mutual friend introduced them at a gallery reception in Richmond on an autumn night. The following weekend he invited Clio to take a daytrip to Williamsburg to visit the restored Colonial Capital. A risky choice, Clio thought, for them both, because they had committed the entire day together. The drive down Interstate 64 allowed them time to get to know each other. They talked of growing up, her in Newport News, him in Falls Church, and of their careers. His interest in history had been the reason for the trip to the Historic Triangle area.

After the tour of the restored Courthouse and a reenactment of a witch trial, they stepped out onto the cobbled street. Distant high-pitched tweets and thudding beats of the Fife and Drum Corps promised a parade within a few minutes. Devin stopped at the edge of the road to look back at Clio. His eyes twinkled in the sunlight. "You bewitch me," he said.

"No such thing," she said and stepped to the side of Duke of Gloucester Street to avoid a steaming pile from a horse-drawn carriage. The bright orange leaves of the trees fluttered in a warm autumn breeze that carried the hint of horse manure.

"Bewitchment?" Devin asked. "No, I think women have a power over men. You just heard in the mock trial how men feared a strong woman."

Sexuality seemed to be the only power she could think of as he talked. Men didn't care for romance or companionship, all their thoughts and actions could trace back to the pursuit of sex. Such a primal urge, such an easy desire to manipulate. Although his attempt at wooing her steamed and smelled as bad as what the horse had left on the street, Cliodhna liked him. Devin's face had the defined angles of a man of physical action, the deep eyes of a man of introspection, the wide mouth of a man of easy laughter.

"Women have no power, other than the obvious," she said.

"Not this, coming from a successful woman?" He acted as if she had said the world was flat. He laughed, took her hand, and led her to a bench under a maple tree, where rich crimsons and golds cast a glow around them. "You have a power that no one else has. You're charming, modest, smart, and beautiful."

Age and experience had taught her to smile when a compliment tossed by a man landed in her lap. Not that she gave it much credit, but she knew he seemed to be working toward a goal of flattery. Why, she thought, am I so cynical? The motivations of other people intrigued her as if she were removed from the social context, just an observer, an analyst of human behavior. "You are balancing between cute and bullshit," she said before she could edit herself.

"Ha!" he let out the laugh in full force. "I need to stay alert with you."

They toured the old stores and homes, the marketplace, the Governor's Palace, and the Capital building. Maybe she had charmed him because she seemed to say and do things that delighted him. Devin could have had any woman that appealed to him.

Cliodhna watched as other women, some with husbands and children at their sides, snuck glances at Devin. His hearty laugh made her smile. His strong chin made his face handsome to her, a kind and satisfied face that she enjoyed.

"What made you move to Richmond?" she asked. They settled at an outdoor table at the Trellis Restaurant. He ordered a beer and she asked for wine, pinot grigio.

"I paid a price," he began, but seemed to hesitate. "Let's just say my ex-wife felt D.C. was the best place to raise a potential child. I didn't. We broke up before we had kids, luckily."

"Sorry," she said. "Richmond is a good place to start new. It's a beautiful city. I live in Carytown, There's an urban feel without the cold, high-rise buildings."

"Carytown?" he mused. "Carytown. I don't picture you as a Carytown girl."

"First off, I'm no girl –"

"Sorry," he said.

"And what exactly is your image of Carytown?"

"Funky. Edgy. Tattoos," he listed.

"Just because I sell software doesn't mean I can't let my hair down," she said. "Besides, I would have thought you would love that neighborhood."

"A bit too quirky for me to invest money in a house there," Devin explained. "I didn't care for the suburbs of D.C., living outside the Beltway, but my place in Westham gives me just the right amount of convenience and anonymity with an easy commute to work."

"Anonymity?" she asked, intrigued that he would admit to such a thing.

"You don't want all your neighbors to know your business," he replied.

"I have nothing to hide," she said, then cocked her head to the side and raised an eyebrow. "You?"

"Deep, dark secrets," Devin said in a low voice, his mouth turned up just a slight bit at each corner as if he really did have a mystery in his past. He reached across the table and took Clio's hand, his index finger tracing across her knuckles and lingering in the spaces between, the valleys and hills of the back of her hand. He moved her hand over and stroked the mounds in her palm at the base of each finger. "I wanted to learn to read palms when I was a kid," he said.

She caught her breath as he pressed his thumb into her palm. The sensuality of his touch caused her to shift in her seat.

"This," he said with his thumb stroking the base of her thumb, "is the Venus mount, your passion, your virility."

The waitress interrupted them with their drinks, but Clio couldn't shake the lingering sensation of his touch on her palm.

"Cheers," Devin lifted his brown ale to her. She clinked his beer mug with her wine glass and thought about how he had changed the subject from himself back to focusing on her.

She thought about sex with him. Would he be a giving lover or a man focused on his own satisfaction? He played the right notes to woo her, a symphony of flattery, coyness, masculinity, and slight sexual aggressiveness. His attention stayed on her as if no one else existed.

As Jessie drove them back to work, Cliodhna checked her face in the mirror on the back of the sun visor. The needle pricks had stopped bleeding and she had wiped away the blood spots before they left the doctor's office. Angry red dots still hovered under her makeup, so she dabbed on more concealer. She concentrated on the process because the injection areas tingled a bit, but she couldn't feel anything more than that.

"Tomorrow," Jessie said, "you won't see a trace of redness. Which is perfect because I'm going to Raleigh to meet with the hospital tech staff. Never know when a handsome doctor might be around," she said and winked at Clio. "God, I need to get married – again."

"Husbands aren't collectibles. Plus, finding one that is compatible is next to impossible," Cliodhna said.

"Has Devin made any moves in that direction?"

"No, and I'm grateful he hasn't brought it up." But Clio wondered if she really was.

Chapter Three

Taliesin's uncles had all retired from their factory jobs, either by age and right or by force to an early retirement by a crumbling economy. His father would have been, Tal counted up in his head, sixty-five years old if he'd lived. Finn had been the youngest, and Grandmaw Roane had given him the legendary Irish warrior's name. Somehow she had named all her sons mythically as if she expected extraordinary accomplishments from each one of them. Machinist, mechanic, middle manager, none aimed for the greatness she had set at their birth. Least of all Finn. Most of what Tal could remember of the man consisted of his smell of metal shavings coated in oil and the grin that never left his face.

Finn had worked in the machine shop along with a few of his brothers. Southwest Virginia winters brought Taliesin and his cousins snow days from school and the kids usually ended up at the machine shop, underfoot to uncles Lionel, Brendan, Oscar, and Brian. The other two uncles had long ago moved their families away. Dylan took his young family out of the mountains and away from the extended family, and Tristan had aspired to the community college, then snagged an ambitious woman. When his new wife took a job in Atlanta, Tristan clung beside her, like a vine to a tree. Talie loved those days of spending time in the company of his father and uncles – their interactions, their skills and traits. Each uncle had his own strengths and insights. Oscar taught Taliesin and his cousin Ricky how to arm wrestle. Brian teased Taliesin with a deck of playing cards backed with pictures of naked ladies. The shop was more of a fraternity house than business.

But that shop, like their lives, was ruled over by the brothers' father. Pawpaw Joe kept his boys in line, except apparently for the baby Finn. The brothers knew Finn was the favorite too. Seventh son of a seventh son. Joe had been the last son of his parents, and it seemed to the family that he and Grandmaw Roane had been aiming for a seventh son themselves. Taliesin had overheard his uncles complaining that they were no more than stepping stones to Finn — the grinning boy.

That Finn 'MacCool' grin seemed to irritate the brothers, as if they thought Finn harbored some secret they should know too, some undisclosed key to happiness, some aspect of life he cheated on. And the wolf... Yes, Taliesin knew there was a wolf in his father. It didn't take a full moon to release it, just a pretty face or a curvaceous figure. Plenty of prey in the hills of southwest Virginia for Finn, and the snare of a wife and son wasn't about to hold him back. Nine-year-old Talie knew that wolf would have gnawed his foot off to free himself from the restrictions of that marriage trap.

Eventually, it did.

"Talie," his mother had called to him in his room, "come down here to the kitchen."

The morning had been cool, but not as frosty as it had been earlier in the month. Still April had a chill, especially in the first rays of dawn. Taliesin pulled on his Star Wars slippers, rubbed his eyes, and flopped down the stairs to the warm kitchen. Breakfast wasn't on the table. His mother wasn't dressed for work; she still wore her nightgown and bathrobe. "What?" he asked.

"Did your father say anything to you last night?"

"About what?" He didn't like the vertical crease in her forehead between her eyes, her bloodshot eyes. "Where's Daddy?"

"That's what I'm trying to find out." His mother's breathing was deep, but steady as if she had passed desperation and had moved to controlled anger – barely controlled.

The smell of coffee didn't fill the room, and on instinct, Taliesin looked to the Mr. Coffee machine on the counter. The carafe sat empty and dry. "Is he at work? Maybe he went to the shop."

"Work's the last thing on his mind," she said and wrapped

her robe tight around her body. "I called your pawpaw. He and Brendan are on their way."

Something could have happened to him, Taliesin thought; he could be dying in a ditch next to his wrecked car. His mother didn't look as if she worried about her husband's health, but worried about herself.

"You think he left us?" The words flowed out of his young mouth without stopping in his mind for him to decide if he should voice them.

"I…" For the first time, she faltered. "I don't know. His clothes are all still here, but his Chevy is gone. He's gone."

"Cigarettes. He just went out for cigarettes," Taliesin said. "A man's got to have his cigarette in the morning," he added the mantra he'd heard from his father.

She exhaled a slow sigh and leaned against the counter with a blank stare.

When Pawpaw Joe and Uncle Brendan arrived, Taliesin went back upstairs to his bedroom and burrowed into his sheets. The air had changed when the men arrived, thick and static with accusations against his father. Even Pawpaw Joe seemed to believe that Finn had run off with another woman.

Why? Why would he? One woman is enough for any man. Taliesin knew the smell of women and hadn't smelled it on his father – well, not often. He was supposed to take Taliesin to his fiddle lesson Saturday at the music store in the Bristol Mall. Then they were going to buy him new Cub Scout pants at Parks-Belk because he'd outgrown his old ones. They were going to go fishing at South Holston Lake, on a boat Uncle Oscar had bought the summer before.

Now, nothing would happen. He began to tremble in the cold, lonely April morning.

Was Grandmaw Roane losing her mind? Taliesin sat on the corner of a low stage in the State Line Bar and Grille in downtown Bristol.

He sipped a beer in the mid-afternoon light. He and the boys had a gig that night, and he wanted to get the equipment set up before the supper crowd came in. He wouldn't even know where to look. If a man wanted to disappear then he sure as hell could. Taliesin couldn't think of one good reason to dig up the past…except for that old woman wanting answers before she died. That trumped anything he could conjure up.

With the cables laid, the amps plugged in and tested, and his guitar tuned, he slid into a booth at the window and ordered the amber ale of a local brewery. Wolf Hills Brewing Company, they had taken their name from nearby Abingdon's history. Daniel Boone's dogs had been attacked by wolves coming out of the caves of the hill that would eventually seat the county courthouse. "Two hundred and fifty years ago those damn wolves drove off Boone," Taliesin said to himself, "then a wolf took Finn. She-wolf," he corrected himself.

He pulled his cell phone from his jeans pocket and dialed his cousin Brigid's number. "Hey, Shaman of Shenandoah, you got a minute?"

"Shit, Tal, this friggin' hospital is running me ragged."

"Geez, Brigid, you kiss your momma with that mouth?"

"Yep. What's shakin' bacon?"

"I'm worried about Grandmaw Roane," he said. "She's got things on her mind that should have been forgotten long ago."

"What?"

"Daddy."

Brigid's silence caused Taliesin to think his phone had dropped the call. "You there?"

"Yeah, once she's got it in her mind," Brigid started, "that's what she'll talk about until something else bumps it out."

"Is that your professional opinion?"

"No, that's my free opinion. You want professional, you can come in for an office visit. Your insurance intact?"

"Insurance? What's that?" He sipped his beer. "Why don't you come down for a couple days and see her?"

"What does Dad say about her?" Brigid asked.

"Uncle Brendan..." Taliesin said, but stopped. "I can't bring this up with him. He gets all red-faced when anyone mentions Finn. I'm afraid of his blood pressure. The other uncles aren't much better."

"Those old boys should just get over it. I'm off Wednesday and Thursday. I'll drive down," Brigid said. "You playing anywhere this week?"

"Tonight," Taliesin said. "I just finished setting up and stopped to have a beer and call my favorite cousin. We start at nine after most of the supper crowd is done and the drinkers come in. If you leave now, you could make it."

She laughed. "I'll be there in a few days. You don't think she's ready for assisted living do you?"

"Her mind is strong. That's what's so puzzling. She thinks he's still alive."

"No offense," Brigid said in a slow, low voice, "but I hope that's not true."

Chapter Four

Brigid's diploma seemed useless. The hospital administration wouldn't let her incorporate alternative healing practices because the labs couldn't replicate the success, only failure. Yet, Brigid added a regimen of herbal supplements to Mr. Hawkins' routine, a list of instructions she had typed on her computer and printed out for his wife. Hawkins suffered from several ailments that the hospital treated: swollen joints, occasional incontinence, chills, confusion, loss of balance. The computer spit out a list of medications that had been programmed for the symptoms, and Brigid had prescribed the drugs, but the combination made Mr. Hawkins lethargic and produced bouts of vertigo that required his wife to monitor his movements, especially when he first got out of bed or stood from his chair.

"Why don't they put these computers in grocery stores like vending machines?" Brigid said to the nurse outside the examining room. "Administration wants us to type in the symptoms and let the computer diagnose the condition and prescribe the treatment." She jerked a pen from the breast pocket of her lab coat. "He's eighty-three years old. These are symptoms of age."

On the printout, Brigid circled the minimum dosage of one of the five prescriptions listed and added some vitamin supplements. She hesitated, then listed the number of a Tai Chi instructor that she liked who lived off Cherry Avenue. "A little movement and balance would do him a world of good." The nurse typed in the updated information and Brigid reviewed the plan with Mr. Hawkins and his wife.

"You can't just go willy nilly changing the recommended treatment for a patient," Bob Wilkerson said. "The staff bastards will have my head."

"Screw management," she said and propped her feet on the edge of Bob's desk.

"You can have that attitude when you've been here for a while, but Brigid, you need to play by the rules until they can see your way works."

Sweat broke out on Bob's upper lip, which he wiped away with the cuff of his white dress shirt. Brigid felt relief that he hadn't used his silk tie the way she'd seen him do before.

"I can't abide by a computer diagnosing patients for me."

"It doesn't. It gives recommendations based on years of experience from a database of doctors," he said. "It's the same as having the advice of thousands of physicians weigh in on your patient. If all the information is not given to the program then it can't give good feedback."

"The drug companies," she said and shook her head, "those bitches are the ones who program it. Bob, it gives me specific brands to prescribe. Not the type of med, but a specific brand name."

"You want to practice medicine like they did fifty years ago –"

"Yes, exactly," she said.

"Well, you can't. It's not a search-your-memory kind of practice. There are tools that ensure consistent and reliable care."

"That's bullshit," she said and slammed her feet off the desk and onto the carpeted floor. "We're trained and tested to diagnose a patient."

"Tools," Bob said. "That's all that computer program provides, tools. You still decide what the best route is."

Brigid paced to the window and back. "Then why do we have to log any departure from the computer-prescribed treatment?"

"It helps tweak the program. Adds more data." His voice rose slightly as if pleading with her to believe him.

"Right, I bet there's a printout waiting for me during my next performance review with the chief of staff." She perched on the side of Bob's desk. "An exception report, I bet that's what they call it."

"They can call it Linda Lovelace if they want to, but you'll have to answer to it," Bob said with a sly smile.

Brigid slumped back into the chair, keeping her expression neutral. "You think I don't know who that is? Not quite appropriate."

His smile dropped as if he had gone too far, maybe a sexual harassment suit too far.

"They should call me Linda Lovelace," Brigid said and kicked her heels back on the corner of his desk, "because I'm the one getting it crammed down my throat."

He raised his eyebrows and shook his head back and forth. "You are pushing me toward early retirement, Dr. MacGuire."

 Greg Lilly

Chapter Five

Spring 1708 – James Cittie Shire, Virginia Colony

The wail echoed through the black night and around the cabin, a shriek of an owl maybe or the cry of an old woman or a bobcat. Whatever produced it, Anna Mayford shivered for it summoned lore from the motherland of banshees. They would come for her. News from the north reported the hysteria of Salem, the blaming of women who did not conform, who would not be docile. But what woman could be docile when she had no man to help raise her son or no one to assist her to hunt or to farm or to trade for the essentials of life?

The small farm of the Widow Mayford clung to the fringes of Williamsburg. Where the other women wore skirts and blouses, Anna had become accustomed to wearing breeches and her dead husband's shirts. A practical way of dressing for a woman who had to tend the fields with her young son, not what she would wear into town or wear for anyone else's eyes, but those other eyes watched her. They watched her queer ways; they watched her work like a man and a woman; from the dusty road, they watched. She knew they did too.

After her husband died, Anna found the spring planting occupied most of her time. When she could, she'd direct her young son Stanton in the field. He planted potatoes while she pulled two loaves of bread from the smoldering embers of the hearth. She turned to find Tobias Hart standing at her doorway.

"Good day to you, Madam Mayford," Tobias said from the

threshold.

She did not step back or invite him to enter her home. "Good day, Mr. Hart. How may I be of service to you?"

One side of his mouth turned up in a lop-sided smile. He leaned his forearm against the doorjamb, blocking Anna's exit from the house. His right hand rested on his hip draping back his linen coat, and she noticed a watch chain hanging from his beige waistcoat's front pocket. His breeches matched her husband's favorite pair, and she wondered if they had come from the same tailor in town. "I felt the need to offer you my services, Mrs. Mayford," he said. "I know with Mr. Mayford gone, you and the boy could use the assistance of a man. For the pasture," he added and glanced over his shoulder to where her son worked in the distance, "I could send over a couple of my field slaves, if that would please you."

A couple of his slaves? Anna thought. As if he had more than a couple to offer, the pompous ass. "No thank you," she said and dipped her chin a bit as the smallest of bows possible and began to close the door.

He stopped the door with his boot. "A woman of your delicate features should not be in the harsh sun," he said, eyes surveying her as he might a calf, colt, or piglet. He reached up to touch her cheek, a gesture, much too familiar, that caused her to jerk away.

"Your wife," she said.

"Is away," he answered her protest. "Her mother needs her. And I'm bewitched."

"No more bewitched than the moon," she said and pushed the door against his foot.

"Anna, you have no man here."

"My son is in the field."

"You know what I mean."

"I do and I care not to think of it. Go home and let me be."

"You will not survive without friends," he said.

"I know the old ways from my grandmother," Anna said. "She survived as a widow."

"In the homeland," he said. "Not here in the colony. You can protect yourself against the Indians?" He nodded his head toward the woods south of her field. "They desire women. Savages," he added with a spit of disgust. "Devils, really. I heard they copulate like bears, the woman on her hands and knees."

"That's quite enough," Anna almost yelled. "I will not have you speak in such a manner to me."

"A blush covers your cheeks," he remarked and stroked the side of her face with his fingertips.

Another jerk of her head caused his hand to fall back to his side. "Please leave before I have to call for Stanton."

"That boy," he started, but stopped to look out to the field where her son drove an ox and plow. "That boy isn't old enough to sprout a whisker."

"Whiskers or not, he knows how to use a rifle."

"The flush of familiarity still colors your cheeks, a familiarity that you miss with Edward gone."

"Do not speak of my husband."

"I will not speak of him if you do not speak of that wretch of a wife I have."

How he could compare the two, Anna couldn't fathom. Her Edward had succumbed to the Black Vomit the summer before. From the time they arrived in the colony, Edward had hoped and planned. Carved out of the thick woods, their little farm sustained them and their child and provided a safe harbor for Edward Mayford's family. Even the Indians that Tobias Hart seemed to despise had been kind and gentle to her and the boy after Edward's death.

The only troublesome people she encountered were neighbors like the Harts. Tobias, with his suggestions about her state of mind and physical needs, darkened her door more than good sense warranted, especially with the townspeople watching and talking. His wife, Parnella, seemed to dislike Anna from the start, maybe from the attention Tobias gave Anna, or maybe Parnella, being barren of child, coveted Anna's role of mother to Stanton. Whatever the cause, Parnella found few comforting words for the recently widowed Anna.

"Please allow me to continue my chores," Anna said.

Tobias stepped back, and after a slow stare moving downward from Anna's capped head to her dress hem, he removed his boot from the door. "Good day to you, Mrs. Mayford."

"She did it," Parnella Hart accused. The boney finger pointed at Anna, and a sneer quivered her face. "That woman conjured a spell and hexed our hens. They have stopped laying." A small woman in stature, but large in voice, Parnella drew her shoulders back and glanced around the crowd that had gathered in the Williamsburg market square. "She has the impudence to appear in the presence of God-fearing Christians, in broad daylight. A wonder the Devil himself doesn't materialize by her side."

"What a mind you have, Parnella," Anna said with a steady and firm voice, although her hands shook from the attention of the ten or twelve people watching her and Parnella. "What a mind to invent such a story. Idle hands and thoughts play into fanciful tales, tales that our grandmothers dismissed long ago." She tightened her hold on her market sack, a supply of sugar and flour. "You scare me with your talk of devils. Get ye to the church and confess your sins."

"Witch!" Parnella yelled in a rage. "Don't pretend purity and innocence."

Tobias walked up behind Parnella, and Anna could see the wild confusion and embarrassment in his twitching eyes. His tense grip pulled Parnella toward him. "Hush woman," he hissed. "You make a spectacle of yourself and of me."

"You," she said, and narrowed her brown eyes at her husband, "you are bewitched by that conjuror, that witch of a woman. She charmed you."

"Enough," he said and grabbed Parnella by the arm, jerking her away from Anna.

Murmurs drifted through the crowd of bystanders. The women held her hard in their stare while the men ambled on toward their home or to the tavern. Anna's face burned from the accusation and public humiliation. Parnella must be losing her wits, she thought.

As Anna walked toward the market stalls, a few women whispered to each other then turned their backs toward her when she passed. The blacksmith's wife had promised to have Anna's bird spit repaired and ready for her on this trip to Williamsburg. The older woman with frizzy gray hair, barely contained by her straw hat, stood up from her stool when Anna walked to the table under the canvas strung between two maples.

"That Parnella is trouble," she said. "She's latched on to you like a leach."

"Any association she has with me is only in her own head." Anna sat her market bag on the table then untied her pocket sack from around her waist, dumping out a few coins in payment for the repair. "Mistress Allerton," she said, handing the coins to the woman, "I know little about Parnella Hart and wish I knew less."

"Just the same," warned the older woman, "murmurs of witchcraft fluster the feeble-minded among us." Mrs. Allerton tied a string on the end of the repaired bird spit nearest the turning handle. The spit tapered down to a sharp trident with the middle prong continuing to a point. "Hang this by the string from your shoulder," Mrs. Allerton instructed. "Mind the points; don't spear yourself instead of a quail. It's strong and stable," she added and nodded to the tip that was repaired.

"Thank you, Mistress Allerton, and good day to you." Anna turned and walked toward the road that would take her back to her farm, the small fowl skewer bumping her hip with each step.

"The Devil's pitchfork," a little girl said and pointed at the bird spit. The girl ran and hid behind her mother's skirts.

A little boy, about eight years old and probably recently breeched, pulled back his shoulders and said, "Nay, silly Lizzy, that's for poking a baby like you." The boy grabbed behind his mother and pulled his sister around to face the road. He pointed at Anna. "That's what a witch will cook you with."

The mother ignored her children, but Anna couldn't shut out their prickly voices.

If I could conjure, she thought, I'd mute stupid children.

"Which way went the witch?" the little boy sang, his shrill cadence rising and dropping with each syllable.

Chapter Six

"Grandmaw Roane, he's dead." Taliesin sat on the aluminum and cushioned glider on his grandmother's front porch, watching the cars drive down Lee Highway. The late morning sun filtered through the rhododendrons along the stonewall railing. "We have all accepted that's the reason he never came back home." The highway was far enough away from her hilltop house that the cars only produced a low roar as they passed, something Taliesin had grown used to during his infant years and now the sound didn't register, just the motion of people travelling north or south, a perpetual flow between Bristol and Abingdon.

"After he left," Grandmaw Roane said, staring at the highway, "you and I would sit up here and rock in these chairs, watching, waiting." She sat next to him in the matching rocker to her porch set, purchased when her children were young.

"He ain't going to roll down that highway and wave at us." Taliesin softened his tone. "Brigid is coming to visit."

"Good, I been missing that girl," she said. "She staying with me or her daddy?"

"I guess Uncle Brendan and Aunt Charlotte."

"Just as well," Grandmaw Roane said and picked at the cushion of her rocker. "Brigid likes to talk too much. When she gets to be an old woman like me, living alone, she won't be used to a lot of jawing."

He had to laugh. "Never thought of Brigid as a chatty girl, but I guess she is. She sure likes to hear her own opinions."

"Children. That's what some of you grandkids don't have. The ones with kids have mellowed. Children sap the energy." She reached over and patted Taliesin's arm. "It didn't weaken your daddy's energy…fathering you."

He knew she was stuck on the memory of Finn. Every time he

tried to steer her away, she found a route back. Maybe Brigid could get her mind onto some other topic. "I'm playing at the State Line in Bristol tomorrow night," Tal said. "You want to come hear us?"

"I thought you just played there. Didn't you?"

"Tuesdays, because they're slow nights, then again on Thursdays and Saturdays."

"You need some money?" she asked.

"No, Grandmaw. I make enough to get by. I'm teaching down at the music store, too."

"I'm glad."

"Me, too." Taliesin knew she was happy he could live from his music. She had always been his champion.

"Before he left –"

Oh, shit, Tal thought, she's driven right back into those Finn 'MacCool' ruts. He must have rolled his eyes because she slapped his arm.

"I'm serious," she said. "I want to find out about your father before I die."

He reached over and took her hand in his, partly to keep her from slapping his arm again and partly because he needed to touch her, to feel her pulse flutter beneath her crepe paper thin skin. She seemed so small and fragile.

"They used to say before a death, you could hear a wail coming from the hills. That's not true. It ain't always a physical death; sometimes it's more a symbolic death, maybe a transformation, like a caterpillar to a butterfly."

"A metamorphosis," Tal offered.

"Yes. That night that your daddy left, just as I was getting into bed, I heard the most painful and soulful yowl coming from the woods. Your pawpaw sat straight up in the bed. 'Banshee,' he said. No, I thought it was Finn saying farewell to us."

"Did it sound like a wolf?"

"No wolves around here anymore," she said.

"If Pawpaw Joe thought it was a banshee, then it must have sounded like a female."

"Who says banshees are female?"

"I do." Taliesin squeezed her hand tenderly and smiled. "I'm the son of Finn 'MacCool'. I know all the legends."

"There's a reason there are legends." She sighed. "Truth shows itself in many ways."

"You, old lady," Tal said, trying to lighten her mood, "are a wise woman."

"You bet your ass I am," she said. "Can't get this old without learning a thing or two."

A Barcelona red Toyota Prius slowed down at the highway and turned onto the driveway with a little whir of sound as it climbed the hill to the house.

"Friend of yours?" Grandmaw Roane asked.

"That's Brigid's new car. She's being socially responsible."

"It will clash with her hair," she warned and pushed herself up from the rocking chair to walk around to the garage. "Redheaded girls shouldn't drive red cars."

"What are you complaining about now, Grandmaw Roane?" Brigid slammed the door of the Prius and rushed up to meet her with a hug.

"She was just commenting on your choice of car color," Taliesin said as he caught up with their grandmother.

Brigid kissed Grandmaw Roane on the forehead then leaned over and kissed Taliesin's cheek without letting go of the old woman.

"Don't crush me between my two favorite grandkids," she said and squirmed out of Brigid's grasp. She walked over to the car and ran her hand along the side. "Hardly makes a sound."

"That's why I bought a red one," Brigid said. "If you can't hear me coming, you better be able to see me."

"Clashes with your hair," Grandmaw Roane said, still touching the car and looking in the driver's side window. "It's almost noon. You hungry? Want me to fix you some dinner?"

"Let's go out to eat. My treat," Brigid said. "We can go into Abingdon for a nice lunch."

"Can we ride in this thing?" Grandmaw Roane asked and patted the Prius.

Taliesin picked a restaurant where he had played a gig once, just on the far side of Courthouse Hill. He hoped to talk with the owner to see if he could book some acoustical performances on Friday nights.

Grandmaw Roane continued to ask Brigid questions about her hybrid car, and apparently, only had a problem with the color choice. "A blue one would have looked nice," she said over her open menu.

Brigid took a slow, deep breath. Tal could tell she was tiring of the red car discussion. Her skin flushed at the base of her throat.

"Grandmaw Roane," he said, "try the grilled salmon. They make some good salsa topping for it."

She looked back at the menu. "Sounds pretty good."

Brigid motioned for the waiter. When he approached, she said, "I need wine. Merlot."

Taliesin hoped their grandmother wouldn't comment on the color of Brigid's wine. "Grandmaw, you want a little vino?" he asked.

"Beer for me." She set the menu down and smiled at the young waiter. "Make it a Bud."

"Sam Adams," Tal ordered. The waiter left to retrieve their drinks.

"Talie says you feel Uncle Finn might still be alive," Brigid said without any sign of cushioning her reasons for her visit.

"Gee, Brigid," Tal said, "you could have waited for the drinks."

Grandmaw Roane laughed. "Ya'll think I'm losing my grip. No, it's been on my mind for a while. Taliesin is old enough to set this straight. He needs to know as much as I do."

A breath caught in Brigid's throat, then she let it out slow with a visible, forced relaxation of her shoulders. "Okay," she started. "Uncle Finn left town years ago with nothing but his car –"

"His Chevrolet Impala," Grandmaw Roane added, "baby blue."

"Nothing but his Impala," Brigid continued. "No one has heard from him since. We assumed, right or wrong, that he ran off with a woman. But," she said and held up her index finger to stop Grandmaw Roane's opening mouth from objecting, "but we don't know anything for a fact. Why would you think there was more to the story than what a million men do on a regular basis?"

"Finn wasn't like a million other men. I know that. He was my son."

"You said 'was' like you believe he's dead," Tal stated. "I, as much as anyone, would like to think he's still alive, but I can't honestly believe that." He didn't want to believe it. If his father still roamed – alive and well – then why had he never attempted to contact him? Desertion by death settled minds easier than desertion by choice.

Grandmaw Roane looked at them both. "He disappeared thirty years ago. I know something kept him from returning to us, something other than a woman. He loved you, Taliesin, and your mother. He would not leave ya'll unless he had to. I'd like to think he wouldn't stay away from any of us without some restriction keeping him."

"What gnaws at me," Tal said, "is that Momma didn't seem surprised. We know Daddy liked the ladies. He wasn't faithful to Momma. Maybe he had another family somewhere; a family that he thought needed him more than us." The hurt of saying it out loud closed up his throat.

"Aunt Kay told my dad that she suspected another woman," Brigid said of Tal's mother, Kay. "Tal could be right that Uncle Finn had another family that he felt he had to attend to."

Their drinks arrived, and as soon as the waiter sat the glasses down, all three reached for them and gulped.

Grandmaw Roane sat her beer glass down, clinking the fork at the side of the placemat. "He would have told me or his daddy or at least one of his brothers."

The waiter hovered nearby until Brigid called him over and ordered their lunch. She sipped her wine slowly and watched her grandmother. "What do you think we need to do to settle this?"

Tal asked, "We? Are you volunteering to help?"

"You think you can do anything without my assistance?"

"Shit, Brigid," he said, "I can get along fine on my own. But," he said as he considered her offer, "I'd be glad to have you help any way you can."

"Yes?" Grandmaw Roane asked. "You are going to look for him?"

"We can't turn you down, old lady," he said. "I don't know how the hell to start, but we'll look into it."

The sound of banshees squealed from the highlands in the night, an octave too high for a human, and the note held too long for a natural breath. Taliesin listened. He wasn't in the hills, but at his kitchen table, late in the night, capturing a tune from his imagination for the band when the piercing shrill came. A signal, he thought, or maybe a warning. Banshee in the woods, or a Siren from the water, he knew the caution the sound should bring.

He closed his eyes to focus on the wailing, the mournful howl. If he were his father, what would he do? What action would this sound cause? Did Finn investigate? Did he even hear such a shriek?

Chapter Seven

"Uncle Brendan." Taliesin grabbed the old man in a hug. "You feeling okay?" He had driven to his uncle and aunt's house, Brigid's parents, to see what they remembered of his father's last few days.

His hair thin and combed over his bald spot, Brendan scratched his head and smiled at his nephew. "I'm keeping upright. That's about as good as I can report. Brigid went out with her mom to Food City, in case you were looking for her."

"Actually, I need some advice from you." Taliesin knew Brendan loved to give his opinion on any subject. "Momma doesn't say much about Daddy anymore. I know," he said – and shook his head as if sorry for bringing up the subject – "that's a sore point with many people, honestly Uncle Brendan, he was my father and I want to know about him. Where should I start?"

Brendan closed his eyes slowly then let out a sigh. "Let's go out in the yard. I need a cigar, and Charlotte would kill me if I smoked in the house."

"Aunt Charlotte is particular about her air quality."

"Can't even fart in my own house," Brendan mumbled and led Taliesin out the back door to the patio under an oak. They settled in wrought iron chairs. Taliesin noticed his uncle didn't move as well as he remembered, slower now that he had retired.

The half-smoked cigar took the flame as Brendan inhaled, orange fire flaring at the crushed end. Puff, puff, puff, exhale. Then again until the loose fragments burned off and the cigar smoldered. He blew a smoke ring that made Taliesin smile. When he was twelve, his uncle let him try it if he'd promised to not tell his mother. Tal had loved it and snuck a smoke with Brendan from time to time over the years, but never found it as a reliable habit, too much puffing, too much work.

"Finn," Brendan started, then stopped, "I mean Tal. Why dig this up now?"

"Grandmaw Roane said I looked like Dad," Taliesin said. "Do I? You started to call me Finn."

"Just getting old. You know how Mom calls all of us by each other's name until she runs down the list and hits the right one. Yeah, I guess you are looking like your father. But a hell of a better personality."

The thought of his father's personality brought a smooth, warm feel, like fur, to Tal. Finn had been a loving father, full of praise and support for his only child. Tal couldn't remember how his parents were together, guessing the awareness of children didn't extend far beyond the self, at least not when he assumed they sailed in calm waters. But today, he knew storms had rocked the marriage. Eventually, Finn abandoned it. "What was Daddy like around you?"

The old man inhaled and blew a stream of blue-gray smoke into the air. His eyes settled on Tal. "I loved him. He was my baby brother. You see it with your cousins, as you grow up, things change. Personalities and opinions start to rub. The kids we were became adults with different priorities. Your daddy's priorities were himself. Oh, he was good to Mom and Dad. But, I know your Pawpaw Joe's heart was broken when Finn left. I could see it in the way he shuffled around after that. Mom became strong for both of them."

His eyes looked red and watery. Tal stood and walked over to the oak's trunk to give Brendan time to recover.

"Damn cigar smoke irritates my eyes," Brendan said, rubbing his wrinkled hands over his face.

"Yep, mine too," Tal said. He sat back down across from his uncle. "Life just ain't fair. I appreciate all you did for me. Momma does too. I know it wasn't my fault he left, but a kid always takes on the blame – warranted or not. Momma said it was her fault. Pawpaw used to say it was Finn's wild streak, his lust for women." Filing the memories away as past experience should have been his strategy, but his grandmother's questions required answers. She had churned up the muck and needed it cleaned out.

"Family was important to him, in his way," Brendan said. "He would have done anything for Mom and Dad, Kay and you, even for us brothers, but something called him, something with a stronger draw." He rubbed the cigar stub around its edge, honing a packed, ashy tip against the ashtray for later re-lighting.

"I'm going to look for him." Leaning forward, elbows on his knees, Taliesin searched Brendan's face for a reaction.

Brendan shook his head from side to side. "No use. I'd bet dollars you won't find a thing. When an adult wants to disappear, he does. Nobody searches long for a man that doesn't want to be found, especially all these years later." Brendan cocked his head and asked, "What do you expect to get from it?"

His throat felt dusty and dry. "Closure." The word rasped out from Tal.

A slight grin flashed across Brendan's rumpled face, maybe a brief flicker of hope or forgiveness, Tal thought. "I wish I knew where to tell you to start," his uncle said.

"I was thinking about trying to trace his car," Tal said. "Grandmaw Roane said it was a blue Chevy Impala. I'd assume Virginia license plates. You wouldn't happen to have any record, maybe at the shop, of his plate number?"

Brendan stared into the oak tree's branches. "Back then we got new plates each year, none of these little stickers in the corners like now. The numbers changed or was that when they first started using those stickers... Shit." He pushed himself up from the wrought iron chair. "There's a Polaroid in the album of Finn and you with that Impala in the background, if I'm remembering right."

They passed through Charlotte's kitchen into the paneled den. Brendan dug through a cabinet in a bookcase next to his television. The television broadcast a golf game. "Here it is." He handed the thick photo album to Tal, and they went to the kitchen table to search through it.

School pictures of Brigid filled several pages then reddish tinted images from a vacation in Myrtle Beach in the 1980s. Tal saw a photo of himself wearing an Indiana Jones hat on the beach and a tall handsome man beside him. "Dad." He smiled.

Brendan looked closer. "Yep, that's Finn. Seems like he drove that Impala to the beach when we went. We used to go to the Outer Banks, but as you kids got older, Myrtle Beach was a better fit. Hell, a whole bunch of us rented a house. Me and Charlotte, Oscar and Loretta, Brian and Cindy, and Finn and Kay – seems like Lionel kept the shop open with Dad while we were there. All you kids ran wild on that beach and the boardwalk. Brigid was about 15, and she looked after you and the other little cousins."

In his head, Tal counted the brothers. "So that was after Uncle Tristan moved to Atlanta. What about Uncle Dylan? Where was he?"

"Dylan was an odd bird. Packed his family up and moved away. He told Lionel that the family was in each other's business too much." Brendan shrugged. "That's what family does. Don't know what he expected."

Brendan flipped the page. "There she is – that Impala. Pretty car."

The images was a little fuzzy and the film had tinged red, but Tal could see his father leaning against the car's hood, arms crossed over his bare chest with Taliesin sitting on the bumper, sand pail in one hand and other hand down the front of his swim trunks.

Brendan laughed. "Sand gets itchy on a boy's balls."

"Nope, I just liked to keep my hand down there, still do." He examined the photo closer, trying to make out the license plate on the bumper, but his eight year-old self had his elbow crooked and partially obscured the tag. "Can I take this? I'll scan it to the computer and bring it back."

"Sure, take it."

As soon as Taliesin arrived home, he scanned the picture into his computer and zoomed in on the image. He made out the letters:

HR-413. The first letter was covered by little Tal fondling himself.

"What the hell? Where..." Tal tried to think of how to search for that car, but he needed the full license plate, as least. "Maybe not..."

He opened up the web browser and searched for the letters and numbers. "Friggin' congress. Nothing but government legislation." The HR had brought up the House of Representatives sites and any Bill that had a 413 as part of its number.

The phone buzzed – Brigid calling.

"What's up Brigid?"

"Dad said you stopped by today."

"Yep, asking a few things about Finn. We're playing tonight. Why don't you come down for a few beers?"

"Can't," she said. "I need to get back home. I have to be at a meeting in the morning. Hey, why don't you come up for a few days? Stay with me. You can scout out some of the Charlottesville bars to see if the band — or just you — can play some gigs. C-ville has got to pay better than Bristol."

He considered the trip. "I'll call you tomorrow."

A phone call to Paul Cullop, his old high school buddy, sent him to another friend who had worked at the Virginia DMV. That led to a current employee of the state, who was willing to do a few searches on the databases. "Can't see anything right off," the man said.

"Not a recent plate, but should have been issued in the late 1970s or early '80s to Finn MacGuire."

Taliesin could hear the guy typing on the computer.

"So you went to school with Buck?"

"He was a few years ahead of me, but we played football together," Tal explained, as if his connection to this guy's former co-worker really made a difference, but as he thought about it, the round-about connection got him this far. "I heard Buck got divorced. Didn't know that girl he married. She was from up north somewhere."

"Yankee," the DMV guy kind of spit the word. "She talked like them Yankees do. No wonder he divorced her."

From what Tal could remember about Buck, he guessed the wife had left him, not the other way around. "That's what I'm trying to do here," he told the DMV man. "Tracking down dear old Dad who took off in that Impala like the hills were chasing him."

"Here we go," he said. "Finn MacGuire, tag GHR-413 last renewed in 1988. Address is on 124 New York Street, Bristol, Virginia."

"Nothing after that?"

"Nope, not for that tag number or from your father's name. That's the last record." The man hummed a few monotone notes. "You know…Try searching on the VIN."

"It was a 1977 model. Did they have VINs back then?"

"The standardized Vehicle Identification Number came later, but all manufacturers put some type of serial number on each car. Chevy was probably already using a standard. It's here on the registration. Got a pen and paper?"

"Yep. Go."

"1J4GA64147L117310"

"Bet I can run this through one of those used car report services to get the history."

"That can go across state records. My sister got one of those reports on a car she was thinking of buying for her son. Damned thing had been flooded during that last flood they had over in Missouri. Lucky she found out. Water damage is hell on car electronics."

Tal's mind was spinning on the next steps to take, so he didn't focus on the story. He thanked the man and promised to let their mutual acquaintance Buck know that all was good with him.

A beer sounded like a solid thinking tool to Taliesin. In his kitchen, he settled at the table and opened his laptop computer. He searched a website that would produce a report for the VIN he'd received from the DMV guy. After a few clicks and a small fee, he had the information displayed on his screen. The printer whirled to life in the next room and spit out the report.

Shit, he thought. He sipped the beer and called Paul Cullop. "Hey buddy, need another favor."

"That grandmother of yours is running you ragged. Just make up a story for her to quiet her down."

"I would, but honestly, I want to know, too. You can understand that."

Paul sighed and his voice softened. "Yeah, I remember how it hit you. You really hadn't talked about it since."

Tal knew with all he'd shared with Paul that they were closer than brothers, yet he hadn't opened up about Finn's leaving. Thirty years after the fact was an odd time to get so intense, but time was limited – Grandmaw Roane's time was limited.

"I understand Grandmaw's question. I want to know what was so damn important to take him away from his family," his voice cracked, "and from me."

"Sit tight," Paul said. "I'm on my way over."

"Oof." Tal let out a breath when Paul grabbed him in a bear hug as he opened the door.

"Man, you okay?" Paul asked, still squeezing Tal to him. When Tal didn't respond, Paul released his embrace then moved his hands up to the sides of Tal's face, stroking Tal's sideburns in unison with his thumbs. The action always calmed Taliesin, a sort of petting motion like Paul would do to a dog – an action they had done in private since they had been in elementary school.

The upper part of his jaw line relaxed from the pressure. His forehead soothed. His temples lulled. It was better than a buzz for Tal, maybe that's what it really was. He smiled and pulled away from Paul's touch. "Dead end on my dad."

"What was the favor you called about? From the sound of your voice, I wanted to get here and see you face to face. I'll do anything for you. Name it."

"You're the best girlfriend I ever had," Tal kidded.

"Fuck you."

Tal grabbed a beer for Paul, and they settled on the couch. He handed Paul the printout of the VIN report.

A quick scan of the pages and he looked back at Tal. "Nothing after the DMV registration in '89?"

"Which confirms that the car was never registered anyplace else, never sold, never scrapped, just disappeared," Tal said.

"Never officially tracked by its VIN," Paul said. "That's all it says, not a dead end."

"Okay, let's say you wanted to disappear – for whatever reason – and officially your existence drops off the radar in 1990."

"That's before the Internet, before cell phones, before satellites tracked our every move with GPS. Well, he did it at a good time." He winked at Tal and took a swig of his beer. "Oh, remember Hitchcock's *Psycho*? Norman Bates tried to make Janet Leigh disappear by rolling her car into that pond."

"You think the car was disposed of?"

"There's no trace of it now. Cars can't just disappear. Could have been disassembled for parts – chop shop."

"Could be." Tal thought for a moment. "Impala parts... Really?"

"Chevy is the poor man's brand," Paul said. "Who else would be looking for cheap parts but a Chevy owner?"

Dead end, Tal thought. "Dad didn't use credit cards. He paid cash for everything, so trying to track that would go nowhere."

"Somebody somewhere knows something," Paul said, then gulped his beer.

"You're a goddamn Battle High School graduate if I ever heard one."

"That's a quote from some wise man, maybe Confucius or George Clooney."

"Okay," Tal said, propping his feet on the coffee table. "Yes, someone has a lead on where Finn went."

Paul assumed the same position as Tal, feet on the coffee table and pushed back on the couch. "Who was the last person to talk to him?"

Maybe he'd been avoiding it. The thought must have hovered in his mind for years, but he'd always dodged it, as if asking would be picking at a scab, a long-time wound that never really healed. "Mom saw him last."

Kay MacGuire had sold the home she raised Tal in after he moved out. "Too many memories and too big for one person," she had said. Now, she inhabited a three-level townhouse that was taller than it was wide. Tal often wondered if it was a facsimile of a castle tower where young maidens paced, imprisoned until their prince rode up to save them.

No prince had rescued Kay. Tal suspected there had been a few courting her over the years, but his mother didn't seem the type to remarry. Maybe the scars from living with a womanizer hadn't healed.

He glanced around the den, big enough for a couch, chair and television on a console table, but Kay had added many little tables, baskets, lamps, so much so that the room was stuffed – not with useful things but clutter. Each room in the townhouse had gathered disharmony like dust. Although Kay kept herself tidy, nothing around her was.

She sat in the rose-pink wingback chair next to the television, still in the floral dress she had worn to work at the Belk department store, a Virginia Slims cigarette in the ashtray tottering on the tiny table beside the chair. Her hair, still dark, but a little out of place, made her seem younger than her late fifties. "Why are you so jittery?" she asked.

"I feel claustrophobic in this room. Its décor is very – complex."

"Thank you," she said, with a tinge of mockery. "I try to impress."

"Grandmaw Roane has been talking about Daddy lately." He let the subject settle as he watched his mother.

She held her breath for a single beat then reached for her cigarette. She held it to her lips but didn't inhale and then, as if she had, she returned it to the ashtray. "You think she's getting dementia?"

"Not sure. Brigid seems to think not. I know Grandmaw Roane's been thinking about dying; she's at that age, so maybe that's why she brought up Dad to me."

"What'd she say about Finn?"

"She wants to know what happened. Why he left. Why he didn't come back."

"Don't we all," Kay said, tarry bitterness dripping from her words.

"Yes," he said, "I want to know too. Why did he leave?"

Kay glanced at the cigarette then snuffed it out. "Chasing some woman – like always."

"No, really, what do you remember? I want to come up with an answer for Grandmaw Roane. And for me."

She exhaled as if she was tired of the conversation. "I can't remember a thing from that night. It was almost thirty years ago."

"You can't tell me that the night your husband left the house and never returned has faded from your memory." The standard answers would not work. "I've gone over it in my head a million times. That's the one morning I'll never forget – coming into the kitchen with you saying he was gone."

"I don't know what you want from me," her voice rose as if he had accused her of murder. "He left. He always ran around on me. I wasn't surprised. I just thought he would have stayed for you." She looked away, at the window.

A punch to the stomach. "I couldn't keep him from straying," Tal said, quiet and soft. "If you couldn't, a son couldn't either."

"I didn't mean that," she said. "I had never seen him as happy as the day you were born, 'I've got a boy' was what he said. The nurse put you in his arms – a pretty nurse too – and he only had eyes for you. I'll never know why he left."

"What was going on back then? When he left? Was he seeing someone?" Tal hated to dig at that scar, but she's the one who would know.

"Someone? Maybe two or three. Tal, your father couldn't

control his urges. Maybe as he got older, he felt he needed a woman's desire to tell him he was still attractive. He was more vain than any woman you could ever meet."

He leaned forward on the edge of the couch. "How long had he run around?"

"Always," she said. "Before we married, Mrs. Hagy pulled me aside and said that Finn was a playboy. That he wouldn't stay true to me. I just thought she wanted him for her daughter, but I soon realized that he chased after every woman that gave him a sideways glance. God, I wish Connie Hagy had got him. But, then I wouldn't have you." She reached for her cigarettes, hesitated before pulling one out of the pack. "All those boys. I should have gone after Tristan. Maybe I'd be living the high life in Atlanta."

"Uncle Tristan depended on Aunt Diana for everything," Tal said. "Probably still does. She's the one who got the job in Atlanta and he followed. Pawpaw Joe wasn't crazy about Diana, was he?"

"You know, he didn't like her that much, but she took control of Tristan and kept him in line. More than I could do with Finn. Don't idolize your pawpaw. Do you know he said it was my fault that Finn left? Like I could have kept that whorehound at home—"

"Mom. He's still my father." Tal felt she had gone off the edge into a Finn bashing session, which she did from time to time.

She took the cigarette, turned it around as if to inspect its quality, placed it between her lips, clicked her lighter to it, and inhaled. "You're a grown man." She exhaled the smoke. "Toughen up. Your father ran off with some whore. Since he never came back, he either found another one after her or her husband caught up with them."

"Why do you think it would have been a married woman?"

"That's what men do. A single girl will press to get a ring on her finger. A married one is in it for the fun."

"So that's what I tell Grandmaw Roane?"

Kay smiled. "I love your Grandmaw Roane as much as you. She's been good to me after all these years without Finn here. She still refers to me as her daughter-in-law and part of the family. But, she's been around. People tend to think old people are cute and innocent. She knows more than you or I will ever know about Finn. She raised him. She saw the stuff he got into. She's seen a lot in her years. And, I tell you this, Mr. Taliesin MacGuire, Finn MacGuire pushed everyone to their limits in devotion and affection for him. He knew damn well what he could get away with and what he couldn't. Your grandmother knows that too."

"She thinks leaving wasn't something he would do."

With mock surprise, Kay held out her hands as if to surrender. "He was here when we went to bed and gone the next morning. I don't think he was abducted by aliens."

"So you didn't see him leave?"

She sighed and took another hit from her cigarette. Her eyes darted around the room, as if trying to find something calm to land on. "He would get phone calls from time to time. This was before cell phones, so the only way women could reach him was either by calling him at the shop, where his brothers would hear, or calling him at our house, where I would hear. I guess he took most of the calls at the shop. Once in a while a woman would call him at home. If I answered, they'd hang up. If he answered, he'd talk quickly then he'd say he had to go to the store for cigarettes. Be gone for hours."

He could remember his father leaving the house, saying he needed to go to the store. Tal would sometimes ask to ride along, but Finn always found a reason to leave him behind.

"Did he get a phone call that night?"

"Oh yeah." A distant haze filled her eyes. "There were more calls a few weeks before he left. I can't remember what he said about them. Time robs us of those memories, or maybe, it shields us from them. That night, late, the phone rang. I was mostly asleep. The doctor had me on Valium. I think there was a phone call. She must have said the coast was clear. They took off."

His memory wasn't any better. The night didn't even register anymore; just the next morning when he discovered his father was gone. He always wondered why. Why did he leave, and as a child, a son, he wondered what he did wrong to make him go. Kay had stressed, over and over that Finn's desertion wasn't about Tal, but he couldn't believe it. It's never just about the husband and wife. It's about the children too. It's a family after that first child is born. The dynamic never goes back to a couple. Tal wondered if Finn or Kay had ever understood that. "Sometimes I thought I didn't ask to be brought into the world. To be put here and then abandoned."

"No, no," she soothed, as she always tried to do. "You weren't abandoned. I'm always here for you."

Tal understood a son has a special relationship with his mother, but an even deeper one with his father. His father was the man he tried to emulate. The man he wanted to be. *Failure or success, I looked to him, his memory, how would he have reacted to me?* "There are times I'm furious, times I'm devastated, but always empty."

"I know," she said. "I used to feel that way, too. But now, I left that behind."

Never will there be anyone to take his place, Tal thought. He wasn't sure if finding the truth would settle anything in his soul. *Truth? There was another woman who meant more than my mother? Another family that meant more than me?* He shivered and tried to steel himself. *It's not about me.*

"No. It's about nothing else but me," he said. "How could he leave us? How could one man be so self-absorbed?"

Kay kept her eyes down, not meeting his stare. "We have to find a way to cope, let it go. His actions can't control our lives."

But, Tal knew that they did. For Kay never remarrying or having a long-term relationship. She had still been a young woman when Finn left. That shaped her from then on.

Tal had never believed he was deserving of anyone's love. Why work for it, why try to maintain a relationship? They don't last. Those thoughts guided his adult life.

"Why didn't you look for him? Why didn't Pawpaw Joe try to track him down?"

She shrugged. "If a man spends his time with other women and one night disappears, would you go crawling to him? Beg him to come back? Throw all self-respect out? No. To hell with him." Her voice quivered. "I'd had enough. Your Pawpaw Joe was burning mad. Brendan and the other brothers said 'good riddance' to their little brother." A tear streaked her face, and she brushed it away with the back of her hand. "I was afraid that you'd be like him," she said. "Have that wolf in you, sniffing around every woman you see." Kay looked at him, straight in the eyes. "I hope you find someone – female or male – who will keep your interest for a lifetime. I don't know if that's possible. Isn't a lifelong love the biggest myth our parents pass along? Sure, a mother loves her child until the end, like Grandmaw Roane loves Finn and I love you. But a life-long romantic love? That's a myth. Try to find someone to make you happy, but please don't believe the fairy tales. You or he – it's usually the men who roam – will fall out of love. Maybe a girl would be better for you. Just promise me you won't tell her it's forever."

He wasn't sure if he thought love could be forever. He knew few couples who made it work. He wondered how Grandmaw Roane and Pawpaw Joe had lasted as long as they had. Some of the uncles were still married to their original wives, but he couldn't pinpoint one couple that seemed devoted and passionate as newlyweds. No, he knew newlywed passion was fleeting, Long-term affection would be enough.

He stood and went to the kitchen, walking away from his mother still sitting in her chair, cigarette in hand. "You fixing dinner tonight?"

"Shit, I thought you would," she said. "I've been on my feet all day. Call in a pizza."

"None of that franchise crap. How about Bella's? I'll go pick it up."

She came into the kitchen, where Tal had his phone out, searching for the restaurant's number. "Let's just go there. I'll change clothes."

He hadn't had a meal with his mother in a restaurant, even a pizza joint, since Mother's Day.

Chapter Eight

1607 Tsenacommacah (Virginia)

Several of the tribe looked to Thomas as he walked into the longhouse of the chief. Simmering heat baked the land, but oaks shaded the village and the clay shelters. The chief's lodge, cool and dusty, held counseling elders who stood as Thomas bent through the low opening.

Over the years, he had learned the Croatan, Cheraw, Tuscarora, and Catawba languages, but he rarely used his native English except with his son. Thomas feared he would forget it, forget his heritage, his ancestors, in which the natives in the new land held their forbearers in great regard. An ancestor possessed more knowledge than a living man could ever accumulate. His son, William, now fifteen, had grown accustomed to the many dialects from his mother's tribe and the neighboring tribes, plus his father's English. Their chief had renamed William to Willow — once Thomas pointed to the tree that had a similar English name. A tree as a designation was easier to explain than the long tradition of Anglo-Saxon names. As a compromise to his wife and his chief, Thomas called his son Will. His son waited outside the chief's lodge as Thomas discussed the Europeans with the elders.

Thomas didn't believe the rumors passed from one tribe to the next. Or maybe, he admitted to himself, he didn't want to believe. His son wished to see the people who looked like him, and to be completely honest, Thomas wondered if they had finally returned. But, why would they not land at Roanoke? To the north, through the land of the Chowanocs and their Chief Menatonon and then the Weapemeocs and Chief Okisko, the curious tribe members explained to Thomas, a man could travel to the location, maybe rest at the edge of the vast swamp then reach the river by the next day.

"If it is true that Englishmen have returned, they may try to reestablish a settlement," Thomas told the chief and his men in their language. "Englishmen can't survive without the assistance of the tribes. They do not know this land, the climate, the resources, or the politics of our people." He claimed the people of the new world as his own now.

"Many have tried before and failed," agreed the chief. "Could these men be a danger to our people?"

"As we did years ago, they come to create a settlement of their own. Just as with any people, there will be good and bad ones. This land has many gifts that the nations across the sea have depleted. They arrive looking for a better life."

Casphanha, a bearish and curdled man, who maintained a counselor position to the chief, grumbled. "Why welcome them?" he asked, glancing to each man in the circle. "What benefit do they bring to us? Deer, bear, and turkey of the earth, fish of the seas, the Great Spirits only provide a limited amount. Why allow these white men to take our share. And they will." He nodded to Thomas. "No offense to you. You have proven yourself as a valuable hunter and warrior."

Thomas told Casphanha that he appreciated his compliment and that the Europeans would not arrive to take their resources, but to introduce new ways – their ways – that may be beneficial to the local tribes. "I brought ideas from my background that have helped the tribe."

"Not all ways that work for one man will work for another," the chief said. The others in the circle nodded in agreement. "Wahunsenacawh of Powhatan deals with these people in his way. The white men are not skilled hunters. They travel these woods and waterways for many years, searching for gold, silver, valueless things for survival. Casphanha, do not worry about them taking food from the mouths of our families. The white man wants trinkets, the shiny playthings of our children. Thomas, scout them. Take Willow with you. He needs to see his people and have the choice of living with his mother's tribe or going to his father's tribe."

"My tribe is here," Thomas stressed. "Those people are not my tribe. They may look like me, but that is the end of the relation." He harbored a deep hurt from the abandonment of the Roanoke Colony.

"Just the same, Willow deserves the option," the chief said.

They walked the edge of woodlands and crossed meadows. Thomas decided that he and Will would go alone, without another scout. Will had grown up as part of the tribe, despite his Englishman father. The tribe took him and a few others from the evil that wiped out the English colony years before. Some of the Englishmen moved inland, perhaps to find riches or more adventure. What more adventure they could want, thought Thomas, than the misfortune of the colony? But, they moved on, and Thomas stayed. He remained because of Neshinnah, Will's mother and Thomas's partner. He couldn't call Neshinnah his wife because they had not been joined by the Church of England or any Anglican minister, but she was more than a mate to him. She grounded him in a time of distress and confusion. She stood by his side when the tribe worried about keeping a colonist in their presence. She kept Kiwasa and other malevolent spirits from their hut. She gave him a son who embodied the best level-headed characteristics of Thomas with the soul and creativity and beauty of Neshinnah. She was the river to his shore, replenishment and motion to keep him stable and focused.

"Fayther," Will said, walking along side of Thomas. "Do these mon worry you?" He had picked up a mixture of English with his Croatan tongue, creating a dialect that made Thomas smile. "What happened with the colony last time?"

"Bad things." He really didn't want to relive the memories as they ventured toward a new colony. Neshinnah would say the talk would summon the evil of the last colony, the failed colony.

"I am a mon, Fayther. I can understand."

He had told Will the tale of the English establishing Governor White's colony at Roanoke Island and the kindness of Manteo, a chief that had actually travelled back to England with Governor White. But, he had never told him about the winter of 1588.

"With the Governor returned to England," Thomas started the story, "we – the colonists – continued our processes of growing crops, hunting and fishing, and stockpiling for the autumn and winter. On the seashore, storms can create havoc from September through March. The tribes of the coast traded with us and invited us to festivals and celebrations."

Thomas talked of the god Ahone and his lesser gods such as the sun, moon, stars, water, forest, and sky. He had rarely mentioned the Christian religion of his upbringing to Will or to Neshinnah, mainly because he wasn't a devout Christian. But, he had found parallels in Christ and in Ahone; the angels, saints, and apostles resembled the natural world gods of the native tribes; the Old Testament creation story matched the creation legends of the Indians; so much so, that he had reconciled the legends of his childhood religion with the lore of his current family, friends, and tribe. The main difference, and one that he fused into his beliefs, was the concept of rewards and retribution in this life instead of in the afterlife. His tribe believed that all people received penalty or bounty based on their actions throughout the years, some affecting the entire tribe. That belief helped Thomas accept the horror brought about by the heretic of the colony.

"At a feast to appease Kiwasa, the English people expressed their disbelief of a malicious entity that could cause lightning, violent winds, crop blight, or stillbirth. I had argued, that Kiwasa was similar to a Christian demon, that all beliefs had the balance of good and evil, something or someone to blame when horrible events occurred to virtuous people."

Will stopped walking and stared at his father. "Do you mean you do not pay reverence to Kiwasa?" He bowed his head as he said the deity's name.

"I respect Kiwasa as do you," Thomas said. "The religion of England has different names for the gods, and the colonists could not suppose that another believe system could exist in harmony with their own. They knew enough to not offend our hosts. Returning to the village, the English people discussed the feast and the 'false idol' of the tribe. The woods teemed with night sounds – chirps, howls, rustling, buzzing – one noise caught my ear: a constant, near-distance stride. The steps walked with us in the dark. When I concentrated on the rhythm of phantom gait, it faded, but returned as I turned my attention to a companion, staying just under my comprehension in the dark of night."

"Kiwasa followed the Englishmen," Will stated. "He knew of their disbelief."

"I don't think it was Kiwasa himself." Thomas straightened his shoulders as they walked. "Since the time the English had been in contact with the local tribes, we heard warnings of witches and their familiars. From our own Europe, tales of a covenant between witches and wolves circulated for many years, so when the English settlers heard of witches in the New World, they worried that the Old World lore wasn't superstition, but fact. The belief in the supernatural is strong in Europe, although most educated people dismiss it."

"Do you believe, Fayther?"

Thomas glanced into the shadowy woods that bordered the vast swamp. "I do now."

The brush ahead of them stirred with the crinkle of dead leaves and dried grasses, Thomas gripped his son's arm to keep Will from moving forward.

"Caution, boy," he warned. They moved behind a pine, sagging from the summer drought and afternoon heat.

Hunched and lumbering, an animal of rugged dark hair appeared along the edge of the woods. It made no sound except from its crushing through the tall grasses. Round, fat ticks had attached to the beast's ears. The young black bear trudged out into the open field. An arrow wobbled from its back hip – a sorry shot by a hunter too far away. The bear stopped and sniffed.

Thomas became aware of the touch of the breeze on his chest. He and Will crouched downwind of the bear. Not all hunters honored the spirit of the bear. He would never have allowed the bear to wander off wounded. No other creature should suffer at the hand of man.

Will shifted his squat as he pulled an arrow from his buckskin quiver, nocked the arrow, drew back and released. The arrow soared strong, straight, and low. The bear fell. They ran to the dead animal. "Brother Bear, we respect your sacrifice." Will and Thomas dragged the animal to an open incline in the meadow, its head down slope, and began to bleed the animal. The process of field dressing the bear and its meat took more of their time, but they could not leave the bear for waste. Drying the meat held the fastest and easiest way for them to gather the bear meat on their return to the village. Thomas and Will worked their knives swift and precise to thin-strip the meat for drying on a high branch of a creek-side sycamore. They also hung the skin to dry so they could take it back as well. Will wrapped a portion of the bear meat – washed and dried – in a tight swath of buckskin for their supper. A campsite farther along their route would keep them safe from any wolves, cougars, or bobcats that might go for the bear meat during the night.

They walked along the edge of the swamp and then headed west, away from the damp ground and the wildlife it would attract as the sun set. Will gathered wood for the fire and Thomas cleared the area for them to cook the bear meat and rest for the night.

In the twilight, the fire lapped at the meat sizzling on the spit. Will stoked the coals of the fire and rotated the meat. "Before we saw the bear, you talked of witches and the Englishmen."

Not sure if he wanted to follow that tale, Thomas attempted to get Will's mind on the next day and seeing the English ships on the river. "The English and Spanish have been here many times, but not stayed. We were told that our settlement would be moved north. This new settlement sounds to me that the English abandoned Roanoke and her people and decided to try again in a different location. Three ships are what the local tribe reported to come ashore. That should have brought about a hundred men."

"Are they as cautious speaking of witches as you, Fayther?"

He had to chuckle at Will's persistence. "Yes, they probably are." He settled by the fire, and Will pulled the bear meat off the spit and laid each piece on a warm rock by the edge of the fire circle. They had cooked enough for their supper, the next day, and their journey home.

"Aren't witches just evil priests?" Will asked.

"No. They gain power from people's fears as much as from medicine. Ways different from the village or rejection of the customary manners distances a person from the colony or tribe. The person becomes an outsider. Little comfort comes from other people, so the outsider grows more distant and strange to the colony. That is when the minds of the people start rumors and tales of that outlier. Nothing good is mentioned of the strange, only distrust and suspicion. Wary minds create innuendo that births horrors that are not real."

"What tracked the Englishmen back to their village on the island – that night of the Kiwasa feast?"

The dark night pulled in toward their fire, hovering just a few feet from them. The sounds of the nearby swamp hissed and clicked with the burning of the soggy wood thrown on the embers. Crimson sparks rose to meet the night, disappearing into the blackness. The odor of cypress wood and roasted meat permeated the campsite. The smell would attract carnivores from deep within the swamp since the wind had died with the setting sun.

The sparks dancing above the flames appeared as many pairs of demonic eyes to Thomas. "A woman is usually accused of witchcraft, but some men become burdened with that too. A young girl of the village had fascination with the spirits and the strange customs of the local tribes."

"Girls find such wild ideas exciting, more so than real life," Will said. His own experience with young women had jaded him to what he considered frivolous pursuits by his female peers.

"You are not a believer in witches and their familiars?" his father asked.

Will hesitated. "Believer or not, I have respect for others' tenet. The land and sea and the creatures that inhabit them are vast beyond my knowledge. Elders know more than me. I have heard wild tales from an elder or two. What did the young girl of Roanoke do?"

"She begged an outlier from the tribe, a strange woman with her own ways, to share her knowledge of potions and spells. The girl, Kazeiah, longed for the attention of a young man, Daniel. His heart belonged to another. The other girl died from a mysterious illness, suddenly. Daniel mourned for months, even as the colony's food situation grew bleak and the young man had to push himself to harvest and hunt. Kazeiah kept company with the strange woman, and with each return, she changed – physically. Kazeiah's beauty faded, her frame thinned, her skin paled, her dark hair dulled. What I remember most was her eyes," Thomas said. "I thought her pale green eyes made a striking feature for the girl, but as the months continued, Kazeiah's eyes transformed to brown."

"Eyes cannot change color," Will said.

"Daniel continued to ignore Kazeiah. She became furious. The night we walked back from the Kiwasa feast, the footsteps following us belonged to the old strange woman, the mentor of Kazeiah. She was no longer old, but had absorbed the youth and beauty of Kazeiah. She trailed our group until with a great leap she landed on the back of Daniel." Thomas stood up from the fireside. He paced back and forth then looked into the flames. "Her teeth tore into his neck. His life blood gushed across his shoulders and soaked into the sand where he fell. Panic seized the colonists and we ran."

Thomas looked to Will, the light of the campfire flitting across Will's face, brows tight, eyes staring. "Fayther. Go on."

"The tale is difficult to tell because it is as if I experience it again. I saw in the brush, chasing a child, a tawny cat. It was larger than any cat of the area, more like a panther of the far south. As I ran to rescue the child, I found the panther had bested me and had the child in its jaws. I heaved a rock at the creature. It dropped the child and met my eyes with its dull eyes." He stopped again. "This I have never said to anyone, not even your mother. That was not a panther or any type of cat. It was Kazeiah."

"The girl who followed the witch?"

"Yes, her mind had accepted the legend, and her body transformed to become her beliefs." Thomas sat back down by the fire. "The frightful experience rattled the colony. Talk circulated that the young witch Kazeiah took her revenge on Daniel for ignoring her and that the old witch had stolen Kazeiah's beauty and moved farther down the coast where she could start a new existence. Some of the women claimed that they saw Kazeiah in the brush, watching the settlement. Any setback or frustration or mishap became the work of the witch. Blaming another is easier than discovering the cause and remedying it."

Will sat quietly for a moment. "We must look deeper. When a snake bites, it is not evil. He defends himself from a footstep. The young bear did not ask for the arrow. He will charge if hurt. This is the nature of the creatures."

Pleased that Will presented thoughtful understanding, Thomas asked, "For the Europeans at the river, are they attempting a settlement because of their nature?"

"Like you did Fayther?" Will smiled. "Man seeks adventure with new places and experiences. Once the water vessel of knowledge is depleted, it must be refilled. I'm not sure if living among the Englishmen would add to my understanding or hobble me. I thank you for allowing me to make that decision."

Thomas wasn't much older than Will when he boarded the ship to join Governor White's expedition to the New World. He knew the time would come for his son to decide his own path.

Chapter Nine

1959 Abingdon, Virginia

"They don't like me," Finn said and crawled up on his mother's lap.

She leaned back to start the rocking chair. Set on the front porch's uneven flagstone floor, it hick-upped with each rock forward. The setting sun warmed the river stone façade of the old house. "Brothers tease," she said.

"I hate them all."

She moved her hands to his shoulders and faced him to her. "You're saying that because you're upset. Brothers are all you'll have when your daddy and me are gone. They love you. The littlest always gets picked on by his brothers, but just you wait. If any other boy tried to look at you sideways, I bet Oscar or Dylan would knock that boy into next week."

The thought brought a grin. "You think I could get Oscar to punch Dylan?"

"Don't go pitting one brother against another. Did Dylan say something mean to you?"

"He said I was a mangy wolf. I'm not mangy."

"But you're okay with the wolf part?"

"Yep. I want to be a wolf. Then I could rip the head off mean people."

"The good Lord sent me seven boys," she said. "Just like your daddy's momma had."

"That's a lot of boys," Finn said. "Who's your favorite?" He snuggled his head up under her chin like a puppy and wiggled his bottom.

"You are the charmer, my baby."

They rocked and watched the cars drive up and down Lee

Highway. Across the road, Calla Motor Court welcomed travelers to its neat line of buildings with parking spaces outside each. The clientele had waned since the interstate highway had been built, but the owners kept it clean and orderly. Finn almost mentioned to his mother that he'd heard his eldest brother Lionel say that was a good place to go with his girlfriend, but he restrained himself remembering how Lionel had whispered it to Brendan. A secret, it seemed. Something to keep between brothers.

"I don't want you and Daddy to leave me," he said.

"Don't you worry about that," she said. "We plan to be around for a long time, well after you have children and grandchildren of your own."

"Wolves stay together, don't they?"

"A pack," she said, "wolves form a pack."

"Will you be in my pack?" he asked, eyes wide with anticipation.

She laughed and hugged his little body close to her. "I always will be."

Chapter Ten

1970 Washington County, Virginia

The girls could not get enough of the MacGuire brothers as each one made his way through John S. Battle High School. Washington County had not seen such a flow of seven boys, one after the other. Each excelling in one discipline or another. Lionel, the star football quarterback set the stage in the 1960s. Brendan played baseball like he was born with a bat in his hand. Oscar was the scholar. Tristan was the social director. Brian was the class clown and could make any girl giggle right out of her panties. Dylan dribbled the basketball against the other team as if they were nothing but mere wisps of vapor. But, the baby Finn had it all – athleticism, brains, humor, compassion, friendly as a puppy and handsome as Elvis and James Dean combined. He hadn't gone into the hippy stage of the late '60s of bell-bottom jeans and shaggy hair. He entered high school with the coolness of his brothers and their long legacy of achievements to live up to.

Expectations were not lost on Finn. He knew what each teacher or coach wanted of him and he became that. Football season he was the best running back in the county. In the winter, he learned from Dylan to get the basketball down the court by passing to the best shooters. Spring brought baseball and track, and Finn mastered both. His speed and long legs took him through the hurdles in record-breaking time, times still not broken in Washington County. That same speed helped him round the bases of the baseball diamond quickly. Even if he wasn't the best hitter, he could steal a base like he stole hearts.

Hearts...Of all the brothers, Finn was the heart-breaker. Not that he intended to move from one girl to the next, but, hell, there were so many flavors out there. He couldn't help his wandering eye. His sophomore year, his eye fell on a girl he'd known all through school, but for some reason at fifteen, she had blossomed.

"Joyce," he called across the hallway. "Wait up." He jogged over to her locker. His jeans, sneakers, and white starched shirt – that Joyce knew his mother required all the MacGuire boys to wear to school – looked old-fashioned to her. She had her beginning of the school year wardrobe from Parks-Belk that included her new miniskirt, as mini as the principal would allow the girls to go, but nothing as short as girls wore on television. Her development in the bust area had taken some time, but this was her year. Her green paisley peasant blouse swirled its design in all the right places as if the pattern circled her breasts.

"Finn, what can I do for you?" She slammed her locker shut and walked toward the science hallway where she had her biology class.

He took her book and notebook from her hand. "Let me help you with those."

"You never offered to carry my books, not since all the time we've been in school – all the way back to kindergarten."

"Gee, Joyce, you used to make McDonald hamburgers out of Play-dough and eat them. That was too much for a boy of five to handle, no matter how pretty you were. Of course, now without the Play-dough, you're downright beautiful."

She laughed. "That's an odd compliment, but I'll take what I can get from you, Finn MacCool. These days I prefer real hamburgers. What about us going to Bristol to get one after school?" With him finally paying attention to her, she wanted to keep it going.

"The Hi-Lo Burger is about all I can do since I have to get home to help with chores." They arrived at her classroom. "You still hanging out with Roger or is that over?"

"Now why would you think Roger and I were over?"

"He's not carrying your biology book, I am."

Soon, Joyce had Finn toting her books between classes and sitting with her at the cafeteria at lunch. His brothers Brian (a senior) and Dylan (a junior) would sit with them sometimes and their girlfriends were friendly to her. It was a big deal for a sophomore girl to have junior and senior cheerleaders sitting with her at the same lunch table.

Wanda, the smartest girl in their class, walked by the table, and Joyce said hello to her. "Wanda's my biology class partner," Joyce told Finn.

"Boy oh boy," Finn said. "You got lucky. I'm stuck with Jeep." The biology of motors was Jeep's specialty, who spent his time in the machine shop and only took sophomore biology because the state of Virginia required it.

Although Wanda was cute, in Joyce's opinion, she could be really pretty if she would wear fashionable clothes and a little make-up. Wanda was the president of the 4-H club and wore a lot of blue jeans and gingham shirts — like Elly May Clampett on the "Beverly Hillbillies" television show. Joyce and Wanda both held officer positions in the Tri-Hi-Y club, sponsored by the Bristol YMCA.

Just as she was thinking of asking Wanda to go with her next time she went to Lerner's in downtown Bristol, Brian's girlfriend, Tina, slapped him and stormed away from the table.

"What?" Brain asked the rest of the table and grinned. "I just asked to feel her pom poms. What's wrong with that?"

Dylan's girlfriend Joanne, the other cheerleader at the table, stood up with her tray in her hand and her nose in the air. "You boys think it's funny to tease us. Well, it's not."

"Hey, don't run off from me because Brian's being a jerk," Dylan said and ran his hand along her arm. She melted to his touch and sat back down.

"You boys are so immature," Joanne said with a pout.

"What's this 'you boys' stuff?" Finn began. "I'm not immature."

Brain leaned over and kissed Finn's cheek. "No, he's our baby brother."

Joyce laughed, but could see Finn's face blush and guessed he was furious that Brian had mocked him in front of the girls. Joyce reached over and took Finn's hand.

His eyes shifted to her, and he smiled. "Let's go to class," he said. He grabbed their books and papers, then led her out the cafeteria's side door and around to the back of the gym.

They walked in the opposite direction of the classrooms. She didn't hesitate, but followed Finn, her hand in his.

He leaned against the brick wall, out of sight of the school's windows and the prying eyes of the faculty and students. The books and papers fell to the pavement like fluttering leaves. He pulled her around to face him, his hands rested on her hips, hers on his shoulders.

Neither said a word.

His eyes held to hers, not quite a stare, but she could tell he had nothing but her on his mind at that moment. She became aware of her own breathing, increasing in speed. Her chest fluttered and her head felt light. His firm grip on her hips pulled her to his body. The cotton fabric of his trousers pressed against her, the satin of her panties slipped to the side as Finn rubbed against her, manipulating her breathing and thoughts.

His right hand slid down her hip to her skirt hem. The touch of his palm on her bare thigh shocked her just as if he had touched a live wire to her skin.

His eyes never wavered from hers.

Trying to speak, she found her throat dry and no sound came. Joyce leaned in to kiss Finn, put he pulled back his head and rushed his hand up and under her panties.

"Oh, God." Joyce almost lost her balance.

Finn leaned into her; his tongue traced the side of her neck and to her earlobe. She felt like she'd lost control of her body as her head tilted to his nibble.

His lips found her mouth. Searing heat moved up her body from his fingers. His hips rocked against her.

The rush of his breath snorted out of his nose. He huffed.

The urge to laugh caught Joyce. The spell had broken as she associated the snort with a bull ready to mount a cow. But she knew not to laugh at Finn's passion. He continued to grind his erection against her, his hand still in her underwear. "Hold on," she whispered into his ear.

"What?" he asked in a voice low and rough like gravel.

"I…I don't want this to happen behind the gym."

He stopped and his hand came out from under her skirt. "You want it to happen?"

"Eventually, just not between lunch and Algebra." She smoothed down his hair and kissed him, then straightened her skirt and blouse.

Finn pulled his comb from his back pocket and stroked his hair back into place. "Are we going together?"

"I think you're supposed to ask me," she said.

He straightened up and tucked his shirt in his pants where it'd pulled loose. "Will you be my girlfriend?"

"Yes. Now and forever." She saw Finn not as he stood there as a fifteen year old young man, but as the little boy she'd grown up with, the boy she had seen mature. The physical part that they'd fumbled into wasn't her goal. She loved Finn. He had been her match since the first days of school. The MacGuire family seemed as much hers as her own, knowing all the brothers and Mr. and Mrs. MacGuire from their volunteering at school events.

The sharp trill of the bell signaled the change of classes. He gathered up their books, and they snuck back into the school through the back door of the gymnasium. Her hand clasped his, and she felt different. His touch, to a place no one had caressed, altered her attitude of herself and him. The childishness of yesterday vanished. The concerns about the heartthrobs on television and magazines lost all meaning. The social cliques, the cheerleaders, the football team, the teachers, her classes, and even her grades, didn't have any relevance to her future. She wanted to be alone with Finn, to explore what God and nature had given them in each other.

He stopped walking and pulled her to him. They had arrived at her Algebra classroom, hovering at the doorway. He kissed her cheek, handed her Algebra book and notebook to her. The MacGuire boys didn't slobber all over their girls in public like some of the country boys did. "Hi-Lo burger after football practice?"

"I'll wait at the bleachers."

She saw him walking up from the field house, gym bag swinging from his hand. She twisted the ring on her finger, hoping she wouldn't scare him off with her token of affection. His smile gave him a spring in his step.

"Hey ya, Joyce," he said and dropped his gym bag at his feet. He reached out to take her hands then leaned in and kissed her on the mouth. She shivered.

"Good practice?" she asked.

"Sure. You hungry? We can go to the Hi-Lo with Brian and Tina." He started to lead her to the parking lot.

"Hold on a second," she said. "I've been thinking about you all afternoon." She let go of his hand and pulled the ring off her finger. "I want you to have this."

"Oh, wow. It's an Irish Claddagh." He tried to slip it on his ring finger, but it didn't fit. He moved it to his pinky. "I'll get a chain and wear it around my neck, so it hangs close to my heart."

"I just wanted you to have something of mine."

"From me to you," he said and bent down on one knee holding her hand, "I give you my love and loyalty and friendship, just as the rings says. I will love only you – for my entire life." Tears welled in his eyes. "I mean it."

She couldn't keep her tears from flowing. "I pledge the same to you."

"Our secret marriage," he said, standing up and wrapping her in his arms. "Always me and you."

Chapter Eleven

"**C**harlottesville is diverse enough to test each module," Clio's manager, Doug Williams, a thin and cramped man in his mid-forties, said, pacing Clio's office in his tightly-wound way. "They're close, so our techs can drive up to tweak the system as we need to."

"I'm not sure any hospital likes the words 'tweak the system' when they rely on it for patient data." She watched as he took three steps then held his foot slightly off the ground as if trying to decide if he should pace the return route or just stand still – he always retraced the steps to the other side of her small office. His turn was just an odd hesitation, like he was out of sync with normal walking or that his thinking stalled his physical movements.

"You should develop a good relationship with the C.O.O." he said.

"Not sure the operations side gets that much say in it. We need a higher power," she said and thought for a moment. "The chief medical officer, Ted Mears, would be the man."

Doug's face tensed into a jackal-like grin. "A man. You can charm him, Clio."

"I'm not pulling a Jesse," she said of her friend's past exploits with the software decision makers at her accounts. When Jesse flirted with the older male management of a medical organization, she had come close to overstepping the consultant/client boundary of professionalism, at least in Cliodhna's mind.

"I'm not asking you to fuck the guy," Doug said without any sign of joking. "Just use your sales skills – whatever that entails."

She hated the concept of sales. Pushing someone to buy wasn't her method, though she knew plenty of successful representatives who did just that. But, for Cliodhna, she talked with potential clients to learn their challenges, to see if her company's offerings met those dilemmas and helped solve their problem. She wasn't always the highest in sales volume, but she placed at the top of long-term relationships with customers.

Watching Doug pace and talk, his wiry body and coyote-hunch, she remembered how he had always yapped about opportunity, when to jump on it, when to scavenge from other vendors. She ignored his yammering.

Treating customers as partners worked well for her – in business. But, in her personal life, she had long ago been accused of being too needy, too motherly, too controlling. So far Devin had not succumbed to that curse. If anything, for the past six years, she had consciously avoided the possibility of getting emotionally intimate with Devin. So far, it seemed to work.

"And, I need you to sign this hospital," Doug said and stopped directly in front of her desk. "I know this was Leslie's client; she sold them; she implemented the software. But she screwed up. She didn't have everyone on-board. There's a bitch of a red-headed doctor there who hates anything that smells of automation. Dr. MacGuire is her name. She's not that high up in the hierarchy, but she's vocal and apparently somebody likes her enough that she can cause waves without getting the boot. Have you met her?"

"No. Did this Dr. MacGuire get Leslie fired?" Clio asked. Leslie had left the company less than a month earlier. She didn't take the time to transition the account to anyone else. Now, Doug was pushing it on Clio.

"No, but MacGuire was a thorn in her side the whole time."

"I hate taking over a troubled client, but the company needs me to do this," she added. She had already agreed to adopt the account. Her style might work for them. Leslie had been all talk and no follow-through.

He sighed. "You're a trouper," he said with a bit of a sarcastic tinge. "By the way, Clio, you seem a little tired. Are you getting enough rest? Just concerned." He left her office without waiting for an answer.

At the hotel in Charlottesville, Clio unpacked her suits and checked her iPad for her schedule the following day. She tapped out answers to several e-mails, then called Devin to let him know she had arrived safely.

"Ready for the big day?" he asked.

She could hear the traffic hum in the background of the call – he must have been on Interstate 95 heading home. "Yes. I still have some white papers to read about the hospital, but I have copies of their strategic planning document and the comprehensive plan for the next five years. This makes good sense for the hospital."

"Don't have to convince me," he said. "I'm rooting for you. Hey, I could be up there in about an hour. Will you let me take you to dinner?"

"Thanks, but no. I have some more homework to do before tomorrow and that's why I booked the room instead of driving back and forth. I need to check in with all shifts to make sure the medical staff gets the benefits of the software."

"All work and no play –" he started.

"Yeah, I know. But I want to show Doug my way works as well as the high-pressure sales model that he pushes. Besides, I think he gave this to me so I would fail. He would like to get me out."

"Well," Devin said, "if you left that stressful job, you could move in with me and have the resources to take a job that's more fun and less pressured."

She massaged her temple with one hand. "I like this job." She had told him over and over that she didn't feel like moving into his house. He hadn't mentioned marriage, just moving in. She wasn't sure that either option was that attractive to her. Marriage seemed frightening and restrictive. Living together seemed less restrictive, but it was a step she wasn't sure she wanted to make. She felt as awkward as she did with Doug's gawky office pacing. "I'll call you tomorrow."

She disconnected the call and set her cell phone on the desk then picked up the pages to read more about the client she had to meet the next day. The words seemed to meld together in front of her eyes, and Devin kept invading her thoughts.

The morning sun streamed through the hotel window as Cliodhna watched it rise over downtown Charlottesville. Her mental preparation had begun with yoga and ended with a quick rundown of the news from the local morning show on television. She wanted to be in the hospital as the 7:00 a.m. shift arrived.

Traffic, compared to Richmond, was kind, and she arrived at the hospital by 6:45. A cup of coffee from the cafeteria in hand, Clio found a chair in the lobby and watched the shift change.

Nurses and interns scurried to and from the elevators. The doctors strode across the floor as if the hospital would bend to their schedules. None hurried, at least not in the public areas.

Patients' families, looking like pioneers who had just crossed the mountain range, collapsed into couches and chairs, some trying to sneak in some sleep before returning to their loved-ones' rooms.

Clio couldn't imagine working in a hospital with sickness and death a daily occurrence, grieving families, frustrated nurses, disconnected doctors. When she stopped to try to take in the full scope of her surroundings, depression crept in. She couldn't process the collective fear and misery. She took another sip of her coffee, and comfort rose from the heat and sweetness.

The elevator delivered her to the administration floor where Chief Medical Officer Ted Mears watched over the hospital from his corner office. The receptionist asked her to wait while she checked to make sure Ted was available. Clio studied the oil painting on the opposite wall. The Shenandoah Valley spread across the canvas in the delicate greens of early spring, the rising sun illuminating the soft ridges with a creamy lemon hue. She knew that mountain paintings usually depicted the colorful autumn, but appreciated the choice of beginnings instead of endings for the hospital's decor.

"Clio Fitz-Adams?" Ted Mears asked, as he emerged from his

office with his receptionist a step behind.

She introduced herself, and they exchanged the usual pleasantries as they entered his office and took a seat at a round conference table. She sat facing a window and could see the hospital parking lot and past it, Thomas Jefferson's home, Monticello, on a distant hill.

"I have to be blunt," Ted started. "When Leslie implemented this, we thought it was a time-saver and a way to achieve consistency from the staff doctors and nurses. Some of the staff love it. Some don't and refuse to use it."

She smiled. "Our software delivers the best results when everyone inputs their patient information. The great part is that a young doctor can access the knowledge of his or her more experienced colleagues on an as-needed basis. For example, if my mother came into the emergency room and her regular doctor was out of town, the attending physician could view her records, enter her symptoms, and the system would cross-check her medications and search the entire database for recommendations from this hospital's staff and others in the system."

"I know," he said and sat back in his chair. "But, some doctors see this as taking away their diagnosis training and skills. 'Automation of the doctor' is what I hear."

"Think what would have happened," she said, "if this had been around when AIDS first appeared or the avian influenza or even back in history to the 1918 flu pandemic. The CDC has information, but we take that and winnow it down to localized and specialized data."

"You don't have to convince me," he said. "I'm on-board."

Clio felt tension drain from her body.

"But, I need your help with the staff. Doctors are a special breed."

"Once the benefits are accurately described, people see the usefulness. Within a few months, many clients say they can't imagine life without it." Clio looked out to Jefferson's home on the hill. "There are formal organizational structures and informal ones. Who is your informal thought-leader for the skeptics?"

Dr. Mears laughed. "That's easy: Dr. Brigid MacGuire. She's a great doctor but is headstrong and stubborn. She has a fan club here, which includes the chairman of the hospital board."

The challenge of winning over this doctor appealed to Clio, especially since it wasn't a man. Doug would imply she had used something other than professionalism to sway a male doctor, but a female doctor had demands as well. She understood that winning a woman's trust was more complicated.

"When can I meet Dr. MacGuire?" she asked.

He scooted his chair back and leaned forward, elbows on the conference table. "She's a bitch when she wants to be."

Not sure if Dr. Mears was being sexist, Clio ignored the word. "Nonetheless, I need to talk with her one-on-one to address her concerns. You said yourself that all the staff needs to be behind this. It sounds like Dr. MacGuire can bring her contingent when she converts to our side."

"Okay," he said. "I understand the business jargon. You want her buy-in to strengthen our core competency and empower our associates without her feeling like she's had to drink the Kool-Aid. To be frank, it's all bullshit."

She exhaled without thinking. "Yes. We need to be frank with her and with you. I doubt she's a bitch any more than I think you are a bastard, but I can make this happen with you backing me up."

He laughed. "I am an old bastard. You got it. I'll do what I can — short of firing her — to get this software running." Dr. Mears stood and offered his handshake across the table. "Now make this happen or we'll pull the whole damn system out and go with your competitor."

She knew he wasn't joking about aborting the installation. Rumors that Charlottesville would dump the software had spread all over the office in Richmond. She bet Doug used this to test her.

Dr. MacGuire's office loomed at the end of a hallway. Clio could see the open doorway and a man leaning against the doorjamb. Not wanting to interrupt, she stopped, found a chair in an alcove and re-read her notes.

A laugh bounced down the hall. A woman's laugh that sounded joyous and uninhibited. This can't be the bitch doctor, Clio thought.

"Tonight," the man said, "I'll meet you at Fellini's." He turned, and until he looked Clio in the eyes, she hadn't been aware she was staring. "Hey," he said as he passed her chair.

"Hey," she managed to get out before he left through the stairwell door.

Maybe a few years younger than her, the man had a handsome face with a strong chin and a confidence that, even though his plaid shirt and jeans didn't fit in with the hospital surroundings, he strutted with the certainty of a man who owned the building. Surely, he did not, she thought, but he wasn't intimated by the doctors' white coats or scrubs. Something about him appealed to her. A glimpse, the plaid shirt and jeans, and, oh yes, the scuffed cowboy boots maybe that had been it. Her history with men usually meant she could concoct a fantasy man from the disparate ingredients she could capture from a split second glance. The remembered features, she knew, she couldn't count on. She might fill in the blanks of her memory with a movie idol's dimples or a rock star's snug-fitting pants or a jogger's boyish waist.

"Back on subject," she muttered to herself and stuffed her notebook into her brief case. She approached Dr. MacGuire's door. The woman typed on the computer with her back to Clio.

"Dr. MacGuire?" Clio asked as she knocked on the door frame to get her attention.

"Yes?" the doctor said and turned toward Clio.

True, the doctor's hair was a blaze of auburn, red, and copper with natural curl that framed her pale face. "The bitch of a red-headed doctor" that Doug had warned her about. Clio recognized the Irish heritage, much more showed in this woman than in Clio's own features. Her eyes showed charm and warmth, but with impatience.

"I'm Clio Fitz-Adams with—"

"Oh, yes, the software wench from Richmond," Dr. MacGuire said without a hint of a smile.

A few beats passed before Clio could decide how to respond.

"And you're the bane of progress."

"Ha! If only… 'What can I do to make your life easier?'" she mocked and stood up from her chair. "That's what your predecessor asked me."

"That would have been Leslie, and she would have asked that stupid question." Clio knew she couldn't try any bullshit, not that she would have. Dr. MacGuire would throw it back at her before she finished a sentence. "I want to know what you can do to make my life easier."

"Funny. What's Mears busting your tits over?"

"You. Apparently, you hold a significant sway over hospital operations."

She stood and leaned over her desk then jerked her chin for Clio to come closer. "They're scared shitless of me," she whispered. "It's taken me years to get the men in this hospital to respect my opinions and take my ideas to heart. So anytime some stupid girl walks into this building and tries to use her perky tits to persuade the men to do things her way — well, that offends me. I'll slam her Victoria's Secret clad ass to the sidewalk before she knows what hit her."

Clio straightened up, then sat in the chair opposite the desk. "Is that what you did to Leslie?"

"Yes." Dr. MacGuire took her seat again.

"Was Leslie the reason you're fighting the implementation?"

She stretched back in her chair. "No. I see what the advantages are. I'm an intelligent person, and believe me, open-minded, but I don't like sheep. I'm not a follower. The other girl didn't even attempt to listen to my concerns or questions because, I guess, my lack of a penis."

"Is the culture here that sexist?" Clio had to ask because Dr. MacGuire obsessed over male versus female control.

She sighed and shook her head as if too tired to breach the subject. "I have work to finish before my morning rounds. Thanks for stopping in to introduce yourself." Dr. MacGuire stood again.

Clio pulled out her business card and handed it to the doctor. "Call my cell, please, when you have a few minutes so we can talk about the implementation and your questions. I'm meeting with the database administrator, but after lunch I'm flexible."

By six o'clock that evening, Clio had not heard from Dr. MacGuire. She decided to try another approach.

The building tucked at the end of the block had open windows to the street, and music flowed out from a piano in the corner of its front room. Clio settled at the small bar just inside the door and looked around for Dr. MacGuire and her male friend. She knew eavesdropping on their plans, and then showing up at Fellini's, wasn't the most professional way to handle her job, but it was all she had at the moment. Plus, the guy had stayed on her mind throughout the day. That's the doctor's boyfriend, she told herself, so get over the crush you've brewed in your fantasies.

The smooth bar top gleamed under the dim lights, and Clio tapped her nails to the jazzy tune from the piano player as she waited for the bartender to finish with another customer. Thinking it a good idea to change out of her business suit, Clio had opted for jeans and the royal blue silk blouse she'd worn with the suit earlier that day — she hadn't packed for socializing.

The young female bartender, probably a university student, smiled and asked for her order. Clio began to order a white wine, but thought Dr. MacGuire would think it was a typical female drink, changed her mind and asked for a Devil's Backbone Vienna Lager. "Have you seen a woman about my age with red, wavy hair about to her shoulders?" she asked the bartender.

"Dr. Brigid MacGuire? She's a regular, but I haven't seen her yet this evening. I love her hair, wish mine had that wave to it."

The bartender's short, thick, blond hair looked cool in her choppy cut. Clio had left her dark hair loose because she thought a bun would make her look too old, a ponytail would make her look as if she were trying too hard to look young. Sometimes she realized being a forty year old woman equated to too old to be cute and too young to be refined.

"A Devil's Backbone lager, please," a male voice said from behind her.

She turned to see the man from Dr. MacGuire's office. "Well, hey," she said and smiled.

"Ah, you're the girl from the hospital hallway," he said and pulled out the stool next to her and sat down. "Tal MacGuire," he introduced himself with a nod.

"Dr. MacGuire's husband?"

"Brigid? Hell no." He laughed. "She's my cousin. You work with Brigid?"

"In a way," she said.

He waited as if she would continue, but she held out for a little mystery.

"You're Dr. MacGuire's cousin."

"Call her Brigid. I can't call her doctor, and it sounds weird when I hear anyone else say it. Maybe it's because she's done some very un-doctorly things over her lifetime."

"Really? Like what?" Clio sipped her beer just as the bartender brought Tal his beer.

"Hey now, I told you my name. What's yours?"

"Clio." She lifted her glass to toast him. "Cheers, Mr. MacGuire. Or are you a doctor too?"

"Shit," he said drawing it out into multiple syllables. "I've played doctor, but never been paid for it."

Was he flirting with her? she wondered. Okay, he's not exactly as smooth as most men, but he's funny in a boyish way.

"So, you live around here?" he asked.

Definitely not a smooth operator. "No, Tal. I'm here for work."

"You a hooker?" he asked too loud. The bartender looked over at them.

She grabbed his arm and dug her nails in. "No. I can't believe you would ask something like that."

He grimaced at her grip and pulled her hand from his sleeve. "Can't know unless you ask. Besides, most women don't strike up a conversation in a bar unless they want something from you. What do you want from me, Clio — if that's your real name?" he added in a film noir / Humphrey Bogart imitation.

She laughed. "You're a nut. I'm in software sales and here to oversee an installation at the hospital. Geez, a woman can't even talk to a man without him thinking she's a prostitute."

"Can't sell what you can't give away," Dr. MacGuire said as she walked up behind them. "Besides, Talie thinks everyone wants him. What a coincidence to find you here." She took the stool on the other side of Clio, who was now sandwiched between them. "What are we drinking?"

The bartender set a scotch in front of Brigid.

She picked it up, swirled it in the glass, sniffed and sipped. "Ah."

"I'm staying at the Omni," Clio said, "and wandered down the street looking for a place for a drink and dinner."

Brigid cocked her head at Clio. "That's the official story?"

"Do you have to travel much?" she answered the doctor's question with her own question.

"No, not often. I like being at home, got my routines, got my friends, got my scotch." She raised her glass to Clio. "Do you like to be on the road?"

"Hate it. I eat alone in restaurants too much."

"Then this is your lucky night," Tal said. "You're going to have dinner with us, and Brigid is buying."

"You're a big spender with my money," Brigid said to Tal then looked to Clio. "Sure, join us, but no talk about software or hospitals."

Clio didn't mind avoiding work discussions. Relationship building meant more than sealing a commitment from the doctor, and from what she understood of Dr. Brigid MacGuire, she needed to trust a person more than any kind of technology. "No work-talk," Clio promised.

A waiter ushered them to a table in the corner, apparently the usual spot for Dr. MacGuire's dining. Low lights, soulful jazz, and a waft of basil and oregano and garlic set the mood for an intimate dinner for – three. Clio laughed in spite of trying to repress it.

"What's funny?" Brigid asked. She settled into a chair against the wall. Tal sat next to her.

Clio chose to sit next to him instead of the other side of Brigid. "Just thinking about this being a romantic place."

"Romance is where you look for it," Tal said. "A roller derby rink can be romantic if you're in the right mood."

She felt her face warm with a blush. He was a charmer.

"So, Clio," Brigid broke the settled silence. "What is it you do for fun in Richmond?" She took a sip of her scotch.

"Richmond is work, but I find time to go out with friends. I really love going to the Outer Banks."

"You fish?" Taliesin asked.

"I have gone a few times on a deep-sea fishing excursion, but it takes the whole day. I'd rather relax with a drink by the Currituck Sound, maybe do a little shopping in Duck or Corolla. Are you a fisherman?"

"I fish from time to time at South Holston Lake down near Bristol."

"But what Tal really likes is playing in his band," Brigid added. "Tell her about your music."

He seemed shy all of a sudden. His fingers bent the corner of his menu, and he tilted his head as if to shrug it off. "Yeah. Got a little band with some buddies. We play around Bristol and Johnson City, sometimes we go up to Boone or Blowing Rock."

"He's checking out some of the places here for gigs – just him and his guitar, not the whole group." Brigid's enthusiasm for her cousin's music impressed Clio. This was the first subject that genuinely brought out anything close to delight that she had witnessed in the doctor. Maybe, Clio thought, Brigid MacGuire wasn't the hard-ass she veiled herself as.

"Tal, do you perform your own songs?" she asked.

He twisted his beer glass a couple of times. "Most people want to hear songs they know. The band does mostly covers of popular songs. Alone, I like to do some James Taylor, Paul Simon, Lindsey

Buckingham, Dave Loggins – do you remember Dave Loggins? He was from the Bristol area, Mountain City, Tennessee, I think. I like performing the old stuff. Things our fathers listened to in the 1970s."

"You and Dr. MacGuire –"

"Brigid," she corrected Clio.

"You and Brigid, of course would have fathers that are brothers because of the last name," she said and felt like the beer was slowing her thinking.

They both laughed. "Yep, that would be the MacGuire boys of southwest Virginia," Brigid said.

"Seven boys drove Grandmaw Roane crazy with their fussing and fighting," Tal added.

The thought made her happy and envious. "Sounds wonderful. I have no brothers or sisters, just me and my mom. Dad left years ago."

"Mine too," Tal said. He finished off his beer and signaled across the room to the bartender to send over another. "I guess the thought of raising a family can be scary to some men."

She must have been staring at him, because he straightened up and put his hand over his heart. "Me?" he said. "I'm not scared of family life, just haven't found the right person to settle down with."

A laugh erupted from Brigid. "Shit, Tal. You and I will never marry. No one can put up with us." She looked over to Clio. "I love men, but I can't live with one. Not yet, anyway." Clio hadn't really looked closely at Brigid. Her radiant auburn hair fell in soft waves around her face, her smooth skin reflected the soft light, her eyes sparked with intelligence.

Tal leaned against her shoulder. "Wait a minute. Are you thinking of veering off the career track? Is there a hot intern that's got you reconsidering your old maid status? You found a looker at that hospital?"

"Uncle Finn, Tal's daddy," she said and nodded to Clio, "was the looker of the boys. I was sixteen when he left. Finn was the one all the ladies loved."

"That's for sure. Momma can attest to him being the horn-dog of Bristol," Tal said.

"How old were you when he left?" Clio asked him.

He thought for a moment. "Guess I was about ten. I remember him well – you know little kid stuff about him. He smelled like the machine shop, oil and metal shavings, and cigarettes. He ate a package of peanut butter crackers with a Coca-Cola for lunch each day. He didn't like air conditioning. He whistled a lot."

Clio's eyes welled with tears, as she heard the details of the man who was so important to Tal, and she thought of how little she remembered of her own father. Her mother had never spoken of her father after he left. Clio had been eleven and filled with the drama of a young girl. She imagined that her father had been murdered by some assassin on a mission from the Soviet Union. But the reality was that her father worked in the Newport News Shipyard, until one day he didn't. He seemed to cease to exist – in her life, in her mother's, and in all aspects around them. Her mother didn't call the police or cause a fuss over him leaving, from what Clio could remember, but acted as if the abandonment was expected.

At eleven, on the edge of young womanhood, Clio had needed her father's guidance to ask about boys and life in general. He was not much of a talker, but when she was younger, he would hold her in his arms and hum some tune that she hadn't heard since – a slow lullaby, almost a psalm in her memory, full of sadness and longing, or maybe she had added those emotions to her recollection after he left them. Her advice about life came from her mother, full of distrust, scorn, disillusionment of the way life treated women. No man was to be relied on. To achieve goals, her mother had taught her, use the needs of one man against the needs of another. Become the prize for the victor.

By the time she left for college, she dropped the princess-in-distress model that her mother advocated, and Clio became an independent, need-no-one woman. She knew she wasn't as aloof as Dr. MacGuire. But she could survive on her own without Devin. Want was the opposite of need – she wanted Devin; she certainly didn't need him.

"What about your dad?" Tal asked her. "What do you remember about him?"

She thought about how much to say, to edit what was in her heart about her father, to simply mention him as a shadow of her youth. "He worked in the shipyard and wasn't home that much. I guess he and my mom never really got along. I can't remember them touching – no hand holding, no hugs, no leaning into each other. I understand now why I'm an only child." She managed a smile.

Brigid stared at her scotch. Tal traced his index finger down the side of his beer glass.

"I wonder," Clio began, "if we become our parents or rebel against what they were?" Shit, she thought, where'd that come from?

Brigid finished her scotch. "A little of both, for me. I like to think I took the best aspects of my dad and mom. Right, Talie?"

"You certainly got Uncle Brendan's ornery ways and Aunt Charlotte's persnickety habits. I'd say you got the worst of each."

"Bitch," she shot back at him. "As the only one at the table with a doctorate, I think I managed fairly well."

Clio noted Brigid's need for recognition of her achievements. Apparently the successes in her life were to be celebrated, while challenges were buds of triumph waiting to bloom. "Yes, you have my admiration," she said and realized she sounded too flattering to be authentic – especially for someone she wanted on her side for the software implementation. Best not to sound artificial. "I wish I had continued my education. But, an MBA isn't appealing to me. I'm not even sure I want to stay in this business until I reach retirement age."

"When you love what you do, there's no such thing as retirement," Tal said. "I couldn't imagine not singing or writing songs. If no one wanted to hear me, I'd head into the mountains and sing to myself and the squirrels. I'll do it until they plant me up at Forest Hills cemetery."

The waiter brought Tal another beer and another scotch for

Brigid then they ordered their dinners. The evening progressed with tales and laughter, a comfortable camaraderie that Clio hadn't experienced since her undergraduate days. At the end of the night, Tal and Brigid walked her back to the hotel. To Clio's surprise, Brigid hugged her good-night and Tal kissed her cheek, like a brother. Not that she had developed any romantic intentions on him, but she hadn't written him off as a buddy.

Not sure how to approach Dr. MacGuire the next morning, Clio decided to walk by her office to say hello on her way to meeting with the technicians in the hospital's Information Technology center.

"Thanks again for dinner and drinks last night," she said, just leaning into Brigid's office from the doorway.

Dr. MacGuire balanced charts on stacks of medical journals, reports, and other medical charts scattered across her desk. "You're welcome. That computer program," she started and nodded her head at the piles of paper on her desk, her auburn hair falling into her eyes, "can it reduce some of this mess?"

"That's the goal," Clio said, trying to keep her grin subdued.

"Let's talk later so I can learn some more about it. Don't tell Mears I'm jumping on the train… I just want to see if this system can make our work more productive. I'm drowning in paper."

"Call my cell when you have a few minutes, and I'll come back to show you some screens."

She left for the ground floor datacenter smiling. The evening before had allowed them to see each other as full individuals, not just people with different views on a solitary subject. Honestly, she had to admit that she liked Dr. MacGuire. Most of her girlfriends worried too much about superficial things like wrinkles and gray hair and dating, so the possibility of talking to someone about deeper subjects, real emotions, felt like relief, as if she had graduated from a high school clique.

Chapter Twelve

Summer 1708 – James Cittie Shire, Virginia Colony

The scratch of footfalls followed Anna Mayford. Not quick and jerky like a squirrel or slow and careful like a deer, but these steps crunched the forest floor's dead leaves with a regular rhythm. The repaired iron spit, hanging from a string on her shoulder, knocked against her hip in its own beat, in the pulse of her stride. Her hand found the long handle and brought the iron skewer to attention in front of her. Anna didn't want to stop or turn around to search for the accompanying movement in case a neighbor or child happened to be going in the same direction as her – she would feel foolish if someone innocent saw her swing around the roasting spit like a weapon. But, a shroud of apprehension enveloped her like the late summer humidity.

Maybe, she reckoned, the accusation of Parnella Hart had distressed her. The mind can conjure worry where there should be none.

She stopped and the pursuing steps ceased.

"You are being foolish," she whispered to herself. Why she spoke low these words of self-advocacy she didn't know, but the faint volume of her own voice undermined the content of the statement. A deep breath and she turned.

No one in sight. She watched for movement between the tree trunks and low branches that lined the path. She listened for rustling in the dried leaves, for the scamper of squirrels, for the jabber of jays, or the rumble of the darkening sky. Not a cardinal chirped.

Silence.

"I must arrive home before the storm. My son is working in the fields and needs his supper prepared." She turned and continued on her way.

"Hoo, hoo, hoooo" floated through the trees.

She laughed and stopped. "Thistle!"

"Ji-hen-yah," Thistle revealed himself from behind an ancient red oak. "Ji-hen-yah I have been following you."

"Don't call me 'Sky Witch' because others in town are calling me a witch and they don't find it amusing – like you," Anna said.

Thistle held his arms in the air, looking to the clouds above the swaying treetops. "Sky Witch, you are the woman all other women fear, the woman all men lust for, the woman all Two-Spirits admire." He took the iron spit from her hand. "I will carry this so that you do not spear yourself or me."

"You are in rare form today, Thistle." Anna had known the young brave for several years, first as a friend of her husband, each assisting the other in farming or hunting. They learned what European or Native ways worked best in their farm or village. Then after Edward died, Thistle continued to visit and help her son.

He had blue jay feathers intertwined in his dark hair along with an emerald green silk ribbon Anna had given him. Anna had taught him to braid his hair in the tradition of the Scots and Irish, thin braids on the sides of his face then pulled back to keep the rest of his long hair from getting in his eyes. Gaelic or elfin was what she thought of Thistle's look, only he was dark not blond or amber like the elf folk.

She tried not to think of such things, but the man in front of her caused her heart to race. He reminded her of Edward. The longing for a dead husband cannot be transferred to a friend of his, no matter the amount of feeling she could recapture from being in his presence, a man that spent many hours with her husband and with her and their son. Thistle was lean and tall, a few years younger than Anna, and this being late summer, the young man wore little clothing. The ways of the local native people intrigued her. Their women gave no mind to allowing their breasts to be exposed. Anna had never had the sunlight touch her pale bosom or her back. Unlike, most of the native men, Thistle had chest hair like her late husband. He also had tranquil green eyes. That was one reason she had given him the emerald ribbon for his hair. She felt too familiar with Thistle's face and body to be alone with him in the woods. Not that she worried for her safety, but for his.

"Ne-o-ga, the fawn, is a better name for you," he said. He leaned against a scraggly dogwood. "You move with grace like the young fawn. But you have a temper like a Sky Witch." Thistle smiled at her, and thunder sighed in the distance.

"I am a widow," she said and turned from him and continued her walk along the path. "I have little time for banter and dawdling in the forest with a handsome brave." Why she'd let the word handsome slip from her lips, she didn't know and cringed as she said it. To her benefit, she had been walking away from Thistle and doubted he heard her correctly.

"Hoo, hoo, hoooo," he mocked the owl. "I have sharp ears like my friend the Great Owl. You said Thistle is a handsome man." He ran up beside her, dancing around her as she walked. "Tell Thistle what I must do to court European woman, like yourself."

Her face burned. She had taken herself too far in familiarity with him – alone in the woods. "Please forgive me. I spoke out of turn, for a recently widowed woman to say such things to a bachelor are too inappropriate. Forgive me and forget what I said. I am affected by the heat of the afternoon."

He reached to touch her hand. Something caught his attention in the woods beyond her shoulder. He stopped and listened. "We are not alone."

Anna glanced around. She saw movement near the path from where she had just travelled from town.

The drab brown of Parnella Hart's skirt made the tree trunks, by comparison, appear vibrant. The woman walked with a scowl on her pinched face. Tobias led the way along the path, not waiting for his wife. They seemed to both see Anna and Thistle at the same moment and jerked to a stop. Parnella's eyes widened. Tobias glanced back at Parnella then continued walking toward them. She didn't follow.

"Good day to you, Madame Mayford," Tobias tipped his hat and ignored Thistle standing next to Anna.

"No good day comes with public accusations from Mistress Hart," Anna said. "Your hens are none of my concern or under any control of mine. They must be startled by the shrill tone of the woman of the house." She stared at Parnella as she walked up to them.

Parnella held her shoulders back with her chin up. "Witch!"

Thistle laughed, hearty and happy.

"And I see she allies with heathens," Parnella said to Tobias.

Thistle handed the spit back to Anna, then skipped around her, hands on his head like antlers and wiggled his fingers. "Me a heathen. You a heathen." He grunted, stopped in front of Parnella, turned his ars toward her and farted.

"Oh, Tobias, shoot him!" she stumbled back from the path. "You," she said to Anna, "I will visit the magistrate to bring charges against you for the damage to our livestock. Oh, yes, I have seen you in the form of a cat, stalking our hens."

Thistle meowed at Parnella.

"Thistle, go home. I can take care of these simpletons." Anna turned off the road to walk through the woods, away from the Harts.

Thistle puffed up his chest. "Go away," he said in his best English. "I do not like you. Anna does not like you. No one likes you. You are lower than ticks on the pirates' dicks." He glared at Tobias, who stepped back from the path to where Parnella hid by a pine.

Thistle caught up with Anna as she trudged through the woods' underbrush. "Do not fret over fearful people. They lash out like a summer storm of hot air and no rain – bluster with no use to the land."

They walked away from the road, creating their own path back to Anna's farm. "The town people thrive on waves of gossip – a sinking canard that could drown a woman already struggling."

"I will not let you sink; cast aside those of ill will." He stopped and took her hand. "I help you, here, in planting, in harvest, in home," he said and added, "like partner if you desire."

Her eyes stung, and she wiped away a tear. "Too soon." She began to walk away, but he didn't let go of her hand. "I need time to heal from losing Edward."

"My friend Edward," Thistle said and released his grip, "a great man. He want you to be safe and content. I want you soothed, joyful."

"I am," she said. "Thank you, Thistle. I must return home to help Stanton."

"At harvest, son needs help."

"I can help him," she said.

"Yes. I help you help him." He smiled and bowed to her. "Hoo, hoo, hoooo, Ji-hen-yah – no, you not Sky Witch, you Ne-o-ga, the fawn. Walk soft and sure." With that he disappeared into the forest.

Once supper finished, Stanton crawled into the sleeping loft. Anna reckoned that the day's work and heat had depleted her son's energy. A cool breeze drifted in through the open windows with a slight odor from her cows grazing nearby. Slander, Anna thought, that's what Parnella has done. But, Anna didn't care for lawsuits or the attention they brought. She only wanted to live peacefully on her farm, raise her son, some tobacco, and a few cows.

Maybe she nodded into sleep, but the screech in the night snapped her awake and fearful. Banshee. No cry of a bobcat. She knew from her grandmother's tales that the banshee messenger delivered the warning of danger in the family. No, she couldn't lose her son.

Could it be her death? Why her mind drew that conclusion, she didn't know. She had survived her girlhood beatings from her mother, a mother possessed by a demon, many of the neighbors had said. At the age of twelve, Anna could take the beatings no more. She left home to find work as a servant many miles from the village of her mother. A few months into her new employment, she heard the banshee. Within a year, she discovered from a travelling minister that her former home had caught fire. The remains of her mother found among the ashes. Had she caused the fire in her heated hate of the woman who repeatedly whipped her with a leather strap? Was she in fact a witch and not aware of it?

Chapter Thirteen

Using strange equipment didn't bother Tal. He could sing into a tin can with string if that's all the restaurant had, but this system looked professional and the testing produced clear amplification and solid tones. He'd called Brigid to come support him and to bring all the people she could because he knew the bottom line for a restaurant and bar was paying customers lured in by the entertainment. The manager stressed that the music should be at a volume where the customers in the restaurant area could carry on a conversation. Too many times, Tal heard inexperienced singers try to make the entertainment all about themselves. Sure that works for a concert hall, but in a restaurant, he knew he was there to create ambience.

"I have a couple of original songs," he told Benny, a heavyset man in his mid-forties with a full head of peppery gray hair and an easy-going manner, an attitude rare for a restaurant manager.

"As long as there's no rap in it. Jeez, I hate to hear bouncing rhyme and women called bitches. Anything else works for me." He rested his butt on the bar stool closest to the four-by-eight foot stage.

"No rap," Tal said. "I watch the people to see if they lose interest when I start into one of my songs. I can always transition into something they've heard before."

"It ain't easy, is it?" Benny raised one eyebrow with his question.

Tal knew the restaurant manager had made small talk with hundreds of singers as they set-up the stage, and he knew that he was giving the weary look of an artist ready to surrender and go work in a factory. "It's a living," he said with a wink. "Once in a while, I get encouragement about my own work. Family and friends keep me going."

"Bristol is a big family town for you?"

"Yep. Between Bristol and Abingdon, we've got family scattered all up and down Lee Highway. My cousin Brigid is up here in Charlottesville. She's coming tonight, and hopefully, bringing a few people."

"As long as they're good drinkers, I'm happy."

"Oh, you'll be happy." Tal laughed and set his guitar case behind a speaker. "We're Irish blood."

"Should have known that from the name, Taliesin MacGuire. It's not exactly Benny Taylor."

"Well, Mr. Taylor, Englishmen are okay, too."

Brigid brought about twelve people from the hospital into the bar, including Clio, the software salesperson, and a couple of her technicians. Tal liked Clio, but wasn't sure if she would be someone to sleep with.

Brigid and her group had a couple rounds of drinks, and the bar tables of hospital compatriots and other happy customers cheered Tal's performance. Before he took a short break, he emboldened himself to launch into one of his own songs. He said into the microphone, "This is for the lost MacGuire son."

Brigid whooped and raised her scotch to him.

Not quite a ballad, but with a slow, steady beat – a heartbeat scratch on the guitar strings – Tal played an intro and then sang:

"Generations of sons, old and young,

"Leading to one, the lost one.

"Never forgot her, but did his wife.

"The price he paid was his life.

"Grandmaw mourns for her last born – Seventh son of the seventh son.

"Shifter, drifter, charmer, reaper.

"He's there. He's here. He's everywhere. But nowhere."

The chorus bounced the beat up.

"Seventh Son. Shifter, drifter, charmer, reaper."

The audience tapped toes, thumped tabletops, and smiled. They were into it, but Brigid wrinkled her brow, and Clio's eyes looked through him as if seeing something from the past.

The set ended, and Tal grabbed a glass of water from the bar and pulled a chair up to Brigid's table. "Thanks for bringing people," he told her. "A full bar is a good omen for my continued bookings."

"You wrote a song about Uncle Finn."

"Yep." He wasn't sure what else to say, not like it should have been a surprise to her. Songwriters write about their lives. His father was an important missing part, and more often than he realized, he attempted to make some sense out of it.

"Tal," Clio said, and leaned toward him from the other side of Brigid, "I enjoyed your song. 'Never forgot her, but did his wife.' Is the 'her' your grandmother or the other woman?"

Impressed she had listened so closely, Tal liked her even more.

Brigid leaned against Tal's shoulder. "I'd say it's the woman on the side," she said without any hint of the bitterness he would have had in his voice, but Brigid could be a bit more objective than Tal when talking about Finn.

"Yeah, my father seems to have dismissed everyone for a woman who lured him away."

He sipped from his glass of water. Her questioning look almost had him start into the story of Finn's abandonment of the family, but he knew he needed to get back on stage. Benny wasn't paying him to sit and jaw a tale with friends. "Got to get back to it. Brigid, you can tell her the legend of Finn MacCool." With that he took his water and headed back to the corner to play a rousing rendition of John Denver's "Country Roads," with the entire bar and half the restaurant joining in the chorus.

As the night grew late, the crowd thinned. Thursday nights ended around midnight, and Tal packed up his guitar and tip jar, then settled his fee with Benny. Clio and Brigid had switched to water, but still waited for him in the corner of the bar. Benny handed him a frosty mug of Legend Brown Ale.

"Ahh, nothing like that first beer of the night just after

midnight," he said, as he joined the women at their table. They made small talk about his performance and the crowd's support.

Clio repressed a yawn. "I'm going to have to head back up the hill to the Omni. I have an early meeting tomorrow. Tal, I'd like to talk to you about finding your dad. Brigid told me about your grandmother's request. There's a lot more you can do than Googling his name, and I know some technicians who can get information most people can't find. I'll be back in Charlottesville on Tuesday. Will you be here?"

Finally, someone who might have ideas for him. "I'm heading back to Bristol on Saturday morning. I play here again tomorrow night. Maybe you can call me?"

She thought for a second. "I tell you what. Ride down to Richmond with me tomorrow and we'll be back here in time for you to set up tomorrow night. My technology guys are at the office, and we'll find out what they may be able to dig up."

"I don't want to put you out." But he did want some assistance. Maybe she was doing it to get in good with Brigid and that hospital project she was working on. He didn't care if that was the reason, he wanted the help. "You don't mind? I really appreciate it."

Brigid sat back in her chair like a queen on her throne. He knew she enjoyed the attention and implication that she influenced Clio's support. She might have, but Tal knew he had his own special charms that worked on women – either way, he'd take the help.

Chapter Fourteen

"**I**'m driving back to Richmond later this morning," Clio placed Devin on speaker and set the phone on the nightstand so she could eat her yogurt. "There are a few notes to go over with the programmers, and then I'm heading back here by afternoon."

"But it's Friday. You're spending the weekend working?" Devin's voice sounded thin and distant. She knew he had her on his car's speaker. Always connected, but never together.

She dropped the yogurt in the wastebasket and picked up her cell. "I don't know if I'll be all weekend. Might be coming back to Richmond tomorrow morning."

He let loose the F-bomb and she thought he might have almost hit another car.

"What?"

"I'm playing golf with a client on Saturday." He sighed loud enough for her to hear him over the traffic noise. "I'll cancel."

"No, no. It's just a busy time with my project. Let me see how things progress today, and we'll talk tonight. Be careful driving." They said their good-byes, and Clio wondered if she had purposely scheduled herself away from Devin. A step forward by him forced her to stumble back. Move in? Too much now. She needed some space. The thought of seeing him didn't hold the excitement of a few weeks ago.

Could that be because someone else netted her attention? Tal MacGuire? Yes, she admitted, he was interesting in his pursuits, handsome in a breezy way, his boldness stretched to an aura of charm. Silly, she thought, I barely know him – just the thrill of someone different.

Devin's future prospects gleamed in the city. He knew what he wanted and how to get it. He'd certainly made her his quest, persevering as a man infatuated, wooing her as if a modern woman could still be flattered and enticed into love. Love? Did she love him? Great affection, respect, friendship…But love? Could she love? She didn't know. Romantic love had never found her.

She slipped into her heels and grabbed her bag. Exhilaration fluttered her fingertips as she reached for the hotel room's door. "Calm yourself," she whispered.

Clio met Taliesin in the hospital parking lot at 10:30 after her morning meeting. His white Chevy Traverse SUV was parked next to her company's silver Toyota Camry. He slid into her car's passenger seat, and she drove them toward the interstate. He fidgeted with the radio, finally settling on a satellite station of acoustic guitar music.

"I like to hear what they play. Maybe I can add some songs to my list. But, regional differences matter. These beamed-down national stations aren't always catering to the local favorites." He took a breath and continued, "For example, the John Denver song was a big hit last night. I know we're not in West Virginia, but we're close enough that people hear it a lot, know it, and sing along. That's what I like – people reacting to what I do."

Wondering if he might be nervous because of his jumpy chatter, she tried to be calming. Although she had to admit she was feeling jittery as well. "You connect with your audience," she said. "People like that. I once went to a concert, and the band played straight through their set like it was their CD. No interaction with us, nothing. Just one song to the next."

"That's your basic nervous band, or it was a jaded performer who was on the road too long. Was it Willie Nelson?"

"I won't say," she said.

"Damn, you're like Grandmaw Roane. That woman won't talk bad about anyone, not even people she doesn't know. You don't know Willie personally, do you?"

She grinned. "No. It wasn't Willie Nelson. And no, I don't know him."

"That would be a kick if you and ol' Willie were friendly." He looked out the window and tapped a rhythm on his armrest. "Maybe I should do a rendition of 'On the Road Again.' People love that one. Of course, that only works if you actually go out on the road a lot."

"I'm on the road a majority of my time, driving from one client to the next." She wondered how she'd fallen into a job that kept her away from home. "Where's your grandmother?"

"Abingdon, on the Bristol side, got the family farm on Lee Highway. You ever been to Bristol?"

"Not my territory," she said.

"Well, hell, that doesn't mean you can't visit sometime. You like NASCAR? Bristol International is a fun place on race weekend."

She tried to hide her cringe. "No, can't say I've given NASCAR a try. I'm more of a concert or theater girl."

"Theater," he repeated, but with three syllables: thee-ate-ter. "I've been to the Barter in Abingdon. You'd like that."

"Yes," she said, "I've heard great things about the Barter Theatre. I'll plan a visit."

"I'm going back tomorrow," Tal said. "Come on and go with me."

She must have flashed him an odd expression because he added that Brigid intended to come along. "I'll think about it," she said. The trip would be interesting, a time to get to know Dr. MacGuire better and to see a place in Virginia she hadn't visited before, but she was away from home so often. And Devin. What would she tell him? No, she knew she couldn't take off to Bristol with Tal and Dr. MacGuire – Brigid.

"Where'd you go to school?" he asked.

"William and Mary."

"Fancy. I didn't really want to go to college, but I guess I should have, then I wouldn't be scraping by."

"You have the freedom that I don't," she said. "I have meetings and reports and quotas and management to answer to. It's a steady paycheck, but not as alluring as it may sound."

Tal tapped the armrest in rhythm to the James Taylor song on the radio. "If you weren't a William and Mary grad with a software sales job, what would you be doing?"

Good question, she thought. Did she have a passion for anything? What if she were suddenly out of work, like Leslie, who had the Charlottesville account before her? Was her fall-back plan moving in with Devin? "That's something to think about," she said.

"Well, now. Let's just talk this out," Tal started. "When you're not at work, what do you do?"

Talking it out with Tal, right then, wasn't something she considered to be the optimum solution. She'd rather play "I Spy" or "Name that Tune" to pass the time. He seemed earnest in his appeal to help. "I enjoy exploring little towns around the region, do some shopping, have a glass of wine."

"What's the most memorable place you've been and why?"

"Besides the big tourist places like New Orleans or San Francisco?"

"Yeah, one of the little places that you like."

"Ocracoke Island, on the southern part of the Outer Banks. It's where Blackbeard hung out."

"Arrr, pirates." He closed one eye and scrunched his face at her.

She snorted and clamped one hand over her nose, certain that she'd exhaled something she didn't want him to see. She wiped her nose with the back of her hand and looked in the rearview mirror to make sure nothing had come out. "Stop that. I'm trying to drive."

"The family used to have a cottage on the northern part of the Outer Banks," he said. "I went fishing down around Ocracoke. You fish there?"

"I'm not much of a fishing girl," she said. "My mom runs a store north of Kitty Hawk. I go to see her when I can."

"Is that why you prefer the southern part? A break from your mother?"

"Partly," she said with a laugh. "Honestly, that area gets a lot of traffic in the summers. Too much for me."

"What was it about Ocracoke that you enjoyed?"

"You can only get to it by ferry, which is nice because it makes it an adventure. Once there, you really don't need a car, just bicycles. There aren't any chain restaurants, stores, or hotels. The businesses are all independently owned and operated. It's not like any other place I've ever been. Completely unique."

"That's rare to find. Every town wants a Walmart, Home Depot, Olive Garden, and a CVS on the corner – homogenize, normalize, institutionalize. If you found yourself in Ocracoke for an extended amount of time, what would you do?"

"I'm drawn to the water. Maybe I'd open a kayak tour company." The thought made her smile: the open ocean, salty spray from cool waves, squawk of seagulls, the slap of the paddles against the water, and warm sun on her shoulders.

She glanced over at Tal; he grinned at her.

She put her attention back to the road. "That would be it," she said. "I'd live on an island, surrounded by water, but not a tropical one. I like the change of seasons, the winter Nor'easters and the late summer hurricanes."

"Well, then Ms. Clio. We need to figure out how to get you there."

The smile wouldn't leave her face as she thought about the possibility of doing what she loved instead of what was expected of her.

Tal and Clio arrived at the manicured strips of grass and ornamental Bradford pear trees of the office park on the outskirts of Richmond that housed the headquarters of Clio's workplace. The building stood three stories, encased in glistening steel and the green glass of windows that did not open. They parked, and she ushered Tal into the building and up to her office on the second floor.

Tal followed Clio along the cool hallway toward a closed door where she swiped her badge causing the lock to slide with an audible clack. Inside the room, pale gray partitions separated desks and hid all but the tops of peoples' heads moving back and forth while they typed on computer keyboards or talked on the phone. He thought they would be more excited that it was Friday, maybe hanging around the water cooler and telling jokes like on television shows. Clio walked down a row of the partitions. People glanced at them as they passed; he smiled and nodded to each one, but they mostly ignored them.

Tal wondered how forty hours a week felt in the little square partitions.

"This is Wayne," Clio introduced a thirty-something man with thick black hair and quick eyes.

"How ya doing?" he asked, a firm hand shake with Tal.

"Fair to middling," Tal said, but then thought it sounded too country for a Richmond professional to receive as an answer. "Good, thanks," he revised.

"Wayne, we have a question that I think you can answer," Clio said. "We're looking for information on someone who disappeared in the 1980s. We know the car he drove and his name, but don't know his destination."

"Hmm." Wayne stared at his computer screen, which held a lot of lines of numbers and characters that made no sense to Tal.

"I contacted the DMV for information on my dad's Impala. Last registered in 1988, then nothing." Tal pulled out a slip of paper from his wallet that had Finn's name, their home address at the time, and the Chevy's model, year, VIN, and license tag number. "That's what I have tracked down so far."

"Your dad, huh?" Wayne nodded his head as if he understood Tal's search.

"Virginia's DMV doesn't have anything else." Clio perched on the edge of Wayne's lateral file cabinet. "Can you search across states? Or hit archives?"

"That's just it," Wayne said. "The data from the mid-eighties was probably on mainframes or AS/400s. By now, that stuff is stored on magnetic tapes, archived off-site of the current datacenters. Even if I could creatively get into the systems, there would have to be a request to load the reels from the tape library."

The chill from the air conditioned office bristled across Tal's cheeks. He reached for the slip of paper.

"Hold on." Wayne glanced at him then to Clio. "What about searching police records across jurisdictions? Not that he might have done anything illegal, but if there had been an accident with the car or incident under his name, we might be able to snag that."

"Is that possible?" Clio asked.

Wayne typed a few things on his computer, clicked some links, and then stopped. "Same problem here. If I can get in, the data is probably archived for that time period. I'll need to pull in some favors, and it'll take some time."

"We'll pay you for your time. I wouldn't want to ask for your expertise without doing that," Clio said.

"I'll make a deal. Does Devin still have his Redskins tickets? I would love to take my son to a game next season, even a pre-season game if you could sweet talk Devin into selling me a couple of tickets."

Tal spoke up, "Clio, I'll pay for the tickets if you can get them for Wayne. It's my request he's working on."

"Oh, no. Let me see what I can arrange. Wayne, go ahead and dig all you can. I'll get Redskins tickets for you and your son."

"So, who's Devin?" Tal asked as they walked out to her car.

"He's the man I've been seeing for a while."

"Is he good to you?"

She stopped. The mid-day sun warmed the shoulders of her navy blue blazer. "Yes," she said. "He's very good to me. Almost fawning even after several years of dating. I'm not sure why he's like that, but he seems to like me."

"Ha!" Tal laughed. "That's no way to talk about yourself. You're very likable. Hell, I'd go so far as to say you're fun."

"That's quite a compliment coming from you," she said. "I bet you charm all the ladies."

"And some of the men, too," he added with a wink.

She smiled then the comment settled in her mind. "Oh, okay."

She wasn't sure what more to say. She'd never thought of Tal as being fluid in his attractions, but why not? She'd found a few women attractive, but not enough to switch for an evening. No, she knew she was boringly straight. But the mental image of Tal and her and Devin surged through her thoughts.

"Didn't mean to shock you," he said with an elfin grin.

"Yes, you did." She laughed. "For some reason, I always assume that people south and west of Richmond are Bible-thumping conservatives. Sorry to generalize like that."

"You don't know the MacGuires. Really, most people I know back home tend to do a lot of things they don't share with their neighbors or their church. Those Bible-thumpers let loose wilder than most New York City partiers do. I think it's because they hold it in for so long – just explodes into carnal behaviors behind the Baptist fellowship hall."

"Let's go grab some lunch. I'll show you I'm not so white bread. You can see my neighborhood."

Clio drove them through the tree-lined streets of the Museum District and into Carytown. At a house on Floyd Avenue, she pulled the Camry into a slim driveway next to a three-story, brick home with a large front porch, ferns hanging from the corners. The oaks and maples filtered the sun in a mosaic of light and shade across the small front yard filled with hostas and ivy.

"Wow," Tal said as he got out of the car and glanced around. "Nice place. This your house?"

"I rent it," Clio said. "Too expensive for me to own, but the rent isn't bad."

He headed for the porch.

"We can't go in," she said. "I wasn't expecting company, and it's a mess. Cary Street is just a couple of blocks. I thought we'd go have lunch. You'll see Richmond isn't so stuffy."

The number of cars cruising up Cary Street and the crowd of people walking along the sidewalk surprised Tal. For early Friday afternoon, the activity level frothed. A group of tattooed girls in short-shorts and tight t-shirts sped by them on roller-skates. A Rastafarian-looking black man, with long dreadlocks and scraggly beard, sold glass bongs and colorful t-shirts from a portable table in front of a bicycle shop. An older Asian man and woman walked hand-in-hand, wearing Birkenstock sandals and tatty jeans. Two college-age boys came up behind them and passed them, holding hands just like the elderly couple – and no one seemed to care. That wouldn't happen in Bristol, Tal thought.

Clio opened the door of a busy restaurant, they went in, and sat at a table near the long bar.

"I like this street," Tal said. "I bet plenty of these places have live music." The restaurant's old brick walls displayed black and white photographs of old Richmond: suffragettes at the Capitol building steps, Robert E. Lee's statue on Monument Avenue, Ford Model Ts on Broad Street, and Arthur Ashe at Wimbledon. Tucked in a corner by the bathrooms, a small stage caught his attention.

"You could probably find some gigs here." Clio ordered them both hamburgers and sweet iced tea. "I like living this close to the restaurants and shops. I don't have to drive after a few drinks."

"Cheers to that." Tal could see the front window from his seat at their table. "Hey, there's a sign pointing down that alley: 'Psychic.' Let's go after we eat."

"What? Do you believe in psychics?"

"Don't you?"

"Honestly, no. I think it's entertainment, like ghost tours at Halloween."

"You never saw a haint?" he asked. "There's more to this world than you think. Pawpaw Joe's momma, Great Grandmaw MacGuire, swore that her father, Hardy, had come to her in a dream to warn about her brother's danger in Germany during the Great War. Well, Uncle Julian didn't make it back to Washington County alive. But, Great Grandmaw MacGuire said Julian showed up one evening, just as plain as day, out there in the front yard.

The crickets chirped and the cicadas buzzed, but then the evening sounds stopped as if the needle had been lifted off a record. She looked out across the porch where she'd been stringing beans — there he was, standing tall in his Army uniform, her brother Julian. He didn't say a word, just grinned at her as if to let her know he's good on the other side."

"You're full of shit," she said with a smile. "You made that up as you went along."

"No, no, I'm telling you the truth as it was told to me."

The food arrived, and Tal ordered two beers. "We need fortification. We're heading to the psychic after this," he told the waitress.

Clio protested about drinking on a Friday, but Tal said he wouldn't tell on her.

Finished with their lunch and a couple of beers, Tal and Clio walked down the alley to the psychic's storefront. The place looked like most of the tall, narrow houses along the street, but this one had a wooden sign that stated "Psychic & Intuitive". Tal pushed the glass door open and motioned Clio in. "If your computer guy can't find something maybe this person will."

The front room reminded Tal of a dentist's waiting room, a few chairs and tables with magazines, but the magazines highlighted New Age subjects from crystals to tarot cards to auras. A tabletop fountain gurgled in the corner. The air smelled of sage. A middle-aged woman, rather thin, with short gray hair, greeted them as she arrived from a side room. "Welcome." Her voice rang soft like a chime.

"We wondered if we could talk a few minutes with the psychic," Tal said.

"Of course," the woman said. She handed Tal a brochure. "I'm Angela. I have an appointment in about thirty minutes, so the longest I can do now is a twenty minute reading. If you want to come back later, we can schedule a longer appointment."

He checked the price list on the brochure. "Twenty minutes works for me."

Angela motioned Tal and Clio into the adjoining room. To

Tal's disappointment, the room looked very much like a massage therapy room, deep blue paint on the walls, a bookcase, soft music playing on the stereo, candles clustered on a round table in the middle of the small room. He had hoped it would look more like a gypsy fortuneteller on a Scooby Doo cartoon. No crystal ball. No heavy drapes. No shawl or hoop earrings on Angela.

He and Clio sat at the table with Angela opposite them.

"What information are you seeking?" she asked.

"I want to know what happened to my father."

She glanced at Clio, who sat still, eyes on the psychic, purse in her lap, hands folded on top of the table. Then Angela stared into Tal's eyes.

"When was the last time you encountered your father?"

"When I was ten, he left one night and hasn't come back."

"Physically, yes," she said, "but he's been with you from time to time over the years, in spirit."

She looked to Clio. "You are not this man's wife, but you care about him. What is your relationship?"

"Friends," Clio said, "if that is really important to his question."

"More than friends, is the feeling I'm getting," Angela said. Back to Tal, she asked, "You are named after a seer, and you have untapped potential. What is your name?"

"Taliesin."

"Ah, yes. Bard, magician, prophet. Your parents named you well. Your father's name?"

"Finn MacGuire."

Clio nudged Tal's knee with hers and nodded at the candles flickering violently beside them.

Angela closed her eyes for a moment, hummed to herself. "Surround us with the white light of love and honesty. Let only pure light beings approach us. I call on the spirits to bring information for Taliesin on his father, Finn MacGuire."

A few moments passed then Angela opened her eyes. "Several voices surround us. Finn MacGuire is not one of them, but a mother from long ago is here. She speaks from centuries before. You are her children. She sends images of family, nurture, and love, but there are hints of accusations and a feeling of choking, under water. Something needs to be exposed, but can't. The truth isn't able to come."

"That's what I want," Tal said. "We're trying to find the truth about my father."

"I'm hearing another voice, more recently crossed over. He knows and loves you. He's proud of you. He loves Finn. Your grandfather? I'm feeling a name with J, a seventh son, to an intuitive and healer. The gift is in the family. There's an indication of regret. Finn may have caused his own transition to the other side, prematurely."

"He's dead?" Tal asked.

"Yes."

Even though he knew the answer wasn't based in fact, but on intuition, the words punched him. He had trouble catching his breath. He felt tears stream down his face that he couldn't stop. Clio wrapped her arms around him. "Of course he is," he managed to say.

"What did he die from?" Clio asked Angela.

"Heartbreak."

"Specifically," she pushed.

"All I encounter are feelings, sentiments, moods, emotions. That's what transitions from the other side."

Tal sniffed back his own emotions and asked, "Where can I find evidence of his passing?"

"Water. I get the texture of water from the mother of long ago and from J, the seventh son." A short cough of air caught her throat. "Finn was the seventh son of a seventh son."

"Yes," Tal said. "Is it true? Shapeshifter?"

She smiled. "We're all shapeshifters. But, yes, he presented different faces as needed."

"What can you tell us about our next steps?" Clio asked.

"Your search brings results. You are not at an impasse. I feel encouragement from the spiritual beings that protect you."

"Pawpaw Joe is protecting me?"

"Among others. Go in peace."

Tal paid Angela and thanked her for the information. He felt a warmth from the suggestion that his grandfather watched over him, actually that the past generations could garner some type of connection to the present. Not that he believed those spirits of the past would intervene in his direction – or maybe they did by reminding him of the road they travelled. His eyes began to water again, but he didn't try to hide it from Clio. He felt emotionally safe with her. Now, he wondered what Brigid would have to say about their psychic encounter. Especially that Pawpaw Joe might have been there. He knew he wouldn't mention it to his grandmother.

Late Autumn 1979 – Bristol, Virginia/ Tennessee

The downtown streets of Bristol had lost most of the stores and restaurants when the Mall opened in 1976. Finn leaned against the facade of the Parks Belk store, empty now, waiting for Cheryl. He pulled his Marlboros from his shirt pocket and shook one out. The brick column's chill seeped through his wool jacket. He flicked his Bic lighter and inhaled the smoke from the cigarette. The prospect of fatherhood should excite him, but another of Kay's holds tightened around his throat. Not so easy to escape now, he thought and leaned forward to search for Cheryl's orange Ford Pinto. A baby girl would keep Kay's focus and leave him breathing room. A baby boy, well that was another story. A boy of his own, what things he could teach him. Finn's six brothers and father had taught him to be a man. A good man? That could be debated. The best role model for being a human came from his mother. She didn't get caught up in the jostling for position in the line of men in the family. Yes, Paw was the boss, but his brothers were nothing but clowns filing out of a tiny car, tripping over each other.

He should have left this dying town after high school. But, here he stood on the withering downtown street, waiting for a woman to make him forget his life for just a couple of hours.

Decay and disrepair hallmarked the town that had once beckoned people from all occupations and classes. Weeds grew along the storefronts. A wino slept around the corner. Nine years earlier, the passenger trains still stopped in Bristol, and the Christmas season packed downtown with shoppers, peddlers, excitement – and the Christmas parade. Joyce had marched in the parade, twirling a baton, her sequined leotard uniform sparkled in the red, green, silver, and gold lights strung across State Street. Finn had stood in this same spot with his brothers Tristan, Brian, and Dylan, each having a girl in the parade.

The beep of the Pinto's horn shook Finn out of his memories. Since Cheryl had watched Annie Hall a couple of years before, she had tried to emulate Diane Keaton. Her gray felt hat and oversized sunglasses topped a smile when she pulled the Pinto to a stop in front of him. She reached over and cranked down the passenger side window. "Hey, mister, need a ride?"

He dropped his cigarette, ground it out with his boot, and opened the door. Inside, he kissed her. Her lip gloss tasted like cotton candy.

"How much time do you have?" she asked and pulled away from the curb heading west on State Street, out of downtown, where the old motels rented rooms by the hour.

Room 137 anchored the Starlight Motel, the stump at the end of the right branch of rooms. Finn liked this room because Cheryl could park behind the building, out of sight of West State Street. No one he knew would recognize her car or conclude he might be with her. She hadn't grown up in Bristol, but had transferred as the manager of a store in the mall that sold fashion jeans: Levis, Calvin Klein, Jordache, Guess. In addition to the latest jeans, Cheryl sold denim jackets, denim skirts, cotton shirts, fabric and leather belts, and thick socks. The only clothing the store didn't sell was underwear.

Finn found his boxers on the nightstand where they had landed when he kicked them off earlier. He considered how many times he'd lain between the stained sheets and stared at the same moldy spot on the ceiling, waiting for Cheryl to emerge from the shabby bathroom, always opening the door with a smile and a kiss. She was too good for him. The matted burgundy shag carpet was too good for him. Kay was too good for him. God and Finn knew as a fact the baby would be too good for him.

The bathroom door squeaked and Cheryl, now fully clothed and make-up applied, climbed on the bed and kissed Finn's lips gently. Her hand tugged at the chain around his neck, moved the ring connected to it over his shoulder and out of her way.

"Time is a thief," he said.

"I know. Seems like we just got here and now it's back to our jobs – just a little 'Afternoon Delight' as they used to say."

"Grabbing and holding on, that's the hard part of living." He propped himself up in the bed, the pine headboard smooth on his back. "The good times get pulled away by a cold tide. I reach out and try to snatch them back." He motioned with his right arm. "But, I'm always, always too late. It's my own damn fault. I say the wrong word or do a stupid thing or forget what's important to other people. Am I so self-involved?"

"No, no, baby," she soothed. "You are a man of high ideas and long-range views. Details aren't you. You're a visionary."

The statement struck true to him. "You really think so?"

"For sure."

Cheryl hailed from just outside Columbus, Ohio. She had a worldly perspective that he didn't. Maybe she's right, he thought, then again, she could be as full of shit as I am.

Finn dropped another peanut into his Coca-Cola bottle, one then a pause then another, watching the little splash of caramel liquid and the fizz caused by the salt.

"Dump them in," Brian said from the desk behind Finn. The office of the tool and die shop held three steel desks, lined up perpendicular to the green cinderblock wall, creating three peninsulas into the room. Finn sat at the first desk, feet up on the edge, his chair facing the opposite wall's windows, between dusty, white, metal blinds he watched the trucks drive down Lee Highway. Brian typed an invoice onto a form with the typewriter, hunting and pecking each letter. "We need one of those computers the VPI kids use. Not this crappy typewriter. They say you just feed cards into a slot and the computer prints out all your forms. Stick them in the mail and go. I tell you, if I was a young man, I would surely learn computers. That's the future."

"Shit, Brian, you're twenty-six years old," Finn said. "Head back to school and learn it."

"Don't get pissy with me. We're short here. You're the one that run Dylan off. All your whoring around. 'Course, if I could get me someone to run around with, I'd do it."

"No one would have you, dumbass."

"You don't know that," Brian said. "I got some moves that make the ladies squirm. But, those moves will soon be off the market." He pulled the form out of the typewriter and separated the original from the duplicate. "Honestly little brother, I'm thinking of asking Cindy to marry me."

Finn dropped his feet off the desk with a slap to the linoleum floor. "Man, I don't recommend it. Cindy's a good girl, but marriage changes them. Hell, it changes you, too. I'm not the man I was when I married Kay."

Brian went to the back wall and opened a file cabinet drawer, stuffing the invoice duplicate into a folder. "That's because you married the wrong girl."

"Not so sure there is a 'right' girl. That's a bunch of crap fed to us in movies and television commercials. You believe Cindy is the only one for you? That if you hadn't met her, you'd be alone the rest of your life?"

"Well, no." Brian returned to the desk, plopped into the creaking chair, and leaned forward, elbows on the desktop. "We can be happy with a number of people. Just getting to know them is the challenge. Take you and Kay. Kay's a pretty girl, pleasant —"

"If you don't live with her," Finn interrupted.

"I bet you ain't no Prince Charming your own damn self." Brian picked up a pen and tapped the stack of papers next to the typewriter. "You cared enough about her to ask for her hand and then get married. Something was there."

Finn took a swig of his Coca-cola and chewed a few peanuts that he'd sucked out of the bottle. "Paw said I was getting to the age to get married. So I did."

"Hell, I'm older than you. He never said that to me."

Finn turned the Coke up and drained the last of the bottle, chomping the peanuts. "You weren't sleeping with your brother's wife."

Chapter Fifteen

Clio drove Tal back to Charlottesville with ample time for him to set up for his Friday night performance. She dropped him at his car in the hospital parking lot and promised to stop by the restaurant that evening to hear him play. Reports needed to be e-mailed back to the office, and she didn't want to appear too eager to spend time with Tal or with Brigid. Professional distance, but with a friendly manner defined her style with clients. She reminded herself that Dr. MacGuire was a client.

The issue that worried her, more than the salesperson/client interaction, was that she had more fun with Tal than she'd had with Devin in years. Maybe she and Devin had fallen into a routine, lost the excitement of discovery that defines new relationships. She could almost predict what Devin would say when they talked on the phone. She'd demanded that he not text her. She hated texts. Short little messages that jingled on her phone until she looked at them, annoying like infants whimpering for attention. So, Devin would call to check in, recapping his day, laying out his next day. She had to breathe deep breaths to keep from asking if she should be taking notes or updating his calendar, snarky remarks that replayed in her head. Not really his fault, she thought. They had exhausted talking about their likes and dislikes, their feelings and emotions on current news, so many aspects to explore in the beginning failed to keep the conversation going years later.

"Novelty, just something different," she said as she walked into the hospital and rode the elevator to the basement where she'd set up a workstation with her on-location programmers. If her only worry was finding someone interesting after several years, then she knew she should be grateful. So many people in the hospital had sick or dying relatives and friends. How the staff could deal with that every day, she couldn't fathom. She settled at her desk with her laptop, but didn't open her e-mail. How would she explain to Devin that she had decided to ride to Bristol with Tal and Brigid for the weekend?

So much for professional distance. She picked up her cell phone and tapped Devin's contact entry. "Happy Friday afternoon," she said when Devin answered.

"Right back at you. Are you still in Charlottesville?"

"Yeah. Listen, one of the doctors – a female doctor – has been talking about her hometown just down the I-81. She asked if I wanted to go this weekend to see the area: Bristol and Abingdon, down in southwest Virginia."

"I've been through there," Devin said. "Mountains and small towns. See if you can get reservations at the Martha Washington Inn. I heard it's nice. Do you mind if I don't go?"

In a quick moment, she tensed then eased in her panic, first because he thought she was inviting him and then relieved by his declining the perceived offer.

"Oh, sure. Dr. MacGuire, Brigid, is part of this project. Maybe you and I can go together some other time. I'll scope it out as a potential weekend get-away."

He proceeded to tell her all the people he contacted throughout the day. She opened her e-mail to check her in-box.

That evening, Clio stopped to have a drink at Fellini's where Tal was playing. With a to-go order for dinner, she headed back to the hotel to finish some work.

In the morning, they each took off separately for Abingdon. Tal would stay at his house in Bristol, Brigid would stay with her parents in Abingdon then return to Charlottesville, and Clio would stay at the Martha Washington Inn then drive back to Richmond on Sunday. The inn, a historic home built in 1832, turned into the Martha Washington College for girls before the Civil War, and became an inn after the Great Depression. In its early inn years, it housed actors for the Barter Theatre where Gregory Peck had begun his career.

They all met again for lunch at Jack's 128 Pecan, a small, popular restaurant in Abingdon. Their bottle of Pinot Noir disappeared quickly, and Tal ordered another.

"This is the old stomping grounds," he said, pouring the wine for Brigid and Clio.

Brigid added, "I'm glad I can make it back here from time to time. My parents are getting along fine, but they're becoming an age where I worry about their health. But, yeah, this feels more like home to me than Charlottesville."

"Will you ever come back here for good?" Clio asked.

"Maybe, but for now, the hospital treats me well."

Clio smiled. "You are one of the stars there. I hear lots of admiration for you."

"I'm admired and condemned based on the people you ask. I push the administration and the other doctors to slow down with the patients. We tend to forget that the health concerns patients have are new to them. For us, it's the hundredth time we've talked about it that week, so we skim over a lot. Think how stunned a patient is when they come in the emergency room. Their comprehension is almost non-existent with so much activity around them, and we just speed through dropping diagnosis and pills on them. Do you realize that when a patient wants clarification after that initial consultation, either that took place in the ER or in my office, I have to charge him again for an office visit. That's not his fault. It's mine that I didn't make my explanation understandable."

"That's like teaching kids the guitar," Tal said. "Breaking down the information is hard when it has become automatic to you. I say to them, 'Play a C-chord' and they just stare at me. Getting back to the beginner level is a rare art."

Tal's phone played a short tune, and then Brigid's rang a shrill alarm. They both looked at their screens and answered simultaneously.

"What? When? No. Okay. On my way." The words jumbled from both their conversations.

Tal glanced at Brigid, then turned to Clio. "We've got to go.

Uncle Brendan just found Grandmaw Roane on her kitchen floor. They're on the way to the Bristol Emergency Room."

Chapter Sixteen

Tal and Brigid rushed to the hospital in Bristol. Clio had told them to call her if they needed anything because she would be there in Abingdon. Tal thanked her as they left the restaurant. On his drive down to the Bristol Medical Center, he knew very little he could do but be present with his uncles, aunts, a few cousins and try to calm Brigid as she buzzed around the doctors. He wondered how much professional courtesy they would allow her in this hospital. The woman had some balls to push her way in another doctor's hospital, but then this was her grandmother. Did that help or frustrate her attempts to participate in the diagnosis?

Uncle Brian paced the waiting room. Aunt Cindy half-watched the home renovation show on the television mounted in the corner of the room. Sitting next to Cindy, Jeannie tapped messages on her phone, ignoring her mother's on-going comments about the flooring choices the TV shows' designer made. Uncle Brendan stared out the window.

"Wonder how long she lay there?" Brendan asked of no one in particular, but since Tal stood near him, he answered.

"Probably not long. Being in the kitchen and dressed, she must have been up for a while."

"The side door was still locked," Brendan said. "It's never locked when I stop by for coffee. I knocked, thinking she might be sleeping late. Then –" Tears filled his eyes. He pushed them away with the back of his hand. "Then the thought hit me that... That she might be in trouble. That old door hasn't had a key in years. Of course, I don't have a key to Maw's house. She's always there. Don't know where I found the strength, but I splintered that door jamb with one hit. Wonder I didn't knock my shoulder out of joint."

"Your shoulder okay?"

"Sore, but working," he said and swung his right arm a little with a slight cringe. "The kitchen light was on. She was on the floor, trying to say something to me."

"Grandmaw probably wanted you to help her up so she could start the coffee pot for you," Tal said. He thought for a moment. "Since the light was on, you think she had been there since last night?"

"I hope not. At her age, can she recover?"

The thought had hit Tal even before his uncle had asked. He knew of grandparents or parents of friends who had suffered strokes and after a few weeks seemed okay, but some had lingering effects or accelerated dementia. He knew that Grandmaw Roane wouldn't be the same. A stroke propelled a body down the path to Forest Hills Cemetery. "She'll be as ornery as ever," he said and turned to the window to watch cars travel along the interstate. He tried to swallow his emotion, but his throat caught it, and he coughed hard and rough.

"Dad," Brigid said from behind them. Brendan turned, and she hugged him. "She's doing better. You and Uncle Brian can go see her. We don't want to overwhelm her with visitors, so the boys can go in first." Even in their sixties and seventies, the sons were still "the boys" and their wives, "the girls."

When Brendan and Brian walked down the hallway toward the patient rooms, Brigid nudged her arm around Tal's waist and laid her head on his shoulder. "I'm worried," she said, words part sigh, part scalpel, sliced across his heart.

He pulled away to look in her eyes. No tears, just weariness. "Are you saying Grandmaw Roane won't make it?"

"No." She shook her head then sat down in an armchair next to them. "She should pull through, but Tal, she's ninety-seven years old. She won't be the same. We'll just have to see if she can still live alone."

"We should be taking care of her." He raised his voice. "She can live with me." He would not let Brigid send her to a nursing home where old people stared at blank walls from their wheelchairs parked in hallways, portals stinking of urine and disdain.

She cocked her head to the side. "Tal, are you going to bathe her and take her to the toilet? We need to start planning. Even if she makes it through this and is independent, that won't last long."

"I have to give her peace of mind," he said. "She has to know what happened to Finn."

"Hell, Tal. Just make something up. I don't know how much time we have left."

He knew Brigid tried to give him a release from his commitment to their grandmother, but he needed resolution, too. He would discover the end of Finn MacGuire.

The warm breeze drifted up Courthouse Hill as Clio wandered in and out of a few shops and then walked back to the Martha Washington Inn. She booked a massage in the spa before crossing the street to see the Barter Theatre. The old building had a gift shop, and Clio persuaded the young man behind the counter to let her peek in the theater to see the vacant stage. She slipped into one of the seats in the back row and imagined the generations of performers crossing the stage, the famous and yet-to-be famous actors and musicians. The building held histories, not just the individuals on and off the stage, but of the entire region. Its long roots united the area and the families who had generations centered around the theatre. Had Tal ever played on the Barter stage? She made a mental note to ask him.

What of her own history? She couldn't remember much from her mother or grandmother. They only talked about people and events of today. If she brought up anything of their past, they would say none of that matters and she should focus on the future.

Her phone rang in her purse, and she hurried out the door, waving to the gift shop clerk, to take the call outside. "Hi Devin," she answered the ring.

"Miss you," he said and sounded as if he meant it.

"Anything wrong?"

"No, no. Saturday afternoon and you're not here. I was just thinking it would be fun to go to Shockoe Bottom tonight for a drink and dinner, maybe walk along the river, but that wouldn't be enjoyable without you. When are you coming home?"

He seldom expressed his feelings; mostly he displayed his physical desires, without the emotional ones. Clio moved to the shade of the building because the sun caused her to sweat. Was it the sun's warmth that triggered a sudden flare of sparks under her skin or Devin? "Well, I'd like to leave right now. Dr. MacGuire's grandmother suddenly went into the hospital, so she's there tending to her. I'm wandering around Abingdon. I miss you, too."

"Come on back, then," he said.

"By the time I get to Richmond, it would be late tonight. I'll leave first thing in the morning."

"I can be there in a few hours," he said with such energy she thought he was getting in his car.

"Devin," she said and glanced around to find a bench in the shade. "We both have to be at work on Monday, so no sense in you driving here and back within hours." Suddenly, she felt like her practical mother. "I'll see you tomorrow afternoon. Besides, I should go to the hospital to see if Dr. MacGuire could use anything for her grandmother."

"That's thoughtful of you. Bet she could use a few personal items, you know all those things older ladies need."

Clio wasn't sure what Devin thought older women needed while in the hospital, but she'd stop at a store on her way to see if there was something to take. "I'll call you tomorrow when I'm leaving for home." She started to hang up, but added, "I love you."

"I love you, too. I can't wait to see you." He hung up, and Clio inhaled a long, slow breath, maybe she'd ignored Devin on purpose to distance herself. With the physical miles between them, she needed to be close, to have the familiarity and comfort that had swelled like a wave over the years. But, like an ocean wave, the crests and troughs of their relationship moved forward, nothing too rough or placid to sink or stall them. An urge to retrieve her car and drive back to Richmond rose but subsided when she thought about Brigid and Tal's distress over their grandmother.

Chapter Seventeen

"For ninety-seven, Grandmaw is doing remarkably well." Brigid set coffee in front of Tal and sat in the hard, plastic chair across the cafeteria table from him. The serving lines and kitchen had closed hours before. The bright skylights above them had darkened from evening lavender to early night indigo. The coffee, from a Starbuck's at the entrance to the Bristol Regional Medical Center, smelled sweet and strong.

"Time's running out," Tal said. He tapped his fingers on the beige laminate tabletop. "How's her mind?"

"Sharp, from what we can tell. Her speech is still a challenge, but she should recover fairly fast. Maybe not as quickly as a seventy-five year old would, but the brain re-routes its circuits swiftly to bring back functioning."

"I always thought she'd be here forever, that she'd outlive me." Tal sipped his coffee. "In my twenties, I never thought I'd live to be thirty. Just the mindset of twenty-something, little vision beyond the weekend. Now, looking at forty, I can't imagine the generation ahead of us leaving."

They sat in silence for a few minutes, the hum of the vending machines lulling them into their own thoughts. Heels clicked down the stairs, not the soft swish of a healthcare worker's rubber soles. Brigid smiled at Clio waving a fast food box and a Belk department store bag.

"Sorry, this is about all I could find," she said and set the box on the table. Opening it and placing chicken clubs in front of Tal and Brigid, she took the seat next to Tal. She reached around and rubbed his shoulder. "Are you two holding up?" she asked.

"We're tired, but okay," Brigid said.

"Thanks for the food," Tal said and leaned over and kissed Clio's cheek. The action seemed automatic to him, but as soon as he did it, he felt embarrassed. "Sorry," he said. "That was too forward of me. My mind and manners have fallen to the wayside."

Brigid raised her eyebrow at him. He received her message: watch the impression you're giving. She had the look that could squelch his impulses. But did he even know what his motive was? Clio, personality-wise and looks-wise, attracted him, but the deep sexual craving hadn't surfaced. Could it be loneliness for a female companion instead of a lover? Brigid always acted as the big sister. His mother was distant and focused on her own life. Grandmaw encompassed the feminine aspect of his existence. Was he looking for her replacement? Yes, he decided, watch the impression I make with my actions.

Brigid explained the condition of their grandmother to Clio as Tal wolfed down his sandwich without making eye contact with Clio or Brigid.

"I bought her this robe," Clio said and pulled a cobalt blue cotton robe from the Belk bag. "Those backless gowns are drafty."

"She'll love it," Tal said. "Why don't you come up with us to give it to her?"

"I don't want to barge in."

"Nonsense, she'd like to have some new visitors," Brigid said. "The parade of old faces, sons, daughters-in-law, grandchildren, and great-grandchildren tend to make patients feel like they're getting the last visits from family – everyone looks grim and worried."

They finished their sandwiches and took the elevator up to Grandmaw Roane's room. A young nursing assistant checked her vital signs and recorded them on a computer attached to a rolling cart. Grandmaw Roane's skin retained a tinge of gray that alarmed Tal, but Brigid didn't fuss over it. He wondered if her skin reflected the color of dying. Maybe, he hoped, the hue was due to the lights in the room.

"Grandmaw Roane, we brought a friend to see you. This is

Clio," he said.

The old woman's blue eyes found Clio. She stared for a while, and Tal wondered if she was trying to place the face.

"She's a friend from Richmond. She wanted to meet you."

"Hello, Mrs. MacGuire. I hate to intrude on you. I brought you a robe. You might need it when they have you up and walking around."

She held out a hand to Clio.

With quick looks to Brigid and Tal, Clio stepped close to the bed and held the robe out so Grandmaw Roane could see it. "Nice," the old woman said in slurred speech, dragging out the word. She reached for Clio's hand. "Come here, baby girl."

She held Clio's hand and smiled the best she could, lopsided and trembling.

"Mrs. MacGuire, you are recovering remarkably well."

"You a doctor?"

"Well, no, ma'am. But I hear you're doing well."

She made a spitting noise as if to dismiss the idea of her recovery. "Hard for old woman, old body, old heart."

Tal brushed a fine lock of thinning hair from his grandmother's forehead. "Just rest. You'll be out of here in a few days, back to your house."

She nodded, still holding onto Clio's hand. "Girl here, she can help you with your daddy. Good you're here, baby girl. What your name?"

"My name is Clio."

"You don't need to worry about anything right now, Grandmaw Roane," Brigid said. "Get some rest. I'm keeping in line with your care team. They're good doctors and nurses. You do what they tell you and don't sass them."

Patting her on the hand, Clio pulled away from Grandmaw Roane's grip. Tal and Brigid kissed their grandmother's cheek before heading for the door.

"The nurses have my cell phone number if you need me before morning," Brigid said.

"Bring his baby girl back tomorrow," Grandmaw Roane said.

"Been too long."

Tal looked to Clio. The memories of his grandmother seemed to be scrambled by her stroke. Clio's resemblance to one of his cousins, Uncle Brian's oldest daughter, might have confused her into thinking Clio was one of her grandkids. But, if having people visit she thought she knew made her happy, Tal was glad to bring a parade through her room to entertain her.

On the ride down the elevator to the lobby, Clio's thoughts scraped the walls of her logic. Should she have corrected Mrs. MacGuire? No, no need to add more conflicting information or stress. Sure, she could be a grandchild. Her own grandfather had passed years before, her grandmother just ten years ago. Her mother's mother – her Grandmother Marian – was never fond of her father. Maybe it was the mother-in-law syndrome that no man was good enough for her daughter, but Grandmother Marian didn't hide her disdain for her father. For many years, her only family was her mother and father, plus harpy Grandmother Marian. She remembered reading about religious cults that kept to themselves, denying outside influences or people who would contradict the cult's doctrine. That would apply to her parents and grandmother if they had been religious or passionate about something, but as it was, they had little enthusiasm for anything. Detachment ruled their philosophy, if apathy could be conviction.

They arrived at the lobby floor and headed toward the front door. She stopped, lost in the shadow of memories. "I'm glad I got to meet your grandmother. She's what I always envisioned a loving grandmother to be."

"She can be a fireball when she wants to be." Tal said.

"She thought I was part of the family," Clio said, then immediately felt a little foolish as if she intruded on their lives.

"Stroke patients often confuse new and old memories," Brigid said. "I'm glad she recognizes us. If she adds to her list of grandchildren, that's fine with me. When I worry is when I hear nonsense coming from patients."

"Hell, she told me to listen for banshees," Tal said. "She swore they'd come for her when it was her time."

"She's always held onto the old tales. Like most legends, the symbolism can help explain bigger concepts. Banshees. Could be the squeaky carts going up and down the hallway."

"Yep, she's confused. But we'll take you as an honorary cousin," Tal said to Clio. "Grandmaw Roane holds her family close. I can see it's on her mind. Yesterday she could have told us the lineage back to colonial times on her side and on Pawpaw Joe's side, but today, she does well to say a few lucid sentences."

"Did anyone close up her house?" Brigid asked. "I'll check on it on the way back to Mom and Dad's."

"That's almost to Abingdon," Tal said. "Let's all go, and I'll buy you both a drink at The Martha's bar."

"Geez, I need a drink." Brigid leaned against Tal and winked at Clio. "Let's go. We'll be back here early tomorrow."

All three of their cars snaked off the interstate and onto Highway 11. The highway snuggled between two hills on either side. Clio drove behind Tal's white Chevy SUV, which followed Brigid's red Toyota Prius. Brigid signaled and turned up a long driveway to a stone house build at the crest of a hill. In the dark, Clio could see a white fence outlining the front pastures, up the driveway and around the house and the detached garage – no doors on either of the garage bays, both empty. Brigid parked to the side of the garage, Tal pulled in front of one of the bays and left the other for Clio.

Brigid stood at the walkway to the house and waited for the others to join her. A jaundiced light in the kitchen lit the window near the door, probably the light over the stove, Clio reasoned. She looked up at the stars spread across the sky – clusters of sparks shining between passing clouds. "Wow, I rarely see the night sky like this in Richmond."

"Pawpaw Joe used to have a dust-to-dawn light behind the

garage," Tal said, "so he could get around to the barn at night, but Grandmaw Roane took it down after he passed. She's a fan of the Milky Way."

The sidewalk led to an enclosed porch on the side of the house where the screen door was unlocked. Brigid walked in and flipped on the overhead light. To the left, a door led into the kitchen. It stood wide open, its jamb splintered around where the strike plate for the lock had been.

"Uncle Brendan still has some force left in that shoulder," Tal said.

"Wonder he didn't hurt himself." Brigid ran her hand over the doorjamb. "You think you can secure this for the night?"

"It's been wide open all day. I'll rig it up for now and then get Paul to help me replace the jamb and plate tomorrow. A new lockset with keys for all of us would make sense. This lock is probably seventy years old."

Brigid and Clio went into the kitchen and flicked on the overhead light while Tal fiddled with the door frame. The sharp smell of bleach and Gain laundry detergent hung around the washer and dryer just inside the door. Around the corner, they came into the small kitchen. White plaster walls showcased souvenir plates from travels around the south. Clio wondered if Grandmaw Roane had visited her part of Virginia, but she didn't see any Williamsburg or Richmond plates. She did notice one commemorating the Wright Brothers' successful flight off a dune in Kitty Hawk, North Carolina, on the Outer Banks, south of her mother's shop and house in Duck.

Brigid kneeled on the linoleum by the sink, wiping a wad of paper towels across the floor. "I'm wondering how long she might have been lying here," she said. "There's urine, but not a lot. That could have been from her stroke and not from the amount of time she couldn't pull herself up. She wears disposable briefs, so I'm surprised there's any urine on the floor. Dad said he found her this morning, and the lights were on in here. Makes me think she got up during the night."

"Was she in her night gown?" Clio asked.

"No, she wasn't. He said she was fully dressed." Brigid pulled the trash can from under the sink and stuffed the paper towels in. "No coffee grounds in the garbage. Oh, God. Tal," she yelled to him, "I think Grandmaw was on the floor all night until Dad came in this morning."

Clio's heart ached when she thought of the old woman, struggling to get up from the floor, throughout the night, until someone showed up the next morning. She looked over to see Tal standing by the refrigerator, tears running down his cheeks. She wrapped her arms around him and started crying as well.

"It's okay," Brigid said. Apparently her profession had steeled her for thoughts of the suffering her patients experienced. "I don't think she was in much pain, if any. I'm sure it was frustrating for her to be prostrate, partially paralyzed."

"Shit, Brigid, 'frustrating'? Of course it was frustrating, maybe even terrifying," Tal said and pulled away from Clio, wiping his eyes. "For a ninety-seven year old woman, that was a banshee screaming in her ear. I have to give her the peace she's asking for – peace with Finn's leaving." He turned, as if searching for something on the kitchen counters. "She has some old photos that I need; some of him just before he left. Maybe there's a hint in one of them." He went through the door to the rest of the house, and Clio followed. The next room, the dining room held a cherry wood table, china cabinet, and sideboard. Tal turned to his right to a long hallway and hit the light switch.

Family portraits lined the solid left wall and bedroom doors scored the right. "Pawpaw and Grandmaw's bedroom is over there." He gestured to the closest door, next to a bathroom that backed to the kitchen. "Then three bedrooms for seven boys. Although the younger ones slept together, the older brothers had their own space. I think it was only a few years that all seven were here together. As they got in their teens, Lionel then Brendan moved to rooms over the garage. Oscar had the first room, Tristan and Brian the middle room, and Dylan and Finn had the one closest to their parents since they were the youngest. All these boys and just one bathroom." Tal laughed a little. "Grandmaw Roane sure had her hands full."

"My father's name was Dylan, too," Clio said. "He was an only child, like me, so I guess in comparison, we had it lucky."

"Not so sure," Tal said. "I'm an only child. Got lonesome sometimes, but the cousins were always around. I probably spent more time here with Grandmaw and Pawpaw than in my mother's home." He went into the far bedroom, at the front on the house, turning the switch on a mission-style lamp on the dresser. "Grandmaw keeps her photo albums in this chest." He pulled out a drawer and rummaged through it, placing multiple albums of different sizes and colors on the bed.

"Do you know what you're looking for?" Brigid asked him as she came into the room and sat on the bedside, pushing the white chenille bedspread to the side. "Grandmaw won't let us sit on her good bedspreads. You better make sure those photo albums aren't dusty and leaving a mark."

"There's one that had photos from the Christmas before he left. Late 1980s. It's the one with Madonna on it – you gave it to Grandmaw Roane for Christmas that year."

Brigid smiled. "Yep, Madonna was my girl when I was in high school. Thank God, Mom stopped me from buying a cone shaped bra to wear to the prom."

"Funny, I was more of a Whitney Houston fan," Clio said. "Tal?"

"Melissa Etheridge and Tom Petty for me." He found the photo album and wiped the cover on his shirt to make sure it was clean before he placed it on the bed. They gathered around it as he turned the pages. "There's Brigid." He pointed to a perky teen with a high blond pony tail. "Me." An elementary school-aged Tal mugged for the camera in front of a Christmas tree.

"Uncle Finn." Brigid tapped a photo.

Clio saw a man in his early-thirties, dark hair cut short in a timeless style – not fashionable like the teens in the other photos, but a standard barber shop cut – bangs combed to the left, short over his ears and the back. He wore a red sweater, no pattern, and sat in an upholstered chair that Clio bet still held the corner in the front room. On the chair's arm, a woman perched. Pretty and more late-eighties fashionable than Finn, she smiled at the activity off camera. Finn looked at the photographer, as if surprised there would be pictures at the Christmas gathering. He was handsome. She could see Taliesin's features in both the man and woman.

"Is that your mom with him?" she asked Tal.

"Yep, she lives in Bristol. Never remarried." He pulled the photo from under the clingy film that kept it in place with the other photos on the album's page. "What's up with that look he has? That's a man ill at ease."

"Looking back now," Brigid said, "I would say he's a flight risk, but hindsight is always spot-on. Then, I thought he was the coolest uncle alive. Clio, the women loved him – young or old, he could charm them all. When you talked to Finn, he would stare into your eyes as if nothing else mattered outside of the conversation."

"I have to admit, he was a good dad to me," Tal said. "He ran around on Mom, but I wonder if that's just a product of growing up surrounded by brothers, not much of a female influence to help him understand what women feel in relationships. I know Grandmaw Roane fawned over him, as the baby in her line of sons and being the seventh son of Pawpaw Joe, who was the seventh son of Pawpaw John Henry and Grandmaw Nunley."

Clio envied their natural ability to recall generations of their ancestors. She barely knew her own parents, who rarely talked about the past. The past didn't matter in her childhood home, just what was happening at the time. Even the future wasn't considered that often.

Tal placed the photo aside and flipped through other albums.

When a page opened with a snapshot of the boys lined up against the white fence that edged the farm, Clio pointed. "Are those all the sons?"

The boys stood in order of height. Brigid tapped each head as she named them. "Lionel, then Dad – Brendan, that's Oscar, Tristan, Brian, Dylan, and Finn. Lionel, Dad, Oscar, and Brian still live around here. Dylan and his wife moved away. Tristan and his wife live in Atlanta and visit on holidays."

She'd seen many children photographed by height, showing the stair-step nature of a child born every couple of years. Working the farm, Mr. and Mrs. MacGuire must have been thankful for seven boys to help. Their little faces, smiling in the aged red-tinged Polaroid, appeared happy and content, but the posture and eyes reminded her of her own past. Maybe growing up close to Norfolk Naval Station, Langley Air Force Base, and Fort Eustis colored the image with familiarity of the square shoulders and straight stance of discipline she recognized from the military families of her childhood neighborhood. These farm boys, with their short hair and white oxford shirts and dark slacks, brought up thoughts of class presidents and honor roll students, probably unpopular with the in-crowds of 1970s elementary and high schools. But, they must have been the pride of the teachers, coaches, and parents.

Chapter Eighteen

1971

"How could you?" Joyce flung the letterman's jacket at Finn's feet. "Karla, of all girls. She...I can't imagine..."

He didn't say a word, which made Joyce angrier.

"Why would you do that to me? I thought I was special to you. Just another notch on your belt."

His eyes averted, but he didn't move away from her. She had him backed against the brick wall of the gymnasium, out of sight from the lunchtime practice of the marching band. The band worked through the Carpenter's "We've Only Just Begun" over and over.

"Two years. No," she corrected, "since we were in first grade, I have loved you. Karla is what you want? You are so stupid. Idiot. Get away from me." She wanted to kick him, scratch his face, knee him in the groin, but she couldn't hurt him physically as much as he'd devastated her emotionally.

He began to move away as she had demanded, slow, without making eye contact. His movement, his retreat, kindled her bitterness. She shoved his shoulder back against the brick wall, stopping him.

With both hands, she jerked his face toward her. "Why?"

No words came from him. A thought flared in her mind, full of rage and fever, to grip his head and shove it back against the wall, banging it over and over, to the beat of the band's bass drum and the sound of the marching shoes on the pavement. He must have seen the hysteria in her face because his eyes didn't flinch, but softened, and began to tear, as if his heart broke. Joyce thought that maybe he understood how he'd betrayed her love and trust, how they could never go back, how they had been each other's first lovers, and Joyce had always believed him to be the only lover in her life. Now, that was ruined. Did he understand?

She dropped her hands from his face and let her body sink to the asphalt. Autumn wind blew a ripped, orange maple leaf across her knee. She caught it and handed it to Finn. "It's done."

Finn didn't want to tell his brothers. But word spread quickly through the school. Dylan had seen him in the hallway before sixth period and just shook his head as he walked by without stopping. He knew Dylan would tell the brothers when they got home after football practice. He didn't have to wait that long to get Dylan's reaction.

The coach never pitted the brothers against each other. In scrimmages or practicing new plays, he'd put Dylan on the offensive line while Finn took the running back position. When the coach called a rushing play, the defense lined up, pawing the ground like bulls. The center snapped the ball to the quarterback who quickly jabbed it into Finn's waiting hands. Dylan took a dive and let the defensive tackle barrel into Finn, slamming him back, knocking the air out of his lungs, and bouncing the football free. All the players scrambled for the ball, except Finn and Dylan. Finn lay on the field trying to catch his breath, while Dylan stood over him.

"Way to go, asshole," Dylan said. "This is just the beginning. Baby brother's role as the chosen one is over. You're a man. Act like one. Don't ever go near Joyce again."

Finn gasped for air. Dylan placed his foot on Finn's stomach and pressed. "I always knew she was too good for you."

Neither brother talked through the rest of practice or on their way home. Dylan drove the farm truck, with the radio turned up loud, so they didn't have to acknowledge each other. Once home, Finn jumped out of the truck with his gym bag and stormed toward his bedroom in the house. Dylan headed for Brian and Tristan's rooms above the garage.

"Whoa," their mother called to Finn as he hurried through the kitchen. "Get back here."

"How'd Dylan get to you so fast?"

"Dylan hasn't said squat to me." She patted out biscuit dough on a floured cutting board. "You two fighting again?"

"Joyce and I broke up." He took his gym bag around the corner and dumped its contents into the washing machine. He waited out of sight to brace for what his mother would say.

"Finn, get back in here. Tell me why?"

He edged around the wall. "Just kid stuff." He hoped she would let it drop.

His mother reached into the cabinet and took out a Mason jar, floured its rim, and started stamping out biscuits. She motioned for him to bring her the baking sheet off the far counter, already greased with Crisco. "Tell me."

"Momma, I'm sixteen. Joyce acts like we're married already. I love her, but how do I know she's the one? I mean, all the girls out there, how can the first one be the right one? What are the odds?"

"Don't worry yourself about odds and if there is a 'right' girl. You'll know when love is there. You won't want to be with any other. Sure, other gals might be prettier or funnier or sultrier, but the one you want to spend the rest of your days with, that's the girl you marry. In my day, a few girls might have had an edge on my looks – not many," she added. "Your daddy had a wandering eye in his youth. When he and I met, we just knew it was to be."

"How?"

"I was staying at a rooming house in Danville. Joe had come to town to work at the same textile mill where I worked. I'd seen him around, but hadn't paid much attention to him." She placed the rounds of biscuit dough on the baking sheet, one after the other with two fingers' width between them.

"Well, one evening," she continued, "I heard a confident knock on the front door. I opened it to see Joe standing there. He asked if I'd like to come out and sit on the porch with him. While he spoke so self-assured, he twiddled with his hat in his hands. He rotated it around by its brim then tossed it up a little and caught it." She stopped placing biscuits. The smile on his mother's face reminded him of Joyce when she would look at him from across the classroom. "Something about that confident and nervous boy stole my heart. Not sure what it was he saw in me. Probably liked my cooking – like his sons do."

"Where's Paw? I need a man's side as well. The brothers are all dumb asses. I wouldn't trust anything they say."

She smiled and handed him the tray of biscuits to put in the oven behind him. "They may act the part of asses sometimes, but they'll always take care of you."

The thought of Dylan's foot pressing down on his stomach as he had tried to catch his breath made Finn shake his head and turn toward his bedroom. "I've got homework to do."

During supper, none of the boys mentioned the subject of Joyce and Finn's breakup. Their father talked about the hay that needed to get into the barn before rain came and the expectation of the tobacco prices at the upcoming market. The look on Joyce's face from that afternoon haunted Finn while he picked at the meatloaf and gravy his mother had prepared.

Tristan and Dylan helped clear the table after everyone had finished their apple fritters. Finn followed his father to the porch where Joe would smoke his pipe each evening. Brian walked past them and up to his room over the garage. Finn settled into the rocker next to his father, matching the rhythm of the back and forth motion, each of them staring forward at the cattle grazing by the fence just past the driveway.

"What's on your mind, Finn?" Joe asked.

"Why would you think anything is hovering in my head?"

"You're my boy. You're my youngest. You're a seven like me. I know. What's worrying you?"

The thought of avoiding the question occurred to him, but he'd come out to the porch for a reason. "I broke it off with Joyce today. Paw, she was so clingy, just always around me, all the time."

"Good," he said. "Getting serious too young is a bad idea. Plenty of time for one woman after you get married."

"The thing is, I can't imagine being tied to one woman for the rest of my life. That's a scary proposition."

"Don't tell your momma, but I felt like that too." He tapped his pipe in the ashtray on the table between the rockers, knocking sparks and singed tobacco out of the pipe's bowl. He pulled his pocketknife out and dug the remnants of the tobacco until the bowl was clean, then handed it to Finn. "There comes a point in a man's life when he knows it's time to settle down, put the chase behind you, find that good woman and make a life together."

Since he was a toddler, Finn had loved the sweet smell of pipe tobacco and had begged his father to let him fill his pipe when needed. Now it was habit, and sometimes Finn wondered if his father could remember how or why he'd given the task to Finn. He inhaled the cedar and clove scents mixed with the musky tobacco, tamping it tight into the pipe's bowl with the butt of his own pocketknife. Handing the pipe back to his father, he asked, "Sounds like settling when the time comes. I don't want to settle. Joyce would be perfect if we were older and ready. But..." He took a slow breath, and added, "I like the excitement of touching an unfamiliar girl, getting to know her skin, the softness, the places that make her squirm, the curve of her hips, the taste of her mouth. I don't mean she has to be a virgin, in fact, I like it better when the girl ain't afraid. It's almost mystical to be with someone I don't know that well. It's the thrill of discovery."

The old man held his Zippo lighter to the pipe and inhaled the flame to flare up the tobacco. Smoke whispered up and caught an evening breeze. "I know what you mean." He turned and winked at his son. "But, you be careful. You get a girl pregnant, and your momma will skin you alive and make you marry the girl. Wear a rubber."

"So you're not mad I broke up with Joyce?"

"You do what you need to do. Now's the time to see what you like. She'll be around."

No one ever left the area, so he knew when he'd had his fill of the other girls, if Joyce was the one for him and if she still felt the same way about him, they would be together again. The heaviness that had held him down now felt like a trail of smoke, floating away with his father's reassurance that his feelings were justified and normal. He hoped Joyce would come to realize that as well.

Chapter Nineteen

Clio flipped through a high school yearbook from John S. Battle High School. Girls in mini-skirts and knee socks, puffed sleeve blouses, straight long hair. Boys in plaid slacks, wide belts, wild-patterned shirts with big collars, and their hair long to their shoulders. The cover of the yearbook, a mossy green, had gold print with the school's name and the year and the yearbook's name: Phoenix. "Wonder why they called it Phoenix?"

Brigid glanced over at it. "Rising from the ashes? A renewal?"

"I think it was a fairly new school back then, so I can't see how a Phoenix would represent anything unless the school came from another one." Tal said. "That's Dad's junior year. Add it to my pile."

Clio set it aside with a stack of photos Tal had picked from the albums. She had never seen any school-age pictures of her own parents. She felt as if they had only materialized on earth when she was born. Even her grandmother didn't take photographs at holidays.

"Sure am getting thirsty," Brigid said, and began putting everything back in the drawers of the chest. "Someone promised me a drink at The Martha."

"Okay, let's go." Tal gathered his photos and the yearbook. "I can look through these at home. Maybe I'll take them in to Grandmaw Roane tomorrow. She might like seeing some of them again."

At the bar in the Martha Washington Inn, they gathered around a table with wine, beer, and scotch. The stack of photos was piled in front of Tal; he sorted and studied them as Brigid and Clio talked.

"You're heading to Richmond tomorrow?" Brigid asked.

"I need to get back for work Monday. I'll be in Charlottesville by Wednesday for a meeting with Ted Mears," Clio said.

"What's Teddy Bear got you doing?"

"Geez, Brigid," Tal said, glancing up from this photos. "You have no respect for authority. I wouldn't call my boss that."

"You have no boss." She sipped her scotch. "Free as a wolf."

"And about as starving as one, too." He nodded to the waitress and motioned to the drinks on the table for another round. "You buying this round, Brigid?"

"No, no," Clio interrupted. "Let me get this round." She looked to Brigid. "I've set up weekly status meetings with Ted to review the progress of the implementation."

"I'll be back at the hospital by midday on Monday," Brigid said. "I want to meet with the doctors here Monday morning to make sure they're treating Grandmaw with more than just the prescribed procedures. There are several homeopathic techniques that I've seen produce excellent results."

Tal drained his beer and set it to the side just as the waitress delivered a fresh round. "I don't know that the doctors in Bristol are going to take kindly to some fancy-assed Charlottesville doctor telling them their job."

"I know what I know," she said. "And I know what works alongside the meds. Clio will agree with me. It takes more than a list of medications to help a patient's body recover."

Not sure if she should weigh in on their family debate, Clio poured her remaining wine into the new glass and took a long drink. She watched Tal and wondered if her semi-infatuation with him was a result of her and Devin getting into a rut.

Back to his photos, Tal didn't try to argue with Brigid. "This one is homecoming with Dad escorting one of the majorettes."

Clio looked over at the photo of Finn, quite handsome in his football uniform, and a tall, pretty majorette, in a short sequined leotard, a cape draped over her shoulders, and long, dark, straight hair, parted in the middle. "Is that your mom?"

"No, he and Momma didn't meet until the Bicentennial. Story she told me was that Washington County held a big celebration here in Abingdon, maybe it was in conjunction with the Highlands Festival. But anyway, Momma and some girlfriends drove over from Kingsport. They all worked at Tennessee Eastman – part of Eastman Kodak. So they ran into some of the MacGuire boys at a dance. That was when disco caught on, so lord only knows what they danced to. Finn's charm caught Momma. They were well past high school. She was out of college by then." He stared at the photo again. "Must be one of his many girlfriends. I think he bedded the whole cheerleading squad and half the band's majorettes."

Brigid tapped her glass and pointed at Tal. "Just like his son. The nut doesn't fall far from the tree."

A short laugh came from Tal. "Except I had a couple of the cheerleaders and the quarterback of the football team."

"Can't make a commitment, Tal?" Clio asked, joking with him about his bisexuality, which she found attractive, but couldn't pinpoint why.

"Something better might come along. What about you? No ring on your finger."

Brigid kicked him under the table with a loud thud.

He frowned at Brigid. "Bri, that hurt. Sorry, Clio. That was too personal."

"Rein the brain back or cut out the beers," Brigid said.

"I apologize," he said to Cliodhna. "Brigid acts as my big sister, again and again."

Clio sat back in the leather chair. "No problem. I bat that around myself. I know I have trouble with commitment. I didn't have the best role models for a successful relationship. My mother and father argued quite a bit. He'd storm out of the house and end up at the bar down the street. I would go retrieve him because Mom would lock herself in the bedroom."

"Oh, Clio," Brigid said. "That's awful. How old were you?"

"I was old enough to walk the few blocks alone. Maybe ten or twelve. Newport News wasn't the greatest place for a girl to walk, but I carried my dad's gun with me."

"Are you kidding?" Tal leaned toward her, across the table. "A ten year old girl carrying a gun down the street to a bar?"

"It was a pistol, and I kept it in my coat pocket. Plus, the hidden gun was reassuring when he came back, with a little too much liquor in him."

"Jesus H. Christ, I thought we had it bad." Taliesin sighed. "So this Devin guy… What is he like? Hopefully, the opposite of your father."

"Devin is very flattering to me. He respects me. He's divorced, no children. He wants to take our relationship to the next level and has been talking about moving in together, but honestly, I can't imagine living with him twenty-four hours a day. I like my alone time."

Tal nodded. "We get set in our ways, the older we get."

"Well, I have a great example of a happy marriage. I can't imagine either of my parents being without the other," Brigid said. "As they age, I'm sure one will outlive the other. Then I won't know what to do. They're the type that they'll probably pass within weeks of each other."

"Like how Johnny Cash died a few months after June Carter Cash," Tal said. "Some people are meant to be together here and on the other side. Then others, like Finn, needed to be the lone wolf. Not sure he ever wanted to have a family, too many ties. I mean, I'm a healthy man, but I don't let lust lure me into dangerous situations."

Brigid raised an eyebrow and took a long sip of her scotch.

Clio thought of her father and how he seemed devoid of any type of obsession or deep feelings – not for her mother, for his work, for any hobby, not even for his own daughter. Was she the same? At times, Devin seemed endearing to her, maybe close to love, certainly passion flamed up, but a deep intensity of affection didn't simmer in her. Would she be depressed if she and Devin broke up? Probably not, she admitted to herself. Was she thinking that because Tal sat in front of her?

Tal needed to find out about his father. She wanted to help, so she would check with Wayne at the office on Monday to see if his computer digging had uncovered any beneficial veins in Tal's search.

After a meeting with her boss, Doug Williams, Cliodhna went into Wayne's cubicle to see what information he'd been able to secure. He had mentioned he'd work on it over the weekend.

"Obsolescence is stealing data," Wayne said as she sat in the side chair in his cube. "I called my buddy over at the state police headquarters after I talked with you. He said most of the information from that period – as I guessed – was on magnetic tape, stored in the tape libraries or off-site, depending on how each state police organization structured their data archives. Unless the reports had to do with a court case or an open case, a lot of it was purged. He also said that getting the tapes mounted for us to search could be a problem."

Wayne explained that he met his contact at the state police headquarters on Saturday to see if they could hit the databases from the states that had responded to their requests to mount the tapes from the late 1980s to early '90s. "We did several searches on the VIN your friend gave me. West Virginia, Tennessee, and Maryland returned nulls. We hit a match in North Carolina's database. It was for a scrapped Impala. No license tag, no paperwork, but it was a light blue color – from what they could make out and put in police report."

"What… Or how was it scrapped?" she asked.

"Pulled it out of the Currituck Sound on the Outer Banks, just south of the U.S. Corps of Engineer's research facility. If you've been down there, that's just north of where the Sunset Grille is today in Duck."

"Yeah," Clio said, as her mind turned flips making connections that shouldn't be there. "So, the car got pulled from the sound? When?"

"November of 1990. No identifying information except for the VIN. The report," Wayne said and pulled a couple of papers from his bag to consult them, "says they couldn't find any owner information – probably because the tags were off of it – so it was considered scrapped."

"But the VIN?"

"When that Impala was built in the late 1970s, the VINs weren't standardized and not used for vehicle registration. It was mostly manufacturer's numbers, for production use. So, the VINs weren't indexed in any database."

"We're pretty sure that's the car. But that doesn't lead us to where Tal's father could have gone."

"If the car ended in the Currituck Sound, then I'd guess the driver would have been close by. Either he went into the sound with it or he dumped it and moved on. They didn't find a body and the car was empty and had no license tags. That spells a disappearing act. Plus, he probably wasn't very familiar with the sound because it's shallow there – deep enough to cover a car but not much more. The lucky part for him is that the sound doesn't have a tidal flow, so it's consistent in its depth and kept the car covered for a while."

"So maybe he was familiar with it, or else it was just the first place to stash the car. Thanks for doing this so quickly, Wayne. I'll get those Redskins tickets for you." Clio took the report printout that Wayne offered her and went back to her office.

She read the report, trying to glean as much from the few facts it offered. She didn't know that much about Finn MacGuire, except what Tal had told her, but her mind couldn't stop making connections to her own past.

The year of 1990 had not been a happy one for her family. She and her mother had struggled after her father left. Left? From her memory, he had been dragged out of their house that spring and never came back home.

Chapter Twenty

Brigid informed Tal that their grandmother would have to spend a few weeks in a rehab facility after the hospital released her. He had an appointment with the facility's administrator to finalize the paperwork before Grandmaw Roane could be moved to the place to start her rehab.

With only two in-patient facilities in the area, Grandmaw Roane's insurance plan placed her in a dingy nursing home where Tal had to maneuver his SUV around potholes that pocked its parking lot. The lawn's assortment of crabgrass and dandelions had gone to seed between infrequent mowings. He pulled the glass door open to the lobby. The harsh scent of urine and shit mingled with spray disinfectant. "Better breathing through chemicals," he said to an old woman hunched in a parked wheelchair by the front window.

The receptionist at the front desk looked up as he walked over to her. "Help ya?" she asked and pushed toward him an open three-ring binder with a photocopied visitors log sheet. "Please sign in."

"I have an appointment with Thelma," he said. "Tal MacGuire."

The woman stretched to look around the corner. "Her office is to your right. The door's open. Thelma should be in there."

He found the executive director in a small office where every flat surface had papers piled. Thelma, a woman of about 60, stood to shake his hand. "Mr. MacGuire. Are you one of the MacGuires up on Lee Highway?"

"That's where Grandmaw lives, but I'm in Bristol."

"Whose boy are you? I went to school with a couple of them, Dylan and Finn."

"Finn would be my daddy."

"My gosh, I just can't imagine his boy being so grown. How time rushes by. I'm seeing my old school teachers showing up here as patients. That's a shock when I still remember them in their prime. How's your mother doing? She didn't go to school with us, but I remember her from her working at Parks-Belk." Thelma leaned against her desk. "She caught the boy that no girl in high school could lasso. We always thought that Finn and Joyce Adams would get married, but then she started dating your uncle."

"Uncle?"

She lowered her voice as if the receptionist might hear. "Oh, yeah. That was like a high school soap opera. Now, I didn't run in the same circles as the popular kids. Finn, Joyce, and Dylan – that was the love triangle of the school."

"Damn," he said before he could stop himself. "Sorry." He shifted his stance and leaned against the door frame.

She laughed. "That's okay. We say worse things here all the time."

"Uncle Dylan married Finn's old girlfriend?" Tal had never met his uncle Dylan since he had moved his family away the year Tal was born. Family members rarely talked about him or his wife. This is probably why, Tal thought. His breathing quickened. "That's odd. How did that happen?"

"The way I remember it, Finn and Joyce broke up, and within a couple of months, around the start of basketball season, Joyce took up with Dylan. Dylan was a senior and Joyce was a junior, so she jumped way up in status with that. Must have turned into true love because they married a few years later. Although that probably made Sunday dinner at your grandparents house uncomfortable. Finn, I'd guess, was okay with it, just puppy love for him."

"I hear Daddy was a ladies' man in his day."

"You got his looks." She smiled and added, "And Finn was so friendly. Even to the ugly girls, he would flirt with them and make them feel special."

A bit taken aback by the term "ugly girls," Tal reminded himself that most people didn't think twice about what they said. He wondered how Thelma would talk to the residents when family wasn't around. A vacuum cleaner cranked up, the roar ebbed and flowed as someone pushed and pulled it across the dark green carpet in the hallway outside the office.

"Now," Thelma raised her voice over the racket. "We have paperwork to sign for – your grandmother, Mrs. Roane MacGuire. Do you have her Power of Attorney?"

He couldn't picture his grandmother in this place, a waiting room for death – the odor, the noise, the people. His stomach felt tight yet roiling. "Yes, but can she get her rehab treatments at home?"

"I don't know if the insurance will pay for someone to watch her twenty-four hours and to have a physical therapist, a speech therapist, and an occupational therapist visit her." Thelma opened a file drawer and retrieved a folder. "Have a seat, and we can go over the admission forms."

A piece of paper had never appeared as frightening as the one Thelma held out to him. He couldn't, he wouldn't place his grandmother into this reeking, grimy, neglected, granny-dropoff. The animal shelter had a better facility.

"No, Thelma. I'm going to keep her at her home. Thank you for your time."

He left the nursing home and took a deep breath in the parking lot. Yes, he would keep his grandmother at her house. But how? Maybe that answer would come to him. He hoped so.

Tal found Brigid in their grandmother's hospital room talking with the doctor on duty, an older white man. They spoke in medical terms that Tal didn't understand, but from Brigid's expressions, he could tell she was fairly comfortable with the discussion. He sat by Grandmaw Roane's bed and held her hand as she slept.

When the other doctor left, Tal told Brigid that he couldn't place Grandmaw in the nursing home, not even for just a couple of weeks for rehab.

"So, are you going to take care of her?" Brigid asked.

"I can find some woman to help her with bathing and to the bathroom and to stay overnight with her, and I'll drive her to rehab. That place wasn't somewhere you'd want her to be."

Brigid pulled her phone from the pocket of her jeans. "Dad, can you line up an in-home caregiver for Grandmaw? Tal says the nursing home isn't good for her. Yeah." She listened for a few moments. "Okay." Brigid walked to the window. "Sure, that would work if you all take shifts. I'll let him know. Love ya." She hung up. "Taken care of – you just have to know the right person to hand it to."

"Uncle Brendan knows someone?"

"If a woman has seven sons, corresponding daughters-in-law, a bushel of grandchildren and a peck of great-grandchildren, there has to be enough family around to stay with her when she needs them. He said he and the boys would take care of it."

Their grandmother stirred and opened her eyes. "What you jabbering 'bout?"

"Your speech is better," Tal said and kissed her cheek.

"Not good, but okay," she said, then looked to Brigid. "Will I live?"

"So far, so good," Brigid said. "You have to do what these doctors tell you. Dad and the boys are going to stay with you so you can go back home. Tal didn't like the place the insurance wanted to send you."

"Bah, insurance," she said. "Crooks."

Tal agreed. "Take the money and give us nothing back. Oh, do you remember a girl going to school with Daddy and Uncle Dylan called Thelma? She runs the nursing home."

"Can't place name." Grandmaw reached over and rubbed her arm where the IV was inserted. "Hmm. Kind of a silly girl? Her family was from over in Mendota."

Tal tried to picture Thelma as a girl. "She might have been silly. She remembered Daddy and Uncle Dylan. Sounded like she had a crush on Dad."

"Most girls did." Her eyes drooped and she yawned.

Tal stood. "You get some rest. Brigid and I are going. I'll be back after I teach my afternoon guitar lessons."

"Grandmaw," Brigid said and kissed her forehead, "I'm going

back to Charlottesville. I'll stay in touch with the doctors and you."

Deciding that all planning should not be left to his Uncle Brendan, Tal stopped by Brendan and Charlotte's house after he finished giving lessons at the music store in Abingdon and before he went back to the grandmother's hospital room in Bristol.

"I made up a chart for staying with Maw," Brendan said. He pushed the paper across the kitchen table so Tal could see. Charlotte stood over the stove, filling a pot with redskin potatoes and water.

"We can take four-hour shifts. Your cousin, Jeannie, will stay with her overnight. That girl don't have a job, so she can at least help her grandmother," Brendan said. "Then during the days, each of us can stay a few hours. I know you have your band and late nights playing guitar, plus lessons at different times, so I left you off the schedule. Just come by when you can."

"I'll be around when I'm not working," Tal said.

"We're all old and retired – or unemployed like Jeannie. Don't know what Brian is going to do with that girl. Probably try to marry her off."

Tal slid the paper back to his uncle. "Do you remember something going on between Dad, Uncle Dylan and the girl Uncle Dylan married?"

His uncle didn't meet his gaze. In fact, it seemed to Tal that he avoided looking at him.

"Joyce? I think that was her name. Is that Uncle Dylan's wife? Where are they?"

Brendan sighed and looked over at Charlotte. She moved the pot of potatoes off the stove and left the kitchen.

"I don't know if Brigid remembers them or not. She was barely in elementary school when they left. Yeah, Finn dated Joyce for about a year before they broke up and she ended up with Dylan."

"That must have been awkward. But I guess that happens – the

MacGuire boys are charmers."

Brendan moved the paper schedule over to the side, then pulled it back in front of him. Tapping it with his forefinger, he said, "Your dad was a strange man. Always a bit ill-at-ease, Finn would act like the world owed him something, then a second later he would be the most charitable and considerate person you ever met. I wonder if he was bi-polar, as they call it now."

"Could have been," Tal said. "Momma never said anything about bi-polar tendencies, but she did say he was a wolf, chasing every woman in town. Of course, that's what she focused on – him running around with other women."

"I've tried to think on that. Men that I know will talk a wild streak about chasing women, but few really do. Hell," he lowered his voice since Charlotte was probably in the next room, "it would be a lot of work, all that hiding and sneaking around. I tell you, one woman is enough for any man to keep up with." Brendan picked up his pencil and drummed the paper schedule for a few seconds. "Something stayed between Joyce and Finn. Everybody could see it years after they broke up, even after she married Dylan. We all thought that maybe the little girl was Finn's."

"Joyce had a baby girl? Was it Dad's?"

He laughed – hushed and quick. "I couldn't tell. Charlotte said she thought the baby was Finn's child."

"Was this when he was married to Momma?"

"Not yet. Kay and Finn married a few months after Joyce announced she was pregnant. Paw told Finn to grow up and get away from Joyce. I'm sure Finn loved your momma, but I think he still loved Joyce."

"And she probably still loved him," Tal added. "Wonder why she started dating Dylan and eventually married him?"

"We all wondered that, too. Dylan was a good guy. Maybe after Finn, Joyce wanted someone who would be true to her. But, Finn's brother, that's what made it so odd."

"No shit."

Chapter Twenty-one

August 1607

Will added more branches to the fire. The flames jumped and sparked. The swamp's wildlife roamed near as Thomas and Will dined on the roasted bear meat.

"Fayther, the colony had rough times that winter many years ago. Was it the witch or natural conditions?" Will asked.

"A combination," Thomas said. "Those who wanted to believe in an external force to blame for misfortunes, chose to fault the witch. I saw our troubles as lack of leadership and our ignorance and weakness to adapt to the new world. The colonists began to turn against each other, bickering with friends and denouncing their neighbors."

"Did you ever see Kazeiah the witch again?"

Thomas thought for a moment. His son's eyes glinted in the firelight. "No. I believe she left or met her fate in the wilderness as retribution for what she had done to Daniel and his young woman. Waves roll onto the shore and they retreat. Sometimes what the ocean gives is reclaimed by her with the next wave. The colonists cast their own lots then blamed each other when the situation declined. As the winter grew bitter, people began to move inland," he explained, "some with friendly tribes, a few of the young men decided that they would travel toward the distant mountains and the fabled passage to the great sea. I stayed. I felt responsibility to the colony."

The night grew still and Thomas tired. "Tie up the remaining meat in that tree," he told Will and gestured to an oak a few yards from their fire. "We'll continue on to the Powhatan River in the morning."

As the sun beat down mid-day, Thomas and Will came upon the river. Its water moved quiet and smooth toward the bay and the ocean. Thomas had not canoed the waters of the Powhatan, but had heard from others that upstream rowing was possible until encountering falls well inland. Trade prospered up and down the river with eager tribes. The English had chosen well in this location. Thomas didn't see ships or a fort. They walked along the shore until they came across scouts from another tribe. The men told them of the English and the location across the river a few miles north. By mid-afternoon, Thomas and Will saw three ships docked by a marshy area at a bend in the river.

"The point is a good place for lookout up and down the river," Will said from their vantage place, "but that's a low, wet ground. They should build farther from the river, at least to keep the storm wash from their beds."

"Yes, they would benefit from our experience." Thomas thought of revealing himself to the Englishmen, but wondered if that was wise for the sake of Will, Neshinnah, and their tribe. He knew he would never return to England or want to live with Englishmen again, but their simplicity and inexperience concerned him – he felt as if he was ignoring children in the wilderness. "Do you want to see them more closely?" he asked Will.

Will hunched behind a thicket of briars. "No, Fayther. I have seen all I care to see." Will rested his hand on his father's shoulder. "They look like us, but that's all. Our family is with the tribe."

Relief felt cool on Thomas's face. Willow chose to stay with his family and tribe instead of the new adventure with the Englishmen. Thomas wondered if he would have made the same decision. No, he had not chosen his family those many years before on the docks of England. He had boarded the ship without hesitation for the New World of Virginia. He believed Will had more sense than he had at the same age. Did these men know what they had ahead of them? Would England support them or abandon them? Standing up straight, he looked to Will and said, "We will not let these men suffer as my colony did. Our allies can watch and warn. I will advise, but not reveal myself. Europeans are not our enemies, but infants in a forest – scared and unaware."

Will smiled. "We act as guide spirits from the woods. Help the innocents without them knowing." He sighed. "I know living among the Englishmen would be a great adventure, and that teaching them the ways would please the gods, but my duty belongs to our tribe and my family. Many years, we watch. My future sons may want to travel to see people of their grandfayther's land." He nodded to Thomas. "But, I am satisfied with my life."

With another look, Thomas said a short prayer to both Jesus and Ahone to allow the settlers good fortune and health and not to be abandoned by their country. He and Will would return, but not interact with the new settlers. He owed it to his own tribe to keep the ways of the Englishmen at a distance.

Chapter Twenty-two

Once back in Charlottesville, Brigid checked on her patients. Just as she returned to her office, an intern called – they needed her in the Emergency Room where a car crash patient was asking to see her.

She walked to the nurses' station. "I've got a fan here?"

"Dr. MacGuire, Room 6. Dr. Jarvik said the patient wants you to consult with him. Apparently she doesn't think Jarvik can help her without your assistance."

"Name?"

"The patient is," the nurse consulted the computer screen, "Sue Henderson, age sixty-seven."

"Henderson? Can't place the name. Is Jarvik with her now?"

The nurse found the doctor had moved on with his duties, but called him to meet Brigid at the patient's ER bed. Brigid pulled back the curtain to the room around the corner from the nurses' desk. The woman, a little overweight with long gray hair, didn't look familiar, but she smiled at Brigid despite her injuries, mostly facial lacerations from her car's air bag being deployed. Dr. Jarvik had written in the records his concern about a possible concussion.

"Ms. Henderson, I'm Dr. MacGuire. How are you feeling? Any blurred vision? Can you remember what happened?"

"My memory is fine," the woman said with a bit of slurred speech.

A nurse came in with her tablet consulting the records for Ms. Henderson. Brigid took it from the nurse and re-read it quickly. "You requested to see me." Brigid looked up when the woman didn't respond.

"Oh, that was a question? Yes, I knew you could heal me."

Pulling her stethoscope up to her ears, Brigid asked the woman to sit up. She listened to the woman's breathing, clear and strong.

"Why did you think I could help more that Dr. Jarvik?"

"You're a healer. He's a doctor. I don't need doctoring."

Brigid placed her palm on the woman's forehead. No fever. Ms. Henderson's body relaxed, almost as if all the tension and strain retained in her muscles from the automobile wreck released at that moment. Her breathing slowed. Brigid looked at the woman's face – eyes fluttered. A glance at the heart monitor confirmed that the patient continued to have a steady heart beat, no sign of tachycardia.

Dr. Jarvik pulled back the curtain, entering the small room. The nurse stepped away from the bed. Brigid liked Jarvik. He respected her opinions even though he worked by the book, a man of strict clinical research and its measured results. "Dr. MacGuire, you have a fan here. Ms. Henderson said she meant no offense to me, but would prefer your consultation. She's a lucky woman. That car crash could have been much worse."

"I'm feeling better," Ms. Henderson said and pushed herself up in the bed. "Dr. MacGuire, can I go home? I know I'll be okay."

"We need to observe you a little longer. But, there's no reason," she started to say then looked to Dr. Jarvik for his agreement, "to move you to an inpatient room."

"Right," he added. "Just try to relax. We'll check on you in an hour."

"Thank you. I feel much assured with the two of you here."

The doctors walked out together. The nurse remained with the patient.

"So, Brigid, do you know her? She was insistent that you check her," Dr. Jarvik said.

"Mike, I have never seen the woman before. Sometimes I get those. Not sure if she wanted a female or just a fabulous redhead to give an opinion."

He laughed, then turned serious. "You're the only doctor I've seen patients ask for," Jarvik said. He nodded for her to follow him over to an alcove with a computer stand for entering notes. The space was quiet and private. "I think some people are drawn to you."

"But, like I said, I never met the woman before."

"God knows, I'm not an intuitive doctor, but you are. Some people pick up on that. I can't explain how she came up with your name, but she told me straight out that she wanted Dr. MacGuire to check her. I'm not offended. It wasn't like she didn't trust me or had anything against me; she just wanted your consultation. You pull people to you and they connect with you on an organic level It's the damnedest thing. You should be in a study to see what that influence is, how to measure it and replicate it."

On her way back to her office, Brigid wondered how Ms. Henderson knew to ask for her, why her and not one of the other doctors in the hospital. Jarvik hit it. Some people came to her for advice and help. As she could remember, that had occurred all her life – elementary school, other children rallied around her during recess; in high school, she often helped the other girls deal with their severe menstrual cramps before a period or eased a sprained ankle or a torn ligament from volleyball. College at the University of Virginia seemed to accelerate the number of lost souls finding her. Her boyfriend at the time – an obsessive/compulsive lacrosse star – would call her the "freak magnet" for all the misfits who found their way to Brigid. Both physical and psychological issues seemed to resolve when she spent time with the people who sought her out. Brigid liked to think she provided a good example for her friends of the harmony of mind, body, and spirit.

Her relationship with her cousin, Tal, proved to be her best example. From the time he was ten years old, she had taken on the role of big sister. Uncle Finn left in the middle of the night leaving Aunt Kay and Talie alone. Her father and Pawpaw Joe stepped in to assist Kay on her way to become more independent, yet supported by the family, while Brigid sheltered Talie and encouraged him to pursue his talents. Brigid had her driver's license and would pick up Talie after school to take him to his guitar lessons. Aunt Kay fell into a deep depression. Brigid's mother and father would say Kay had been a fool for not seeing Finn for what he was. Now, as Brigid thought back, she understood Kay's reluctance to name the illness that shrouded the marriage – infidelity. When the monster is named, it becomes real.

Her work in her practice and at the hospital confirmed that a diagnosis of cancer, Parkinson's disease, or dementia recorded on the patient's chart rooted the course of treatment. Her attempts to introduce other complementary treatments and methods that could ease the symptoms of the ruthless drugs and invasive surgeries, were met with rebuffs and grumbles. Brigid recognized that her Aunt Kay didn't want to confront Finn about his womanizing because that would set the marriage on a course of action Kay sidestepped.

But it happened anyway: Finn released, Kay wilted, Talie drifted.

Brigid saw that she should intervene and ease the pain wherever possible. Talie bloomed in his early teens, becoming a person Brigid admired and loved. Finn never returned. Kay strengthened, eventually became tough and independent, but she never opened herself to another.

Brigid walked down the hallway to her office. A young doctor spotted her and changed his route. Okay, she thought, some people avoid me. She'd adapted a bitch attitude to reduce the number of people clinging around her, but – as she considered it – some still sought her out.

Chapter Twenty-three

With the July 4th week past, Joyce readied for continued tourists through Labor Day. The sun peeked over the rooftops between her front deck and the Atlantic Ocean. Gulls squealed while a crow hopped across her neighbor's roof to rest on the chimney. She loved the quiet of the morning before the vacation rental houses around her woke to the delighted cries of children and grandparents heading for the beach. Parents and teenagers slept late then made the trek down to the main road to a coffee shop and bookstore for caffeine and the morning newspaper. The murmur of a truck approached from Route 12 and the rumble increased as a pool maintenance truck pulled onto her street and passed her house. She waved to Skeeter. He stayed on a weekly routine servicing the pools on her street each Tuesday and Saturday.

Mid-week blessed the town with less traffic. The weekends were the turnover days for the rental houses and brought bumper-to-bumper travel with a new batch of vacationers. Shop browsing as a pastime resulted in spontaneous sales for her shop. Her store had a prime location at Scarborough Lane, close to a couple of restaurants that served strong drinks. People tended to find more things they wanted to buy after a margarita or a martini. Joyce had new inventory in the shop's storage room. She needed to go in early to get it entered into the computer and priced.

To the back of her house, she noticed the clouds over the Currituck Sound looked purple in the early morning, a sign that the day could be rainy. She decided she'd drive the quarter mile to the shop that she usually walked.

After her last sip of coffee, she headed back into the house and grabbed her keys to get to the shop early and restock with her new inventory. She checked her phone to see if she had any missed calls or texts. Nothing.

The houses around hers dwarfed her little cottage, one of the original beach houses in the village of Duck. Other homes like hers had been torn down and replaced with nine-bedroom monstrosities, filled with bunk beds, teal couches, and left-behind romance novels. She remembered the days when the Outer Banks meant drafty cottages and no air conditioning and eating fish that was caught that day. But, the waves of visitors and swell of high-end accommodations, eateries, and retail had allowed her to live in the family cottage and earn a living at the beach – a situation that she would have never thought possible thirty years before.

A small community of full-time locals managed the town's council, boards, and committees. Joyce served on the Jazz Festival committee and knew most of the residents in town. She pulled her sea-glass-green Jeep onto the highway and waved to another shopkeeper walking along the bike path. The Currituck Sound to her right looked choppy, whitecaps flashed under the plum-tinged clouds advancing low over the mainland across the water. She loved the water. When she went inland for a buying trip or to visit her daughter, she longed to return to the sand and saltwater.

She parked behind the Scarborough Lane Shoppes and climbed the steps from the parking lot to the main level. Her store faced Route 12 and offered one-of-a-kind items that she had picked up from local artists, consignment shops, estate sales, or auctions. She had an eye for the unique and rare. "Quirky" is what a fellow shopkeeper had labeled her store, but Joyce took that as a compliment.

Joyce's own appearance embraced the distinctive as well. She kept her silver hair cropped short and spiky. She favored loose, flowing garments in shades of lavender, copper, or sea green. Secondary colors suited her as she considered these coastal years her second life. Sandals of cork or leather were her favorites. Most of her jewelry consisted of items from the ocean: shells, pebbles, bones, pearls, sea glass.

With a greeting to the woman who owned the toy shop around the corner, Joyce unlocked the side door of her store and started pulling bubble-wrapped hand-blown bottles from three large boxes. The artist lived on Ocracoke Island and shipped the bottles to Joyce. The wavy glass reminded Joyce that everything in life wasn't flawless or clear, but could still be useful and beautiful in its imperfections.

With the inventory stocked and a quick dust of the merchandise and a sweep of the wooden floor, Joyce decided to go ahead and open the shop early. Tourists wandered in, moving to their right and making a circle through the store, picking up things to take a closer look. A few sales helped start the day on a good beat. By lunchtime, the customers had increased and the shop was busy. Her assistant, Darcy, arrived to help mind the shop for a few hours. Two of them could handle the hectic times.

"I need to get to the hardware store," Joyce told Darcy. "We could use more batteries for those lantern candles." Once outside, Joyce pulled her cell phone from her canvas bag, punching the first name on her Favorites list.

"I haven't heard from you in a while, Sweetie," she said when the line was answered. "Is everything okay?"

She listened while the excuse was given, which seemed reasonable to Joyce. People didn't communicate as they used to, now everything was short messages, leaving the depth of communication for in-person visits. Just as the thought came into her mind, she heard the request. "Sure, yes please, I would love to see you. You know you don't have to ask. This is your home." They agreed on a date and Joyce disconnected. The morning clouds had drifted out to sea. The sun looked brighter and the breeze felt cooler and the tourists spent generously.

Chapter Twenty-four

"Yes. Great," Taliesin said into his phone as he pulled the yearbook from the stack of photos he had at his grandmother's side table. He listened to Brigid and paged through the yearbooks.

Grandmaw Roane tapped the remote for the television mounted on the wall across from her hospital bed; channels flew by as she seemed to search for a program that might interest her. Clicking off the television, she dropped the remote on the bed and looked at Tal. "What?"

He had finished his phone conversation. "We're taking you home today," he said. "Your speech has recovered remarkably well. Brigid is impressed with your progress, and God knows, it's hard to impress that girl." He winked at his grandmother.

"Good. I'm tired of this place. Ready to get back home."

He set the high school yearbook on her lap. "Can you show me the girl Dad dated and that Uncle Dylan married?"

"Your aunt Joyce. She came close to being your momma." Grandmaw opened the book and flipped pages to the junior class.

Tal recognized his father's class picture. Many times, as a child, he had looked at the copy his grandmother had framed and hanging in her hallway. Grandmaw Roane flipped the page and pointed to a black and white photo of a pretty girl, straight dark hair parted in the middle, a flowered vest with puffy sleeved shirt underneath. A flower child of the early 1970s, if Bristol could have hosted such a person then, Tal thought.

"There, that's Joyce," Grandmaw said. "Finn's girlfriend at the time." She turned a few pages toward the front of the book. "Finn and Joyce on the Homecoming Court." Finn stood next to Joyce in a line of couples on the football field. He wore his football uniform and she wore her majorette outfit. They both smiled wide. She held onto his arm with her right hand while holding a bouquet of mums in her other arm.

"What happened that they broke up and she ended up marrying Uncle Dylan?"

"Kids are crazy. Bouncing back and forth to each other as if there ain't enough people to go around. Back then, and I guess now, many of the young people thought they needed to marry up early. Some of them rarely left home."

"Our family has been in Washington County since the Revolution, so we're not much of exploring people," Tal said. "Uncle Tristan and Aunt Diana moved to Atlanta. Uncle Dylan and Aunt Joyce moved… Where did they go?"

"Don't know exactly, now," his grandmother said. "Dylan took off and rarely communicated with us again. He was always an odd bird, but Joyce wedged between him and us. Well, not 'us' but Finn. He shouldn't have married her. Why introduce that into a family?" She looked at Tal with a stern stare. "Don't get involved with the exes of any of your relatives. I tell you, there are plenty of fish in the ocean. No need to fish in a brother's pond."

"Did you and Pawpaw Joe try to dissuade Dylan from Joyce?"

"Sure, your pawpaw didn't like the idea at all. Things were so tense that before they moved away Dylan and Joyce would only visit us when the other brothers – especially Finn – weren't going to be at our house. They would come to see us on Christmas Eve, instead of Christmas day. They stopped by Thanksgiving night after everyone else had left. The only times we could get them together was during family reunions – when Pawpaw Joe's brothers would bring their families to visit."

Grandmaw Roane explained how the seven brothers of Joe's generation had liked to gather at each other's homes every summer to get the extended family together. The brothers' sons and daughters had children of their own, so Joe and his brothers had become the grandfathers, doting on their next generation. Joe had been the only brother to have seven sons. His brothers had opted for smaller families with their wives.

The cousins of Lionel, Brendan, Oscar, Tristan, Brian, Dylan, and Finn brought their children to play with their second cousins. Brigid, one of the older kids at five, took the toddler cousins to see the cows at the barn just as Dylan and Joyce drove up and parked by the barnyard fence.

"Uncle Dylan," Brigid yelled, and ran toward him as he opened his car door. He patted her on the head and held her hand as they walked around the Oldsmobile to open the door for Joyce. She had some difficulty getting out of the low car and Dylan helped her to her feet.

"Grandmaw," Brigid hollered and ran to her grandmother standing at the picnic table under a maple tree by the side yard. "Pawpaw, come see Joyce. She's going to have a baby!"

The crowd of about fifty relatives all stopped their conversations and turned toward the cars. Joyce, barely showing her pregnancy, but wearing a maternity top, smiled, but kept her eyes to the ground as she and Dylan came to the picnic tables where he seated Joyce at a bench. The women crowded around, making over Joyce and offering maternity and baby clothes that they no longer needed. The men sauntered off with their cigarettes and pipes to the front porch – all except for Finn. He and his girlfriend, Kay, stood whispering by the garage apartment where he still lived.

The sons of Joe and Roane had married and began their own families. Small children chased each other around the yard. Dylan and Joyce adding to the mix seemed only logical.

"Grandmaw," Brigid said and tugged at her grandmother's sleeve. "It's wonderful, a new cousin."

Grandmaw Roane bent down and kissed Brigid's cheek. "Yes, honey, another MacGuire is just what the world needs." Her fears kept her from enjoying the moment. Joe caught her eye when he nodded for her to meet him at the garage. "Go play, Brigid." She shooed the child away.

When she stood next to Joe at the bottom of the steps to Finn's apartment over the garage, he shook his head back and forth, avoiding her eyes. "You think what I think?" he asked then glanced up the stairs to the closed apartment door. "We can't ask him in front of that girl."

"I can ask Kay to help me in the kitchen while you talk to Finn," Roane suggested.

"Not sure he would tell me the truth. He might be more open with you."

"A boy won't tell his mother if he is slipping around with his brother's wife."

"He knows I'll take him to the woodshed," Joe said and sat down on the steps. "Maybe he'd be more willing to admit it to you. Go get Charlotte to ask Kay to help her with the meal. That way you can get Finn alone."

Charlotte knocked on the apartment door and asked Kay to assist her in the kitchen. Finn came down from the apartment and stood alone watching the crowd from the shade of a maple. His mother approached him and asked him to follow her into the garage. The old Cadillac parked on one side, the other side of the garage held ice chests of Coca-Colas and jugs of lemonade and tea. She pulled out some paper cups and started filling them with ice. "Finn, pour some tea in these." He complied. "You're awful quiet since Dylan and Joyce showed up. What's going on in your mind?"

"Just happy for them, you know, the new baby and all."

"Shit, Finn. Don't lie to me." She slammed a cup down and the ice scattered across the tablecloth and onto the asphalt floor of the garage.

"Maw, what do you reckon I should say?" He kicked the ice out the bay door. "It hurts."

"I know you've been messing around with Joyce. This baby yours?"

"You think that? Does Paw?"

"I'm willing to bet, most of your kin out there is believing Dylan's a fool fawning over a woman carrying his brother's child."

"Dylan is no fool. He knows that kid is his. I'm surprised you think differently."

She came around the table, wrapping her son in her arms. He

set down the jug of tea and hugged his mother back. "Baby boy, I know more about you than you imagine. Joyce is married to your brother. Respect that and leave her alone."

Grandmaw Roane closed the yearbook and handed it back to Tal. "We never got a solid word on it. You might have a sibling out there. Finn and Kay married a few months after. When the baby arrived, Dylan piled them into his car and took off. Probably for the best."

"How long was this before Finn disappeared?" Tal thought he might have a lead.

She considered it for a while. "That was probably eleven or twelve years before. They were long gone by then and most likely forgotten by Finn. By then, he had married Kay and you were in elementary school. Of course, I couldn't forget my boys. Dylan is happy wherever he is. He left on his own terms to take his family from all the whispers and looks that would have hounded them to this day. That was his decision and I respect it."

"Don't you wonder what happened with them? They could be easier to find than Finn."

"Finn was taken away," she stressed. "Dylan and his family left of their own accord."

Tal felt like his father had left of his own free will, but Grandmaw Roane felt differently. How could she so easily let Dylan and her own grandchild go, yet continue to fixate on why Finn left? Tal wondered, too, about the phone call and what he would find when he went to Charlottesville.

Chapter Twenty-five

1708 – James Cittie Shire, Virginia Colony

Through the barred window, Thistle whispered, "Europeans not smart in their reasoning. Tie woman to a stick and duck her in the river. Their Jesus going to release her and push her up to surface? Stupid people."

Anna trembled on the bench, her back to the thick stone wall of the public gaol. "Thistle, don't loiter here. You will attract trouble, probably more trouble than I am in." Her mind kept going to Stanton. If convicted, she would be sentenced to death. Who would take care of her son? After her husband died, Anna felt very little concern about her own existence, but recovered her sense of purpose for her son. Sitting in the gaol and waiting to be accused or set free, Anna had little hope of walking out to resume her life.

Women's voices chattered down the hall, clanking against the walls like metal chains. Several of the town's women appeared at Anna's cell door, along with Parnella Hart.

"Madame Mayford," Leatha Tucker, a mid-wife of advanced age, said, "we are appointed by the magistrate to search your body for the mark of the Devil." She had the gaol keeper open the thick oak door to Anna's cell. He lingered by the door until Leatha jerked her head and frowned to get him to leave them alone.

"The indignity!" Anna withdrew from the five women. "I will not allow one hand to accost me."

"You allow the Devil to bed with you," Parnella accused.

"You vile woman. Such ideas can only come from a witchy mind. The panel should search you for a Devil's mark."

The women glanced at Parnella, but focused back to Anna. "We have enough evidence that the magistrate convened this panel to report back on our findings," Leatha said. "Do us the favor of removing your shift."

With a jut of her chin, Anna crossed her arms in front of her chest in defiance. The women moved forward and Anna narrowed her eyes. Parnella slunk behind a larger woman.

"We can beckon the gaol keeper if we need," Leatha said. "I do not want to resort to force. Cooperate and I will inform the magistrate of your helpfulness in resolving this matter."

Anna sighed and relaxed her arms. With hesitation, she slipped her shift off her shoulders exposing her chest and back. The women began to inspect her skin. Parnella stood back from the women, but watched them closely. Finding nothing of interest along Anna's shoulders, bosom and belly, Leatha instructed her to turn around.

The memories of her mother strapping her as a young girl overwhelmed Anna and she began to tremble. She heard one of the women gasp when she turned. She knew the scars ran from her right shoulder down her back to the left side of her waist. Multiple, thin lash marks created a grim weave across her skin.

"The Devil left many marks on this witch," Parnella hissed from behind the stout woman.

"No, a wicked mother, not unlike your character, Parnella," Anna said, head down against the stone wall. She didn't want to face the women for the shame she felt, more for her mother than for anything she might have done to bring on the beatings as a child. The only other to see her scars was her late-husband. Edward had tried to reassure her that the marks added to her beauty, but she cringed when he touched her back.

Humiliation squeezed the breath from her.

The women whispered.

"You may cover yourself," Leatha said. "We have seen enough." They summoned the gaol keeper and left Anna in the cell shivering.

The magistrate visited Anna's cell door. He did not come into the cell as the women had, but stayed a few steps back and spoke through the barred opening. A man of about 50 years old, thin gray hair capped with a magistrate's wig – shoulder length, curled, and of the modestly price goat hair – he explained to Anna the process of her trial.

"The courts of Queen Anne charge you with witchcraft," he said, his voice strong and determined.

"I protest."

"You have no say in the matter. The panel of good women, having inspected you for the Devil's mark, have discovered evidence of such. A search of your house revealed a wax doll of Goodwife Hart."

"She placed it there!"

He continued. "Your familiar, a black tomcat, captured on your farm attempted to scratch and bite the court clerk."

"This is nothing that you would not find on any farm in the county. A farm harassed by a shrill neighbor."

"On that account, the charge arises from impaired chickens and cattle of the Hart farm. The waning marital interest of Goodman Hart to his wife. And most importantly, the witness of you changing into a wolf to attack the newborn colt at the Trent farm."

"Wolf? If I were able to transform, do you think these bars could cage me? Why wouldn't I become a crow and fly to my freedom?"

"Talismans against witchcraft are embedded in these walls. Your conjuring has no effect here."

She moved toward the door and the magistrate stepped back. His fear and ignorance could be used to her advantage, Anna realized. "I am a struggling widow with a young son." She pushed her long dark hair away from her face and coyly eyed the man. "Tristan Hart attempts to court me. His wife knows this, and she makes me the focus of her rage. I have no powers other than those that all women possess over lonely men."

He moved closer to the door, but kept an arm's distance. "No widow should have to distress. There are men in the community who would make fine husbands." He glanced toward the gaol keeper's desk. "I am a widower several years now. I understand the struggle and loneliness. My children have grown and started their own lives, but I still know the toil to raise a boy into fine young man."

"How did I get into such a situation?" She shook her head and paced back from the door. "My neighbors do not like me – because of the interest of their husbands or their bad luck in crops and livestock – Parnella tries to blame me. She has enlisted another woman to witness for her and add to the rumors. I am not a witch. Those are the tales of our grandmothers. I trust that our majesty, Queen Anne, does not hold to the old beliefs." Anna turned away from the door then looked back over her shoulder. "How do I get released from this gaol and go about my life in peace?"

The magistrate gripped the window bars of the oak door. In a quiet voice he said, "Confess."

"I will do no such thing." She walked to the door. He did not back away. "I am not guilty. I cannot confess to such a rumor."

"Your actions have brought these charges," the magistrate said.

She searched her memory. "I have not transformed into a wolf. I did not mold a wax doll. That old tomcat is as any other feline in the county, not a familiar. I don't take any notice of other farms' livestock or crops. I invite no interest from other women's husbands or sons. You will not find me roaming the countryside during the night –"

"You consort with the heathen Indians," he interrupted.

She felt the blood rush to her face. "They are people, not savages. No different than Scots or Welsh or German or African."

"Again," he almost yelled, "you show no regard for our society. Slaves and Indians, barbarians with their worship of idols and black magic, do not compare to the good Christian people of Williamsburg. To survive this, you must conform. Confess, denounce Satan, comply with the community standards. With this exposed through a trial, you will receive a petit punishment and then go about your life."

The trial held in Williamsburg drew a crowd to the courthouse, so many people arrived that a hundred or more stood outside the door to listen. Anna's son, Stanton, squeezed into the back of the courtroom to watch the proceedings.

She refused to confess.

The magistrate listed the accusations from two neighbors.

No one rallied to defend Anna – the Widow Mayford, the peculiar woman who worked in the fields wearing her dead husband's clothes; Anna, the woman who moved with grace and strength about the farm, sweat clinging to her bosom, her hair in disarray, eyes sparking with fire; Mistress Mayford, the potential seductress of good husbands, the collaborator with the pagan Indians and the idolatrous slaves.

She stood alone.

The four justices of the peace ruled to test the Widow Mayford – as she had feared – by ducking. Aligning with the Devil meant throwing off baptism. With witches rejecting the holy water, the water forsook witches.

"If the water accepts you, you are innocent," one of the justices explained. "If the water rejects your body and floats it to the surface, you are guilty of cavorting with the Devil and doing his bidding as a witch."

A sob from the back of the room broke the silence. Stanton ran out the door.

Chapter Twenty-six

Brigid's house in Charlottesville seemed more modest than what Cliodhna would have expected for a medical doctor. The bungalow sat in a tidy neighborhood of similar homes with picket fences and wide sidewalks; short driveways led to detached garages or to side carports. The evening sun filtered through the elms and oaks lining the street. But as Clio drove up to the address Brigid had given her, she noticed the luxury sedans and SUVs parked by each home. So close to the downtown, the small homes must be pricey, she thought.

Her hands, cold and a little sweaty, gripped the steering wheel as she pulled in front of Brigid's home. Taliesin's SUV sat behind Brigid's Prius in the driveway. Clio parked on the street in front of the house. Visions from her childhood swarmed in her mind – an argument, the quiet, the early morning sunlight, the man who left with her father. "They are going to think I'm insane," she said to herself then took a deep breath, exited the car, and walked up to the front door.

Brigid welcomed her and led her into the kitchen where Tal sat at the table with a beer in front of him. "Let me get you something to drink," Brigid said.

"Yes, wine – anything you have open."

With white wine for Clio, Brigid poured herself a scotch.

"Tal, they located the car."

"What? Where is it?"

"Long gone, but the records say it was found in the Currituck Sound in 1990. The authorities labeled it as abandoned, disposed of, in the water. I think we need to go down there. My mother lives in Duck, North Carolina, near the place they found the car." She didn't mention more.

"You think we could find people who might remember

what happened? Was there anything in the papers about the car wrecking?" Tal asked.

"Not sure," she said. "My mom has lived there for a while, but not back then. She may know of some people around town that would remember. I thought we could drive down tomorrow and check with Mom and some of the old-timers in Duck, then hit the sheriff's office to look for records that aren't on-line."

"I can bring the photo of Dad and the car. That would show I have a connection to the car and finding out what they found – just in case they seem hesitant about letting us dig through their files." Tal looked to Brigid. "Could you clear your schedule to go with us?"

"Yes, I have a couple of days. Clio, your mom doesn't mind us piling in on her?"

She thought for a moment. The beach house was small in comparison to the vacation rentals around her, but her mother's house had enough bedrooms to accommodate them. "Let me call her to make sure. I didn't mention I'd be bringing friends."

Her mother answered on the first ring. "Mom, I'd like to bring a couple of friends with me tomorrow. No, not Devin. Friends from Charlottesville – that's where I am now. Right. We're trying to find some information from the… I guess it would be Currituck County. Wait; is Duck in Currituck or Dare County? Okay, the Dare County sheriff's records. They're in Manteo? Okay. See you tomorrow… Love you." She added that for the benefit of Tal and Brigid. She couldn't remember the last time she'd told her mother that she loved her. The exchange of words of affection had never been a habit in her family. It felt rough coming out of her mouth, like undercooked grits.

Clio had asked Tal to bring the yearbooks they'd found at his grandmother's house. Being careful not to make any crazy connections until she had evidence, she only told him she might know someone who had attended school with his father.

She sipped her second glass of wine. "My mother's maiden name was Adams. I think there might be a connection to your family." Clio opened the yearbook and searched the photos. "My mother's mother – my grandmother, Marian Adams – lived in Richmond and then in Florida. I barely remember going to see her, maybe I blocked it out. She was always very critical of my mother and of me. I had always assumed my grandmother had lived in the central part of the state her whole life, that Richmond was where my mom grew up. It made sense that we stayed close to my mother's family. My father's family wasn't discussed." She stopped flipping the pages. It could be, she thought.

"When I first applied for my driver's license at the age of sixteen, I had to have my birth certificate, which had been re-issued."

"Re-issued? Did your parents lose it?" Tal asked.

"My mother said they changed my name when I was a toddler – as if Cliodhna was a better choice than what I had been born with."

"Why did your mom change your name?" Brigid asked.

Clio looked at her wine glass and took a sip. "I think my father had changed our name – our last name."

"You're not Clio Fitz-Adams?" Brigid asked. "Your mom was an Adams. Your father's family name was Fitz?"

The idea that for forty years she didn't know who she really was seemed absurd, comical, insane. Of course, she knew herself as a person, but her fit into the world by way of a lineage didn't exist. For many years, especially as a teen, Clio toyed with the idea that she had been adopted as a baby. She didn't want to claim blood relations with her father or her mother. They acted more as housemates than parents. Each had their own world, barely intersecting with each other. Not sure how to say what she wanted, Clio pushed the open yearbook across the table to face Tal and Brigid.

"This, I feel, is my mother." She pointed to the homecoming photo of Finn standing next to the majorette.

Tal squinted.

Brigid sat back in her chair and drained her scotch.

"But," Tal started to say. "Can't be. That's the girl that came between Daddy and Uncle Dylan. She married…"

Clio's hands twitched as she pulled the book back to her. "Dylan?" She peered at the black and white photo of the two teenagers – Finn and a young girl who looked like her mother, a young girl whose name was listed as Joyce Adams. "My father's name was Dylan. My mother…could be this Joyce Adams."

"Joyce married my uncle, so her last name would be MacGuire now. She wouldn't be a Fitz-Adams or even an Adams anymore." Tal bent over closer to the page, straightened up, and stared at Clio. He huffed through his nose like a bull. He flipped the pages back to the senior class pictures. "There," he said and pointed to a picture of a clean-cut young man in a wide-lapelled tuxedo jacket and a ruffled shirt with a fat bow-tie. "That is Dylan MacGuire at eighteen. Does he look like," he hesitated before saying, "your father?"

The eyes. She could see her father in those heavy-lidded eyes and the way the boy had his mouth pulled into a closed, vague smile. Her tears started flowing.

"Oh, Clio, I'm sorry." Tal rushed around the table.

"My mother, Joyce, she can tell us. I hope she will. Must. Has to." Clio's words stumbled out, and she took another fortifying drink of her wine. "I think that if the two of you are there with me, she might be more inclined. More inclined to tell the truth." She knew the truth had never played an important role in their house, and she doubted that her mother had changed much since Clio had left for college years before.

Brigid poured herself more scotch. Before she took a sip, she asked, "Who's driving to the Outer Banks tomorrow?"

Tal raised his hand. "I got it. We can all fit in my Chevy."

Brigid took a long drink from the scotch and patted her mouth with a paper napkin. "I should be able to recognize Aunt Joyce, but then she looked damn close to that yearbook picture the last time I saw her, except pregnant."

"When was that?" Clio asked.

Brigid calculated the time that had lapsed since she saw Joyce at the reunion. "That was just over forty years ago."

"I'll be forty-one in January," Clio said.

They left Charlottesville early the next morning, missing the Richmond rush hour, but hitting the brakes in Newport News traffic. Clio looked for her old neighborhood as they drove toward the Monitor-Merrimac Bridge-Tunnel, and then they crossed to the southside of Virginia.

Memories of her time in the area – her father at the shipyards, her mother working at a daycare, then at a department store – didn't bring many warm feelings. Each had a job to do. Her job was to get out of the house and away from her parents. At the age of eleven, Clio had been relieved of her father. She often thought of his leaving as a relief, but it had barely changed the household. Maybe the habits he had caused in her mother, and in her, lingered because they knew of no other way to act. Not that her father had been a monster, but he was usually angry, better yet, she thought, his mode of operation was to be moody – swinging from anger to sadness to helplessness. As a young girl, she tried to make him laugh with jokes she'd learned in elementary school. He would have moments of amusement, but they never lasted for long.

He seemed happiest when he was busy working. In the mornings, as she readied for school, her mom fixing lunches for them before she left for work, her father would talk about the current project – maybe a battleship or aircraft carrier that he had a part in. The sense of purpose would drive him, please him, hearten him. If only she could have done the same.

Clio's skin bristled when she considered her earlier feelings about Tal. He could be related to me, she thought. She tried to dismiss the assessments she had made about him as a potential romantic partner and how she'd thought more about him than Devin. In the car for a couple of hours, and none of them had trespassed into the possibility of their kinship.

"Grandmaw Roane and Pawpaw Joe had a place down on the Outer Banks," Brigid said from the back seat. "Pawpaw would take the boys fishing, or some of them took their families for a few days at the beach. I remember going the last time when I was about thirteen, not much there, and it took a long time to get to from Abingdon. Later, we went to Myrtle Beach or Surfside Beach in South Carolina because it was a shorter drive."

"I remember that cottage in Surfside," Tal said. "Aunt Loretta's people left it to her. She and Uncle Oscar would let any of us use it." He turned to Clio, who sat in the passenger seat. "Aunt Loretta's maiden name was Byrd. So the cottage was named the Byrd's Nest. It wasn't much more than a cinderblock building."

"Painted pink," Brigid added from the back seat. "I guess they thought that made the cinderblock tropical looking. Three bedrooms and one bathroom."

"Lord, the mosquitoes would eat you alive. That place sat about six blocks back from the ocean, in the pines," Tal explained then started singing in a high tenor bluegrass style:

> *In the pines, in the pines, where the sun never*
> *shines,*
> *And you shiver when the cold wind blows.*
> *My love, my love, what have I done*
> *To make you treat me so.*
> *You've caused me to weep, you've caused me*
> *to mourn,*
> *You've caused me to leave my home.*

Clio's hands and arms tingled. She angled the air conditioning vent away from her.

"Daddy would help do a few repairs when we stayed at the Aunt Loretta's place," Tal said. "I remember him and me getting on the roof to patch it one summer. Flat roof. We had to use tar."

Clio rubbed her hands over her arms to warm up. "Mom's place is closer to the beach, just a few blocks. It was a one-story, but she added another floor because, during storms, the overwash would flood it." Clio couldn't remember much of the house, since they rarely went to it when she was young, and her mother didn't move there until Clio had graduated from William and Mary. She wondered if the money to add the second floor came from her father's life insurance policy.

Travelling south on Highway 158, Tal could see glimpses of the Currituck Sound to his left. The water seemed cool and inviting. The dashboard's outside temperature read 88 degrees. Late July and eleven o'clock in the morning, that 88 degrees seemed too hot for comfort to Tal.

Okay, he thought, Clio could be my half-sister – or hopefully – a cousin. Could Dad have fathered a child with his brother's wife? He considered it. No. But, then again, how well did he know what his father did all those times he left home for hours at a time.

Signs along the highway, every fifty yards or so, alerted drivers that peaches, corn, tomatoes, watermelon and boiled peanuts would be available just up the road. He diverted his attention to the billboards. "Will we be at your mom's by lunchtime?" he asked Clio.

She pointed at the GPS display. "That's the Wright Memorial Bridge that takes us to the Outer Banks. Once over it, we'll be in Duck in twenty minutes."

The timeline would work for his lunch schedule. Food made a good diversion from his worrisome thoughts. He had picked up a lunch routine from his grandfather, father, and uncles' regular lunch times at the machine shop. During the summers, when he was out of school, he'd hang around the shop with his father and Uncles Lionel, Brendan, Oscar, and Brian. When noon arrived, they shut off the lathes, grinders, drills, and screw machines where they had jobs going; the quiet settling through the building, only accented by the laughter or the jaw and jabber of the men. They retrieved their lunches from the refrigerator next to an old Formica table Grandmaw Roane had discarded years before. Then they settled on overturned buckets or the table's cracked vinyl-padded chairs by the shop's open garage door for the breeze and to watch the cars go by on Highway 11. The noon hour, instinctively, brought hunger pangs, and now Tal wanted to have in mind and in sight his lunch. Plus, thoughts of lunch kept reality at bay.

The Currituck Sound appeared between wooded areas from the driver's side window. Tal caught a glimpse as he drove. Too long since he'd been to the beach. The expanse of green-blue water lured him. Whitecaps called. South Holston Lake appeased him for short intervals, but the breathing up and down of the ocean or bay or sound could not be replaced. The waves and tides, to Tal, reached to the land, foamy fingers traced across the sand to pull back what the water could reclaim.

A summer beach day, hazy in his memory, his parents sitting under a wide navy-blue umbrella, Tal played at the surf. The new red plastic pail and shovel swinging in his hand, he scooped wet sand and dumped it in the bucket. Packed down, forming turrets for his wall, the sand pail flipped and pulled up to reveal a perfect tower. The accomplishment made little Tal dance around the sand castle, grit rubbing against his legs and in his saggy swim trunks. Finn joined his son with a handful of scalloped shells and a cracked lightning whelk – its edge broken open to show the delicate inner spiral. The shells capped the towers. The whelk acted as the fortress flag. Running back to the waves, Tal didn't see his pail. His father dug a trench around the castle with his hands. The shovel gone as well. His eyes searched, salt and sand pelted his face. Tears started, but he tried to be big and not cry. Scanning the waves, Tal couldn't find any sign of the pail. He wanted to blame another child for stealing it, although he knew it was his own fault. Suddenly, he was lifted into the air and onto his father's shoulders.

"What's wrong, Talie?" Finn's voice soothed his son.

"The wave took my pail." He held onto his father's head,

behind the ears, for balance, fingers intertwined in Finn's hair. His knees over his father's shoulders, feet resting over a ring hanging from a chain around his father's neck. He hunched and rested his chin on the top of Finn's scalp – a crisp and fruity scent from their Finesse shampoo. "I want my pail back."

Finn's hands held his son's legs. "I'll get you another one. Don't worry."

Easily replaced. He wondered now if that was the lesson from the surf. When something floated away, a back-up was readily available. Had his father felt that about his wife and son? Had they been replaced?

Grandmaw always called his intuition a gift, but Tal wasn't buying into it.

In high school, he could feel the other kids' motives. His father and uncles had graduated from the same high school he attended, and they had left their marks. Tal and his cousins were expected to achieve in academics and sports. Some of the cousins did – Brigid graduated at the top of her class; Kathleen ranked fourth in the state in tennis; Fiona took the crown in beauty pageants; Selby came home with all the 4-H prizes for his livestock; Werner set records in the regional wrestling matches. Other cousins stayed out of the light, but Tal knew when one of them had petty intents on their classmates. He would intervene or call Brigid at college to crack down on them. Brigid took no crap from anyone: child or adult, classmate or teacher.

In football games, Tal could sense his opponents' insecurities and hesitancies. He'd pick the mousy cornerback and run toward him. The guy would panic and misstep while Tal pivoted and flew down the field, catching the football that Paul lobbed.

In romance, by instinct, Tal knew when a woman wanted more of a commitment. The warmth of her gaze told him she had thoughts of fidelity, obligation, and duty. A fire blazed in him for autonomy, respite, and decampment. His mother knew of his exodus inclinations, but had told him he inherited them honestly. Another dig at his absent father…and at him.

Sure, men couldn't stay. *We are meant to sow our seed in as* many furrows as possible, he thought. But then tending life had its rewards. Some like his Uncle Brendan, were nurturers and others, like his father and himself, were tillers.

The SUV followed the road through a deep left curve, and Tal saw the bridge ahead. The waters of the sound billowed and pulsed around the bridge's piers.

"It's been years since I was down here," Clio said. "The water is beautiful."

"So, what happened between you and your mother?" Tal asked.

Brigid reached from the backseat and slapped his head. "Talie, mind your own business."

"No, that's okay," Clio said. "We're just an independent family. We go our own way, but stay in touch."

He felt she was skimming over a lot of emotions. "Joyce Adams. Dylan Fitz-Adams. Fitz," he pondered."Fitz means 'son of' – son of Adams. Don't know of any family called Adams, except Aunt Joyce's." That sounded odd coming out. He had never met his Uncle Dylan or Aunt Joyce, only heard vague things about them from family, as if even mentioning them was taboo. He tapped the steering wheel in rhythm to the tires thumping over the bridge decking's expansion joints. "So, if they changed their last name, why keep a reference to her maiden name?"

Brigid pointed to the highway signs for north Highway 12 to Southern Shores and Duck. "Hang a left," she said. "If the name is close to the previous name, then that might have made things easier, at least for her. But Dylan changing his name would be hard to believe. Clio, you've seen enough of Tal to know the men in the MacGuire family have mighty big egos."

"Hey!"

"I can't imagine," Brigid continued, "a male in the family giving up his patrilineality. Family jewels? The family name is the jewel for these boys."

"It could be coincidence," Clio said. "Maybe I'm trying to

fill-in the blanks in my family with the blanks in yours. After we spend some time with Mom, you can judge. My mind could have made all these crazy connections, links that don't exist. I thought most families were like ours, and that the families on television concocted a perfectionism that no one had."

They arrived at the small town of Duck, where sprawling live oaks reached for their neighboring trees and dappled shade danced over the bike path. The Currituck Sound paralleled the highway, just yards from the road. A boardwalk weaved along the sound's shore, connecting restaurants and stores. Clio directed Tal to the Scarborough Lane Shoppes across the road from the sound, built on piers with parking underneath. "Mom's shop is up there," she said and pointed to the corner.

Tal checked his watch, 11:40. They could meet Clio's mother, and then grab lunch and a beer with her. He smiled.

Joyce pulled her phone from her bag behind the counter. No calls. Clio had said she was arriving before noon, yet she hadn't phoned to say they would be late. Joyce considered the reasons – maybe she changed her mind or something at work stopped her from getting away. But, then again, Clio wasn't the type to talk on the phone. Neither was she, when she admitted it to herself.

Darcy walked a customer to the counter to ring up the sale of a concrete gargoyle, an addition to the shop that Joyce found kept evil spirits at bay. The gargoyle, more cute than scary, was about the size of a cantaloupe, but five times as heavy. Still it made a good garden statue for the tourists. Joyce found a cardboard box to set it in for its ride home with the Pittsburgh couple.

Joyce considered Darcy to be a perfect fit for the shop. Probably about fifteen years younger than Joyce, Darcy worked for extra spending money and to keep busy. Her youngest son had recently left for the university at Chapel Hill and her husband ran a consulting business out of their home in Southern Shores. Darcy had said she needed to get out of the house on a regular basis. She and Darcy saw each other enough that they were friends without spending after work time together, which suited Joyce.

"I can handle the shop when you're ready for lunch," Darcy told Joyce after the Pennsylvania couple left with their new gargoyle.

Joyce checked her wristwatch. "Clio said she would be here soon with her friends. I thought we'd walk across the road to Aqua. Kayleigh is holding a table for us on the deck."

The door swung open as a young man held it for Clio. She was followed by a red-haired woman in her mid-forties. The man, probably close to Clio's age, had a familiar face, but she couldn't place him.

"Clio, how good to see you, sweetie," Joyce said and moved in for an awkward hug. Clio patted her on the back a couple of times and squeezed a little, then released and stepped back.

"Mom, these are my friends, Brigid and Tal."

"From Charlottesville? How nice to meet you. Please call me Joyce." She introduced Darcy, who stood behind the counter. A few more customers came in the shop, so Joyce led her daughter and her friends out and toward the restaurant across the road. "You'll enjoy Aqua. It's a day spa and a restaurant, so while you're visiting if you'd like a spa treatment, let me know and I'll get you in."

"We're here for some research," Clio said, as they walked up the driveway to the large house that contained the business. "I doubt we have time for a massage."

"Now hold your horses," Tal said. "Don't discount the advantages of a good rub down, no matter how quick."

That made Joyce smile. The man had a drawl that reminded her of childhood. "That's not a central Virginia accent. Where did you grow up, Tal?"

"Bristol."

She stopped suddenly. Clio bumped into her.

"That means something to you?" Clio asked with a sharp tone.

His face had the familiar look of Finn, if she had ever seen Finn in his late thirties. She could see Dylan in the man's face as well. He was definitely a MacGuire. Then Joyce looked to the red-haired woman. "Brigid?" The little girl was there; Joyce knew her.

Tears welled up in Brigid's green eyes. "Aunt Joyce? You?" They hugged, tight as if they might not see each other for another forty years. Brigid straightened up and sniffed back her tears. "Let's get out of the driveway. We look like a hillbilly reunion."

Joyce led them inside and requested a table in the corner of the sound-front deck. They settled around the weathered wooden table, capped with an emerald-green umbrella, the wind from the sound fluttering it. So much to ask, so much to say, Joyce didn't know where to start.

Clio took a deep breath. "Why didn't you tell me? I mean, there's a whole, huge family that you hid from me. I've felt alone all my life."

Joyce could see Clio's face flush. She realized her daughter headed for a fury. "There's no excuse," she said. "Your father was the brother of Brigid's father." She looked to Tal. "Who is your father?" But she thought she had a good idea.

"Finn," he said. "You're Joyce Adams...Aunt Joyce. Uncle Dylan's wife. Daddy's girlfriend."

The man who sat in front of her was the incarnation of Finn. The same mouth, nose...even his forehead reminded her of Finn. Reaching across the table, she took his hand. Memories rushed over her. Days and nights in high school, riding around in Finn's pickup truck, cruising West State Street by the K-mart parking lot, looping around the McDonald's drive-through and back to K-mart. His family. "Your grandparents?" she asked, worried about the reply.

"Grandmaw Roane had a stroke, but she's doing better. Swears the banshees were calling to her. Pawpaw passed maybe twenty years ago."

"I'm sorry to hear that." She looked to Brigid. "The boys?"

"Dad is good. He's seventy-three. Lionel, Oscar, and Brian have all retired from the machine shop. Some of the cousins took it over – Oscar and Brian's sons. Uncle Tristan is still in Atlanta," Brigid explained. "When you left Bristol, you came here?"

"No, we moved to Newport News. Dylan had read that the shipyards needed welders –"

"Hold on, this isn't old-home-week," Clio said, her eyes hard. "My entire life," she pounded the table. The approaching waiter turned and retreated back into the restaurant. "My entire life I have had a family that you kept from me. How could you?"

"More things were happening than you were aware of," Joyce said. "I tried to shelter you all I could from your father's accusations. We all made mistakes." She looked at the three people around her at the table – the generation that had come from their confusion, missteps, and entanglements.

Chapter Twenty-seven

1985 Abingdon, Virginia

Finn sent Talie across the street to the Stop & Shop to buy an Atomic Fireball and a pack of Reece's Pieces. The kid was crazy for anything from the movie *E.T.* With his feet up on the corner of the desk, Finn watched little Talie wait for a break in the traffic on Highway 11, then sprint across to the convenience store. Finn enjoyed the last summer days he had with his son, before Talie started first grade in a few weeks.

"Finn," Joe said when he came in the front door. "You think Tal would want to ride with me on the tractor this afternoon? Got that back field to mow."

"He'd love it, Paw. Make sure he's got his hat and shirt on. Kay had a fit when he came home sunburned last week."

Joe made a dismissive noise with his mouth, and Finn was sure that if his father hadn't had a moustache, he would have spit across the room.

"I'm serious. Tell Maw to put some of that sunscreen lotion on Tal's face and arms before he goes with you."

"Sun ain't never hurt me," Joe said. "A little sun is good for a body."

"His little body is under Kay's rule, so please do as requested." He pushed his feet off the corner of the desk. "We got that Westinghouse job. Brian did a spot-on estimate for the dies they need. Of course, Wayne, the head man over there, is your buddy Leon's son."

"Leon was always a kiss-ass. I can see how his son got a high-up job with a big company. He's probably a kiss-ass, too." Joe walked to the window, parted the blinds to look across the highway. "Tal's coming." He turned to stare at his son. "Finn, you heard from Dylan?"

"Shit. I'm the last one in the family he's going to call."

"Then let me clarify that: Have you heard from Joyce?" The look he gave his son had Finn glancing down at the desk.

"You know I ain't in contact with her. That's long over."

"What did you just say to me?" The question felt like an accusation.

"Daddy," Finn started, then stopped and took a long breath. "I might get a call from her from time to time. She just wants to check on us – all of us."

"You have a wife and a young son. They are your responsibility, not Joyce. She made her choice years ago."

That statement sliced through Finn. "You mean she made her choice and I wasn't it."

"Women are hard to understand. They do things for complicated reasons. I will never get in my head why she went to Dylan and then married him. He's my son, just like you, but Jesus Christ, he's not of a temperament for feeling like second best. Maybe that was your mother's and my fault for doting on you so much, maybe it was because he wasn't the oldest or the youngest or the star at any one particular thing. He was a good boy until Joyce came between the two of you." He turned toward the door as it opened.

"Pawpaw," Tal yelled and ran to Joe. "Want some Reece's Pieces? They're the best."

"Naw, that stuff gets stuck in my dentures." He winked at Tal and laughed. "Put that chocolate in your daddy's desk drawer because we're going to mow the back field and chocolate melts in the heat."

"Me? I get to ride the tractor?" He looked to Finn. "That okay with you?"

"Sure. Get your grandmaw to put sunscreen on your freckled face and keep your shirt on. You go home blistered and your momma will skin us both alive."

Tal tossed the bag of candy to Finn, who placed it in his drawer.

"Have fun," Finn said. "Paw, I'll come up the hill after work. You and Maw can handle him until then?"

"He's our little troubadour. We'll sing the whole time we're on the tractor." Joe took Talie's hand and walked out the door. Tal turned and waved at his dad as they left the office.

Up from his desk, Finn checked the shop floor. The men ran the machines or adjusted them for their next job. Brian had the screw machine humming, cutting metal into small screws that dropped into a metal bin with a clang every few minutes. Finn turned back to the empty office, hesitated, and then closed the door to the shop floor. The noise of the machines muffled to a low roar. He checked the clock – 1:23 p.m. – then picked up the receiver of the phone. He dialed carefully and reminded himself to get the phone bill before Brian, Oscar, or Brendan opened it.

The phone rang several times before she picked up.

Tal steadied himself on the fender of the John Deere by holding onto the rod of the shade umbrella his grandfather had secured to the back of the tractor's seat. The massive treaded tire rolled underneath his perch, running through a pile of cow manure, churning it up the tire and under Tal's fender then dropping it back to the ground. The attached mower chopped the manure, along with the grass and clover and left clumps behind them to dry out before raking and baling.

"Pawpaw," Tal yelled over the clatter and rattle of the tractor's engine. "How do you keep from getting a bunny caught in the mower?"

He glanced at Tal, then smiled. "Don't worry about that. The noise of the tractor scares them away. They know to get their little cotton tails out of our path."

"Here comes Peter Cottontail," Tal began singing.

"You're a little late for an Easter song."

"Don't know no August songs about rabbits."

"Then let's make one up." Pawpaw Joe scratched his forehead underneath his straw cowboy hat. "Well... There once was a bunny called Sonny."

"And he didn't wear pants, so he had no place for his money,"

Tal added.

"The ants in the garden thought he was funny." Joe pointed at Tal to get the next line.

Tal thought for a beat, then sang, "He showed them where to find free honey." He began to bounce on the fender. "Bunny Sonny. No money for honey."

His grandfather turned the tractor to mow along the fenceline. Pawpaw Joe steered close to the zigzag line of stacked rails. "My grandpaw, your great-great grandpaw built this. It's a Virginia rail fence."

"We been here a long time?"

"Generations," Pawpaw Joe said. "We settled here after the United States became its own country – it has been a colony of England."

"Where did we live before?"

"Way over near the Atlantic ocean. My grandpaw told me that we had some Indian mixed into our family. A long way back grandmaw – maybe thirteen generations ago – was rescued by Indians after some skirmish with the colonists."

"Indians?" Tal snuck a look at the woods along the edge of the fields.

"Sure. The Irish, Scots, and English tried to settle, but the Indians already lived here. That made them mad."

"Well, yeah. I'd be mad if somebody tried to move on my land."

"Not all were mad," Joe clarified. "Some were friendly and helped the new neighbors like old Grandmaw Mayford. But, then others attempted to scare off the white people – usually by chasing them off with a tomahawk."

Tal thought on this for a moment. "They probably had a point – a sharp point on that tomahawk!" He laughed at his own joke,

"Talie, you're a character."

Tal reached over and patted his grandfather's back. "You are a character, too, Pawpaw. My daddy is the best character. You and Grandmaw raised him good."

Pawpaw Joe sighed and said, "I hope we did."

"Oh, Finn, it's so good to hear from you," Joyce said and settled on the couch, propping her elbow up on the armrest to hold the phone to her ear.

"Can you talk? I guess you can since you said my name," he said, sounding edgy to Joyce.

"Clio isn't home from Brownie Scouts yet. Dylan won't be home until late, if at all."

When Dylan had left for work that morning he was in a good mood, kidding with Clio about her scout project of a diorama of Winnie the Pooh's Hundred Acre Wood, complete with Christopher Robin, Pooh, Piglet, and Eeyore. Joyce wondered why she had added "if at all" to her answer. Did she make things sound worse to prompt sympathy from Finn?

"How is he doing?" Finn asked.

Taken a bit aback because he asked about Dylan before asking about her well-being, she waited a second and then said, "Dylan is Dylan."

"He's holding his temper, isn't he? Is he drinking?"

"No problems in months," she said. Her cigarettes sat on the table next to the recliner. She reached for them, but the phone's cord wouldn't stretch that far. She sat the receiver down and grabbed the pack and Bic lighter. Back on the couch, she picked up the receiver and said, "I think your brother is completely occupied with work. He doesn't pay much attention to me." The flick of the lighter blazed up and lit the tip of the cigarette dangling from her lips. "Speaking of little attention – how's Kay?"

"Now, I don't want to talk about Kay," he said. "This call is to make sure you are getting along. Dylan knows that he can bring you all home, doesn't he? Maw would love to see that little granddaughter. Maybe for a short visit. She would like that…Me, too."

She exhaled smoke. Was he really playing the concerned brother? The kids at the daycare that morning had been irritating her with their excitement over the zoo visit to Norfolk the day before. One little boy kept crawling on all fours, claiming he was a tiger, growling at the other children. Even putting him in the corner didn't help settle him. She needed to find another job. "Oh, Finn, I can't imagine us coming for a visit anytime soon." She wanted to ask him if he had finally decided that he could live his life with one woman, but she knew the answer. At least with a tiger, his stripes stayed true. Finn hunted like a wolf, his hunger never satisfied.

"I know. You and him are a big part of my life," Finn said. "I feel a loss not seeing either of you for so long."

His voice moved her to think maybe he did have deep feelings for her, like when they were young. Her mother had warned her about Finn slipping around with other girls. If she brought up his name, even now, her mother would say: let him be and treasure what you have. What I have, she thought, is a melancholy man jealous of a decade old teenage romance. She wondered, as she had wondered for years, why Dylan wanted her. Did he even love her, or was she just something to show Finn that he lost the hunt to another. Did Dylan even see her as a prize? He treated her more as a hindrance to his life. "Maybe we should divorce," she said out loud, a slip, a blunder.

"Oh, now Joyce," he started.

She interrupted. "No, I was thinking –"

"You were thinking," he cut in, "that I was calling to romance you. You're just having a blue day. Tell Dylan what he means to you. A man needs to be needed, to have a purpose, to feel he's making a difference in his family's daily life, to feel he's a success."

"Does Kay make you feel that way?"

The delay in his response told her more than the words he came up with. "Yeah, she… She knows I work hard to put food on the table and to be a good father."

"What about a good husband?"

"Now, that," he said, "is a tricky aspiration." She heard mischief in his voice.

"Oh, Finn, what happened to us? I know… My mother turned

me against you. The other girls said scornful things, but boy oh boy, did they go after you when we broke up." She ground out her cigarette in the ashtray. "Finn, I still –"

"Now hold on," he said as if frightened of where she was going. "You take care of that little girl and of my brother. They mean more to you than anything else in this world. I gotta get off this phone and get back to work. You take care. Bye now." The line clicked. He had hung up.

Typical. She knew he would always back down if a hard emotional decision came up. Could the two of them be happy one day? If Dylan and Clio were out of her life? If she could be a single girl again with no ties? What was the combination that could make that a reality? How could Finn shed his entanglements? The tears streaked down her cheeks, hot, streaming off her chin and blotting the front of her blouse.

Finn placed the receiver back in the phone's cradle. A movement from the corner of his eye caught his attention. Michelle, the secretary from the Westinghouse plant, leaned against the door jamb, lightly fanning herself with a file folder. She smiled. The woman's deep brown eyes, softly hooded with half-closed lids, gave her the appearance of indifference while her white shirt-dress, cinched at the waist with a silvery belt and just a few buttons left undone – at the top and bottom – conveyed the image of just crawling out of bed. With each fan of the file folder, her butterscotch hair fluffed off her shoulder, then settled back.

"Hey Finn MacCool," she said, not moving from the doorway. "When you boys going to put in an air conditioner?"

"We like it hot." He winked at her.

She smiled and pushed herself from the door. Walking into the office, she balanced on high heels.

Finn looked down and let out a low wolf whistle. "How do you steady all that on those spiky shoes?"

She flung the folder in front of him. "Not hard." She perched on the corner of his desk. "Where are your brothers?"

"Back on the shop floor."

"You got time to take a ride?"

His breathing quickened and he had to adjust his work pants under the desk. "Naw, I got work to do, Michelle." He reached for the folder. "This the contracts? Besides, Wayne will be wondering where his secretary is. And honestly, you wore that dress to work?"

She reached one foot over to his desk chair and tapped Finn's arm with the toe of her shoe. "Those old boys like to look."

He could look, too, from his vantage point. "Come on, girl. I got a business to run, and it's not good to be messing with a customer's secretary."

"But it's good business to keep her happy." She slid closer to him and placed her hand against his cheek. Her touch, cool and soft, ignited his urge. "Same place. We can park back in Oakhill Estates where no houses are built yet." Her hand moved to his, and she led him out of the office to her car.

Michelle slipped her Ford Probe out of the gravel parking lot and onto Lee Highway, heading north. She shifted gears, then let her hand rest on Finn's knee. Windows down, breeze blowing her hair, he watched her drive. She handled the stick shift like a lover. What was he doing? Did he care anything about this woman? No. Neither of them wanted to spend any more time together than what it took to get off. He leaned his head back against the headrest.

They passed the Moonlite Drive-In. The car swerved onto Westinghouse Road and toward the new subdivision where they had parked before.

"Aren't you afraid that someone from work will see your car pulling off into Oakhill?" he asked.

"They got no business being away from the plant." She slowed and made the left just past the entrance sign to the neighborhood.

He wanted to find that feeling, like a chase, or honestly more akin to a hunt. It was a sensation that eluded him. He needed to capture it, hold the euphoria inside of him for longer than a few minutes. At times, he felt like a starving animal, a hunger so big and consuming that nothing mattered but the craving then the fervor of satisfaction – no social pressure, no shame, neither morals nor decency could keep him from the pursuit. The wolf pulled at his soul, ripping out what propriety his mother had instilled in her boys. For Finn, the wolf desire broke through any logical or societal barbed wire. He would take the chance; bear the slashes, cuts, and scratches. Before they could heal, the yearning always returned.

Michelle stopped the car. Her hands moved up and down his body. Her nails scrapped across his chest. His keys clanked, hitting the floorboard, and the breeze from the open window tickled across his thighs causing his eyes to snap open. The interior of the car seemed hazy. He stared at the tan upholstery and the plastic dome light above them. The passenger seat, reclined flat, creaked as she rode him. For a moment, he seemed outside his body, watching, but then she ground down, and he thrust, bestial, rough – the frenzy quickened to delirium.

The phone rang and rang triggering a buzzer on the shop floor. Brendan looked toward the closed office door. He hit the Stop on the punch press then walked to the office. "Finn, answer the damn phone," he said as he opened the door, but Finn wasn't there. He grabbed up the receiver. "MacGuire Tool & Die, this is Brendan." He listened. "Yeah, I can get that. Let me find it and I'll call you back." Why am I doing Finn's job as well as mine? he thought as he hung up the phone.

She returned Finn to the shop, just stopping in the parking lot, not even turning the car's ignition off. A smile was all she offered before driving off, not that he cared for any conversation or an empty promise of a next encounter. The next time would occur the same: Michelle would be in the mood, Finn available and willing.

He opened the door to the office, and Brendan sat at one of the desks, searching through a roll of blueprints.

"Where you been?" Brendan glanced out the window as

Michelle pulled onto the highway. "Oh."

"Don't need your big brother shit right now," Finn said. He thought it would be better to go out onto the shop floor than be closed up in the office with Brendan.

Just as Finn headed for the shop door, Brendan said, "Get back here. What is going on with you? Christ, I can smell her on you. We're not trash. Why are you out chasing women in broad daylight?"

The old guy would never understand, Finn thought, he hasn't had a hard-on in ten years. This brought a grin to Finn's face.

"What's so funny, wiseguy?"

"Brendan, you forgot what it's like to be young. I'm not some old man, I have needs."

"I haven't forgot. You have a wife. What's wrong at home? Why are you fooling around with that girl?"

He sighed and sat down across from Brendan, the large desk covered with blueprints between them. "Nothing wrong at home. I'm just itchy. Is this it? Damn, man, is this the rest of my life? Kay is fine. We're good. Talie is my world."

"You risk losing him when you keep whoring around. Kay wouldn't think twice about taking that boy and leaving your sorry ass. What if you take the clap home to her?"

"Shit. I won't."

"How do you know? That girl is messing around with you; she's messing around with a lot of other men."

God, just get me out of here, Finn prayed to himself. He didn't want to go down this road again with his brother, lectured by Brendan. Only Jesus could claim to be a better man than Brendan. Still, Finn did feel guilt after being with another woman. He had promised himself years ago, along with his love and devotion, to one woman, but things don't always work out the way he'd planned – seldom did. "Hey, just keep this to yourself," he said to Brendan.

"You stopping?"

"No one needs to know my business. Not Paw, not you or any of the brothers, certainly not Maw. Not Kay."

Brendan stood up from his chair and started rolling the blueprints back up. "You're a piece of work." He shook his head and tapped the rolled paper back into a cardboard tube. "You think no one knows what a whorehound you are? Hell, little brother, the word's out all over Abingdon and Bristol. I won't have this reflect on Charlotte or Brigid, Momma or Daddy, or the other brothers and their families. You can't control your dick, then just take it away from the rest of us. You're running the MacGuire name into the dirt."

The thought of being away, free of the disapproving looks and scolds of his self-righteous family didn't sound like a bad prospect – except for not being around Talie. But, was he causing his son more harm than good being around?

Joyce heard the front door open and Clio came bounding in the living room with her Brownie Scout uniform's sash flying off her shoulder. Clio seemed to take the Brownie projects very seriously.

"They said I had the best diorama in the troop," Clio said and set the cardboard box on the kitchen table. "See, Mrs. Balderson really bragged on it in front of the other girls. That made me a little uncomfortable – to be singled out – but not too much so. Jenny wanted me to show her how I made the trees three-dimensional. Hers were just cut-outs taped to the bottom of a shoe box. They flopped over like little lifeless things. I told her my daddy had shown me the way to cut slots and slide the cut trees together to have them stretch in all directions."

Damn, Joyce thought, can the girl take a breath? "Yes, honey, I see how excited you are, but can you put that in your bedroom? Go change and help me set the table for dinner."

"Okay," she said, grabbed the diorama and skipped down the hall.

Why couldn't she be happy with what she had? Joyce thought. Cliodhna had all the enthusiasm of youth, but her own had been lost. "Whose fault is that?" she said. The empty kitchen felt stuffy, but the afternoon was too humid to open any windows. Back home, she remembered, the windows stayed open all summer with the breeze like a soft caress across her skin. The cool evenings, clear and bright with stars, set the stage for front porch after-dinner visits with neighbors or car rides with Finn, maybe out to South Holston Lake. This town, busy with people, wasn't a place where she felt comfortable opening windows or going out at night. But during the mornings, before the heat became so intense, she enjoyed going to the James River or over to Fort Monroe and the Chamberlin Hotel. Sometimes she would go up to the hotel's widow's walk and look out over the Chesapeake Bay, searching the horizon.

The thud of a car door alerted her that Dylan was home. "Hey Joyce," he said as he walked in the front door. He set his lunch box on the kitchen counter and gave her a quick peck on the cheek. "What's for dinner?"

His breath smelled sharp with beer.

"We have a tuna casserole that will be ready in about twenty minutes. Why don't you go see Cliodhna? She's excited over Brownie Scouts this afternoon."

He walked down the hallway to the bedrooms, and Joyce watched. Dylan's drinking had caught up with him. Where he had been rather lean and agile, his weight was now more than forty pounds heavier than when they married. She had been able to get back to within ten pounds of her pre-pregnancy weight, although the last ten plagued her even after trying Jenny Craig for a year and Richard Simmon's Deal-a-Meal deck of cards for another year. Dylan moved like a man with a burden, shoulders slumped, heavy steps, head down.

She had thought that having a baby would have made their life happy. It did for the first year or two, but after Clio began to toddle and talk, their situation didn't get sunnier. The child demanded more attention as the years went by, and neither she nor Dylan could focus on a child all the time. He muttered about the child costing more than he'd thought. "How did Paw afford all of us?" he would ask. "Guess boys aren't as expensive," he would answer himself when Joyce didn't comment. She knew that as Clio grew and got into more activities, the money would fly out the door. That was one reason she took up a part-time job as soon as Clio went to kindergarten. Ballet and tumbling classes cost money. New school clothes and the latest must-have that her friends touted added to Clio's expense. But, Joyce thought, didn't her own parents go through the same with her?

"Daddy, you're so funny," Clio said between giggles, running up the hallway with Dylan following behind her stiff-legged like Frankenstein's monster, arms out in a mechanical reach.

"Little girl, little girl, you created me. Give hug to me."

She hid behind Joyce. "Mom, the monster is after me!"

"Give him the hug; hugs turn monsters into daddies," Joyce said just as Dylan wrapped his arms around both of them.

"I love my girls," he said.

"We love you, Daddy."

Joyce barely nodded.

Clio watched her mother talk with Brigid and Tal. This woman, caught between two brothers, managed to get away from both of the men. Had she defined herself by the value they placed on her? Never, Clio thought, never will I let Devin or any other man dictate my self-worth.

She remembered her mother working part of the day at a job, then cleaning their house – with her help – later both of them getting dinner ready for her father. He waited in his easy chair, ball game on the television, as they hurried around the kitchen, preparing a meat and two sides. Clio never cared much for their meals together. The atmosphere always felt thick. She found life, after her father's leaving, a morsel of relief with a bitter aftertaste. Not that he made life difficult, but just the combination of Joyce and Dylan created a sour flavor. Alone, either parent was fine – like cheddar cheese or bananas, but taken together the flavors produced vomit.

She remembered the arguments. Joyce complained about his drinking, his staying away from home, and his lack of attention.

Dylan yelled about her coldness, but used words like devious, lying, deceit, and mendacity – a word which Clio didn't hear again until her college years when she saw a production of Tennessee Williams' *Cat on a Hot Tin Roof*. Even at the age of eleven, she knew that her mother's deception led to her father's drinking. His drinking led back to her mom's deviousness. Then Dad's disregard. Deception – drinking – deviousness – disregard: a ring of doom.

He was obsessed by something, she could remember that. As if he thought her mother hid some secret life from him. Even when Clio and her father were alone, he'd make comments about her mother that didn't seem like the television families.

The re-run family dialogue: "Meatloaf again?" "Why bother?" "Typical." "Drunk." "Lazy." "Back home." "This IS home." "Not for me." "Just go." "Stay out."

She tried to be good, not cause more stress in the house, but she still held her own guilt from those nights she prayed.

Prayer, a sharp sword.

When they thought Clio was deep asleep, her parents argued and raged and cried. Clio would bury her head in the pillow, praying and bargaining with God to make her mother leave.

Please, make her stop.

She couldn't pinpoint a particular reason why she chose her father over her mother. Girls tended to idolize fathers. Maybe because mothers made the rules for daughters. Maybe because fathers delighted in daughters, while mothers were watchful, maybe even a little jealous of a young girl – a young girl with all her potential still ahead of her.

But nonetheless, she prayed that her mother would just disappear one day.

That atrocity to God, pleading for the demise of a parent, was met with His fury. Her mother didn't disappear. It was her father who was taken from her.

Chapter Twenty-eight

As Clio thought back, she vaguely remembered the day her father left. "Where did Dad go?" she asked Joyce, interrupting the conversation between Joyce, Taliesin, and Brigid on the deck of the restaurant.

The look on Joyce's face hinted at disbelief.

"Really, Mom, we never discussed him after he left. Was he abducted by aliens? My friends at school never asked. Grandmother didn't mention him at holidays. I know he existed. I remember him."

Tal gulped the beer that had been delivered to the table. "That's a MacGuire tradition: vanishing."

Joyce looked at him. "What do you mean? Finn?"

"Yep. That's why we're here. The trail stops at the Currituck Sound." He gestured to the lapping water at the edge of the restaurant's deck.

Joyce's eyes moved from Tal to the water and back. "When?"

"April 5, 1990," Tal said.

Clio wouldn't let her mother get diverted. "How did you get rid of Dad?"

"Me?" Joyce said. "It wasn't up to me. He left. We never heard a word from him again."

"You were there. I vaguely remember it – early in the morning. I thought I was dreaming. Doors slamming. Voices." Clio stared at her mother. "Was there someone else in the house that morning?" The memory bobbed to the surface. "Another man? Were you having an affair? Was that why Dad left?"

Joyce didn't say a word. She stared at Clio, as if to challenge her to keep going.

The waiter stopped by the table. Brigid ordered a scotch, Tal another beer. Clio focused on the rough planks of the tabletop.

◇ ◆ ◇

1978 – Bristol

Finn's brand new Chevy Impala parked in the farthest stall of the Blue Circle drive-in restaurant in Bristol. The waitress dropped off their order – two Coca-Colas – on a tray hooked over the driver's side window. Finn lit a Marlboro cigarette and offered it to Joyce. She accepted, but didn't take a drag, just held it in her right hand to dangle out the passenger side window. He lit another and took a long, slow inhale, the smoke tingled the back of his throat.

"You want to drive around or sit here?" he asked.

"This is fine. I'm tired." She took the Coke he passed to her and unlatched the glove compartment door, laid it open flat, and set the cup down on it.

"You sure you don't want something to eat?"

Her hand went to her stomach. "No, I just ate something before leaving the apartment."

Flustered that he couldn't find the words, Finn looked out the windshield at the Putt-Putt golf course's orange fence that neighbored the Blue Circle. The morning sun flashed off the putter a grandfather used to demonstrate a putt to his toddler grandson. "Is Dylan treating you okay?"

She sighed, looked at him, and nodded. The woman she had grown into was more beautiful than he ever thought she could be when they were in elementary school together. They always had so much to say to each other, insights to share, thoughts that sounded trivial to others, but deep connections when expressed between the young boy and his little girlfriend. She would get mad. He would apologize. Then they were back together, single-hearted, single-minded. The girl who loved David Cassidy and Glen Campbell – and him – grew up and married his brother.

"I heard from Tristan," Finn said. "He likes Atlanta. Diana snagged a job with a bank down there. They're thinking about buying a house in a neighborhood called Virginia Highland. He and Diana liked the area because it's that same name as the community college here where they met. They thought that coincidence had significance in their life together. 'Good Karma' is what Tristan called it."

"I always liked Tristan," Joyce said. "He saw bigger things than most of us. He's a dreamer."

"Well, he got lucky with Diana. She's a go-getter. Of all of us brothers, Tristan was the one who needed a strong woman."

"What do you mean by that?" she said with a sharp edge.

He winked at her. That always made her smile. But this time, she didn't. "All I meant was that he could use some guidance from time to time."

"A marriage is an equal partnership. It's 1978." She tapped the ash off the end of her cigarette onto the pavement. "Men and women have to work together to make a good marriage."

"How's that going with Dylan?"

"He's learning. Mom says it may take a man a while to catch up with modern times."

He laughed, then apologized. "Our momma made us think of girls as more than equal. They are special."

"Girls are more than a man's playthings."

"Whoa." He held up his hand in surrender. "I didn't want to get into an argument. I just wanted to see you and make sure you're doing okay. We've been together most of our lives. Now, you're my… sister-in-law." The words were hard for him to say and to hear.

Joyce twisted on the seat to look at him with intense eyes. "Do you still love me? No, don't answer that. I can't know."

His voice caught in his throat. "Well, what about you to me? That's just as important."

"What are we doing here?" She turned back to sit straight ahead, took a drag on the cigarette, then flicked it out the window. "Dylan is my husband. We can't change that – can we?"

Shit, he thought. Is this why I asked her to meet me? "I, I, we shouldn't be going down this trail of thought."

Her eyebrows gathered in a frown, and she cocked her head toward him. "You've met a girl."

"I'm getting older. I should settle down, too."

"You asshole. You brought me here to tell me you're going to get married?"

"That's just rich for you to be upset about that," he said, trying to control the volume of his voice. "I mean, you married my brother. Now, you think I should stay single just in case you get the guts to leave him – like you should."

"Oh, now it comes out. Why didn't you saddle up like a man a couple of years ago? You could have kept all this from happening."

"You said 'yes' to him. I didn't have a damn thing to say about that."

She took a long slow breath. "You said it all, every time you took some little hillbilly girl to the Moonlite Drive-in, steaming up the windows, wearing out the back seat. Is that why you bought this new car? Old one's springs shot?"

He knew she had a right to be angry, but he did too. "We were too young. Why'd you have to go to Dylan?"

She stared at him. Teardrops pooled, but she didn't blink. "He was good to me. Made me feel as if I was the only girl in the world. I didn't have to compete for his attention or love." The tears dripped down her cheek when she looked at her lap and straightened her blouse.

He wanted to say that she was the only girl for him, really the only one he had ever loved or could imagine spending his life with, but how was he to know back then? He was just a boy – a boy playing with adult feelings, but not knowing how to act like a man. Now, he knew it was too late. He couldn't walk back the years, undo the hurt or the missteps.

The pack he ran with wasn't the marrying kind; he'd aligned himself with girls with easy heat and temporary comfort. Would he ever be reaccepted into the virtuous, Christian flock? He'd preyed on those nubile, young lambs beginning in his Sunday school years through the Tri-Hi-Y club during his teens and the church's Young Couples group, offering the wives a distraction while the husbands attended the weekly Men's Prayer Breakfast. Those feminine conquests never brought him closer to glory. Only one girl had touched his heart, but he'd been too preoccupied with not settling. He had scouted beyond her, and she didn't wait for him to turn his attention back to her – his greener pasture was now bare and deserted.

He reached for her hand, but she pulled away and crossed her arms over her stomach.

"Take me back to my car," she said. "I need to get home."

He moved the serving tray off his window and placed it on the call box. "I'm sorry," he said.

The beer buzzed Taliesin's mind a little, just enough to not take the tension between Clio and her mother too seriously. A glance at Brigid told him the scotch had honed her interest in Clio and Joyce. She looked down to her glass as if giving them some privacy, but he saw her brow twitch as she listened.

"Uncle Dylan took off?" Tal asked. He'd rarely heard anything about his father's brother. Grandmaw Roane might have said a few things here or there, but overall the man had been a mystery to Tal.

Joyce turned her attention to him. "He had a way of retreating," she said.

"He came here," Clio said. "The beach house was where he would go."

"All through school, I was with Finn," Joyce began. "When we were in high school, I found out he was running around with other girls. That hurt me. I thought we were meant to be together and one day would marry. Of course, that's what sixteen year old girls think of their first boyfriends – I was no different. When I found out about the other girls, we broke up. I ended up dating Dylan."

"Damn," Tal said. "From one brother to the next."

She sighed. "Yes, that was my mistake. I thought it would hurt Finn the way he had hurt me, but Dylan treated me like porcelain. I had known him all my life, just like the rest of the MacGuire boys, but hadn't regarded him as anyone more than Finn's brother. Then with his attention on me, I felt cherished – for the first time ever. What girl wouldn't fall in love with that?"

"I remember you both being happy," Brigid said. "But I also remember Uncle Finn and Aunt Kay avoiding you."

"Oh, yes. Finn married soon after I became pregnant with Cliodhna."

"Dad," Clio said, her voice now softer. "Why did Dad, no offense, but why did Dad ask you to marry him?" She had calmed somewhat from Tal's view across the table. "I can see him thinking you only dated him to get back at Finn, but why marry?"

"He loved me. I loved him." She said it simply, as a matter of fact that they should have known.

"Bullshit," Clio said. She was not calm now, and Tal caught the eye of the waiter.

"Please bring this girl Chardonnay – a bottle," he said. The waiter hurried back into the building.

"I cannot remember any intimate or loving times between you and Dad. All three of us lived in the same house, but I don't remember any affection."

Joyce ran her fingers through her short hair. "At first, we had a wonderful marriage; you were a blessing to us."

"Oh sweet Jesus, you didn't?" Brigid said then clamped her hand over her mouth.

Tal knew the scotch had now loosened her up.

"What?" Clio asked.

Joyce didn't wait for Brigid to respond. "I know what the whispers were," she said and shook her head from side to side slowly as if to erase the memories. "Since all our friends and families had seen me and Finn together all our lives, then I married his brother. One of the sisters-in-law whispered that my baby was probably Finn's."

Clio stared at Tal.

Maybe, Tal thought. "But Grandmaw would have known, right?" He looked to Brigid. "She saw Clio. She would have recognized her or at least told me I had a sister."

"I'm not your sister," Clio stated. She looked to Joyce. "Right?"

"Of course not." Joyce started to say more, but the waiter arrived with the bottle of Chardonnay and placed two glasses in front of Clio and Joyce.

"Would you like some food to go with your drinks?" he asked.

They opened their menus to pick something to help absorb the alcohol, ordered, and then turned their attention back to each other.

Joyce reached over the table to rest her hand on Clio's. Clio didn't pull back. "I was true to your father – physically. But emotionally, I have to admit I always loved Finn. I loved your father just as much and although he made it difficult sometimes, I did love him. As for Finn, it's easy to keep love going with a memory. I made Finn the Finn I remembered. I kept the good traits in mind and ignored the bad. So, your father had a hard time living up to my Panglossian memory of Finn. No, maybe I didn't love Finn as much as loving the memory. That wasn't fair to Dylan."

Clio's face relaxed. "I bet that was difficult for Dad," she said in a quiet voice.

"Nothing against Finn," Joyce said to Tal, "but when your trust is shattered in the one person you have given everything to, you gravitate toward stability and faithfulness." She looked to Clio. "Dylan epitomized security for me after Finn and I broke up. He had always been there – one of Finn's brothers, just a year older and doting on girls. Finn was always your grandmother's favorite. We all knew that. The older brothers didn't care so much by the time Finn was born because they were moving on to sports, school, or girlfriends, but Dylan was just a toddler and his mother's affections moved to Finn. That carried on to school. Dylan was never quite good enough for his parents, brothers, teachers, or coaches."

Brigid leaned back in her chair. "I remember some girls in school who would date one brother then the other one. Switching like that amazed me. Wasn't it difficult to not call one by the other's name? Or, honestly, in an intimate moment, not think of the other one?"

A blush spread over Joyce's cheeks. "They were different enough. After the skirt-chasing Finn, I welcomed the dutiful Dylan. But, for all that he wasn't like Finn, he held the same intensity. His faithfulness became persistent attention. This was way before cell phones, so if Dylan called my house and I wasn't at home, he would get in his truck and go looking for me. Dylan graduated a year before me and Finn. My senior year, Dylan hung around the high school, waiting for the final bell. He would pick me up after majorette practice. At the time, I was happy with the show of dedication and loyalty, but a seventeen year old girl needs some time with her friends. We talked it over. He understood and gave me some room to hangout with my girlfriends. All this time, Finn dated several of the cheerleaders and half the flag corps girls with the marching band. If she wore a skirt, Finn had his hand on her thigh."

"Ha!" Tal laughed before he could stop himself. "That sounds like something Momma would say about him." He looked to Brigid and Clio. "Not that anyone today would condone such aggressive behavior."

The waiter arrived with their food, and they jumped in, all hungry from the discussion, tension, and drinks.

"Mom," Clio said. "You married Dad soon after high school. Were there good times?"

"Of course, we loved each other. You were a blessing to us," she said again, but added no more.

Tal could tell that Joyce had tired of the intense discussion, so he changed the topic to life on the Outer Banks and Joyce's store. As they finished their meal, Joyce suggested they go to her house to freshen up. She took the rest of the day off from the store to spend time with them.

Chapter Twenty-nine

Clio rode with Brigid and Tal as he followed her mother's car back off the highway into a neighborhood of tall beach homes on winding streets. She pulled into the cottage's driveway and parked her car under its pilings. Clio couldn't remember the last time she'd been to her mother's house.

Just as they parked and pulled their bags from the back of Tal's SUV, Clio's phone rang. Devin's name popped up. "Let me take this, I'll be right up," she said to Tal and Brigid.

She walked to the end of the driveway and answered. "Hey, Devin, we just arrived at my mom's house."

"Hope she's doing well," he said.

"A lot unfolding here –"

"Great to hear. Listen I have a client that may turn out to be a big deal. I'm staying in D.C. for a few days. Could you run by my condo and meet with the electrician tomorrow afternoon?"

"Devin, I'm in the Outer Banks. I won't be back in Richmond for a couple of days," she said. Her patience had run dry with Devin not listening. "Did you hear anything I said?"

"Of course, don't worry about it. I can ask my neighbor, Tony, to get the door open and hang out there while the electrician runs the wires for the surround sound."

"I have to go," she said and hung up before he could respond.

Brigid and Tal stood on the deck at the front of the house while Joyce pointed at the ocean in the distance. She knew Devin could get wrapped up in his work, but the longer they dated, the more he became self-focused. She tried to remember the last time he'd done anything specifically for her. She couldn't recall, either, when she had last surprised him with something unexpected – a weekend trip or even a dinner at a new restaurant. Now her world felt tugged from its routine.

"Hey, Clio," Brigid yelled from above. "Come see the dolphins with your mom's binoculars. There's a school of them heading north."

She could tell by their excitement and awe at spotting the dolphins that the lure of the Atlantic had caught Tal and Brigid. Where had her wonder gone?

Clio joined them on the deck. Brigid excused herself and roamed downstairs, the original cottage part of the house. When she came back up, she said, "I can see it. The old cottage's shadows are still there. Tal, you don't remember this place, but it was Pawpaw Joe's fishing cottage. He and the boys would come in the fall and early spring. Dad brought us here in the summer, and the house had no television or phone, though luckily it had electricity and plumbing. I guess the last time I was about 13."

"Damn, that was a long time ago!" Tal laughed.

"Your grandfather gave Dylan this cottage. Dylan worked at the shipyards just a couple of hours away. Your grandfather said with us being so close that we could get more use out of it than he did." Joyce walked over to the deck's railing and stared out at the ocean. "I think he knew we wouldn't be coming back."

"Well, that might be why Dad's car was here," Tal said.

Joyce turned to him. "You said the trail stopped here at the Currituck Sound. What did you mean?"

He explained how his grandmother wanted to know what happened to Finn. She didn't believe that he had run off with one of his girlfriends, a conclusion that everyone else had accepted. "I tried to find all I could, but it being so long ago, all leads evaporated. Uncle Brendan gave me a picture of Dad and me sitting on the front of his Impala at Myrtle Beach. That gave me part of the license plate. My buddy, Paul, helped me connect that to the VIN on the car. Clio's friend at her workplace did some fancy computer searches across state agencies and found a police report of an abandoned Impala pulled out of the Sound, just up the road from here."

"You said he disappeared in April of 1990?" Joyce asked.

"Yep. Then the car was found here that November." He went

inside to his bag and pulled a sheet of paper from it. He brought the paper out on the deck and handed it to Joyce. "That printout is all we have to go on."

Clio stood next to her mother as both of them read the information.

"No license tag and no registration papers – nor any documents in the car," Clio said. "But, light blue Chevy Impala."

"He loved that car," Joyce said, her voice breaking. Her eyes welled up. Clio reached out and hugged her mother.

"We plan to go to the Duck Police Department and the Dare County Sheriff's Office tomorrow to see what records they have on the car when they found it." Taliesin leaned against the railing, looking north. "Does that report give the exact location? I'd like to see where they found the car."

Joyce drove her Jeep north on Highway 12 for a few minutes and parked in the lot of the Sunset Grille. They crossed the road to the bike path and walked up the highway about a third of a mile by Tal's estimate. They waited for the traffic to wane then crossed the highway back to the Sound side. The narrow strip of land was wild with live oaks, red cedar, and wax myrtle tangled along the water's edge.

Under the summer mid-afternoon sun, Tal forged a path through the thick brush; the women followed him. They came to the Currituck Sound; the small waves tapping the sandy ground. As Tal gazed into the green-blue water, the roar of cars fell into the distance. Is this where his father had died?

The afternoon heat pulsated on his skin. He closed his eyes, and then he could smell the scent of his father: tobacco and machine oil. The sound of Finn's voice rode across the water: "Talie. I miss you, boy." Tal pulled off his shoes and shirt, dropped his wallet and car keys on the sand and began walking into the water. Brigid called after him, but he kept going.

The water, cold at first, warmed as he waded farther. The

bottom's muck enveloped his feet, confined his progress. A slippery edge of silt pulled his weight out into the Sound's rippling waters. He sank under the water, peaceful, no sounds. Velvety decaying marsh grass stroked his back. Tranquil, detached, soft, he let his arms float up as he drifted down and his feet contacted the bottom. Come home. A figure in the murky water beckoned. Was that Finn? Tal reached out.

Hands grabbed his wrists and jerked him to the surface. Joyce wrapped her arm around his chest and towed him back up to the shore. He coughed and sputtered water from his mouth and nose.

"What are you doing?" Brigid yelled, kneeling next to him and patting his back. She stuck a finger into his mouth and gagged him until he spit up more water.

"Dad," he managed to say between coughs and chokes. "I thought —"

"He's not there," Brigid said and stroked the side of his face.

"Called. He called to me." He looked at Joyce, who sat beside him on the sandy shore, her clothes and hair wet from going in after him. "I'm sorry. I don't know what happened. I just felt pulled, as if there was no other option than going in." He knew the explanation sounded foolish to them, but he couldn't articulate the need, the absolute obligation, to submerge himself in the waters where his father had been.

They drove back to Joyce's home and changed into dry clothes. No one mentioned Tal's descent into the Sound, but as he sat on the deck with the sweep of the ocean's warm breeze across his face, he couldn't shake the sensation that he'd encountered his father that afternoon.

The next morning over coffee, Tal called Paul in Bristol to get his advice. Over the years, Tal found that talking things out with Paul helped to reinforce his decisions. Besides, he missed Paul.

"Hey buddy," Tal said. He explained about Clio, referencing Brigid's history of attracting "those who search" and how he'd almost pursued an inappropriate relationship with this newly discovered cousin.

Paul laughed. "Man, you lucked up there. You are usually the seer. How'd you miss that?"

"That's just it. I feel Clio was drawn to Brigid and me. I found something in her that clicked. Things didn't fit right for a romance, but I perceived a relationship."

"New family," Paul said. "Congratulations. When are you coming back?"

"You miss me?" Tal teased.

"Yes. I do." He said in complete seriousness. "You're not thinking of staying there, are you?"

"At the Outer Banks? No. I can't leave my family… Or you."

"Good." Paul hesitated a moment. "You know I love you, don't you?"

"Yeah, and I love you. We're together always." Tal cleared his throat. "Enough of this emotional stuff. Thoughts on confirming Dad was with the Impala when it went in?"

"Check with the municipalities. There might be a paper trail of reports if the records haven't been destroyed by now."

The first step was to check the Town of Duck.

Joyce made a call to a friend at the town offices. "There wasn't a Duck Police Department in 1990," Joyce explained after hanging up with her friend. "The county had jurisdiction then. She says to try the Dare County Clerk of Court for traffic infractions."

"I guess a car going into the water would warrant a traffic ticket," Brigid said.

"Yeah, but they wouldn't be able to issue a ticket since no one was there." Tal sipped his coffee and grabbed another donut from the box that Joyce had placed on the table. He hoped they weren't at a dead-end with the physical trail.

Clio used her phone to look up the number for the Clerk of Court. She confirmed the hours they were open and hurried her friends toward the door. "Tal, if we get there soon, we'll be able to go through the records before the staff heads for lunch – we may need their help to sort through things."

He crammed the rest of the donut into his mouth. "Let's go," he managed to say while chewing.

Joyce went to her store, while Tal, Brigid, and Clio drove through the towns of Kitty Hawk, Kill Devil Hills, and Nags Head to Roanoke Island where Dare County had its offices. Clio pointed to a sign that advertised the Lost Colony theater. "Some say that the people of the Lost Colony, the first attempted English Colony, went inland and assimilated with the Indians, the Croatan."

"When was that?" Tal asked.

Brigid dug into her purse. "Let me check the phone." She held down the button and asked, "The Lost Colony – when was that?" The phone's mechanical voice began giving her show times for the play at the theater. "Bitch, no," Brigid said and sighed. "I hate these things." Tap, tap tap, she entered her question into the phone's Internet browser. "Here it is: In 1585 the Roanoke Colony was here on the island. When the supply ship arrived three years later, they found one skeleton and the word 'Croatoan' carved on a gate post."

"So, about twenty years later, Jamestown colonists arrived in Virginia," Clio said. "That was the first successful colony. I went there many times for school trips."

"The settlement succeeded at Jamestown, but not here on Roanoke Island," Tal said as he pulled into the parking lot for the county offices. "At least the Roanoke Colony left a clue carved into a post. Wonder if we can find a lead on Finn in the records here."

Inside they talked to several people, and Tal showed the printout of the report and the photograph of him and Finn with the Impala at the beach. A young woman led them back to a file room.

"That number," she said and pointed to a code in the corner of the printout, "indicates the physical file folder that may hold any additional data. The good news is that it's there at all. Most don't have a cross reference number, especially for an incident that old." She went around the corner and down an aisle, pulled open a file drawer and dug through the folders. She slammed the drawer closed. The adjoining cabinet caught her interest. She studied the printout again. "Maybe," she muttered. With the bottom drawer pulled all the way out, she scavenged in the back of the metal drawer. "There it is." She produced a manila envelope with a small bulge at the bottom. "It was dated to be destroyed since it is not associated with an open criminal case. Surprising that it's been stored this long since it is considered found objects. You say you think that car belonged to your father?"

Tal held up the photo again. "Yep. That's me with my hand down my swim trunks. Plus, the VIN numbers match."

She opened the envelope and pulled out a folded report. "This says the car's windshield was cracked and blood was found there. The front of the car showed damage as if from a head-on collision. They wrote here that the car probably wouldn't run from damage they observed. The officer writes that's a ninety percent probability. The Impala wasn't claimed, and it didn't run, so it was eventually scrapped." She jiggled the envelope to produce the sound of metal clinking. "This is all the contents of what was in the car when it was pulled out of the water. Not much. I'd guess the paper documents disintegrated or floated away." She read from the file again. "The Impala was thoroughly checked before it was disposed of. For some reason there was no license plate on the car." She started to hand the envelope to Tal, but then stopped as if to wonder if he was trustworthy.

He grinned, trying to look honest and upright.

"He's my cousin," Brigid said. She showed the woman her hospital id badge.

Clio gave her one of her business cards. "He's my cousin, too. We can vouch for him."

"No one has signed for this since it was filed thirty years ago," she explained. "There you go." She handed the envelope to Tal. "I'll be at the front office."

Tal, Clio, and Brigid went to a small desk in the corner, where he dumped the contents onto the desktop. A ring bounced out of the envelope, along with forty-six cents in coins and two Magnum condom packets still attached to each other.

Brigid picked up the ring. "A Claddagh ring. That's something a good Irishman would have. And the condoms, for a non-Catholic Irishman." She gave the ring to Clio.

"That's it?" Clio asked. She set the ring on the countertop and spun it around. Its silver surface dull with age showed the Claddagh design of two hands holding a heart, the heart topped with a crown. She handed the ring to Tal.

"Love, loyalty, and friendship," he said. He thought for a moment. "I remember seeing Dad wear a ring on a chain. He never wore his wedding ring on his hand because, he said, there was a risk of it getting caught in a machine at the shop."

Brigid picked up the condom packets. "Now these, I could see in Uncle Finn's car."

"We know this was his car," Tal stressed. "The Claddagh ring had to belong to him. But, I thought it was his wedding ring he wore on a chain." Then he considered how the ring could have been in the car for years before the accident, but didn't want to muddy their thought process. He looked around to the door where the county worker had gone back to the front desk. "I want to take this with us," he said in a low voice.

Brigid started to say, "I don't know –"

"Do it," Clio urged. "Put it in your pocket and let's get out of here. It's not stealing because it was in your father's car."

He weighed the options then slipped the ring in his pocket. "Let me take this envelope back to her." With a wipe of the countertop with his hand, he pushed the coins and condoms back into the manila envelope.

"Hold on," Brigid said. She pulled a Hershey's Kiss chocolate candy from her purse and flattened its teardrop point to create a round disc. "Put this in as a placeholder for the ring."

He returned the envelope, protruding with its contents, and they thanked the woman for her time.

Once back in the SUV, Tal pulled the ring out of his pocket and slipped it on his finger, his pinky finger – the only one it would fit. "Were Dad's hands smaller than mine?"

"I can't remember," Brigid said. "I think he was thinner than you. You drink too much beer."

"Bitch," he said, looking a Brigid in the rearview mirror, and then he winked at Clio. "She's one to talk about drinking."

"Was that a dead end?" Clio asked. "We're sure that was the car? The VIN had matched, right? The contents seemed to describe a male of Irish descent had been in it. But no registration papers survived and there were no license tags."

"Yes, those were my father's things, and the car was his. But where did he go?" Tal asked.

Back in Duck, they stopped at Joyce's store, where Darcy had come in to relieve Joyce for lunch. Joyce joined them back at the house and made sandwiches. Around the kitchen table, Clio told Joyce what they'd found in Manteo.

"Most of the car's contents," Clio explained, "must have drifted away, especially things like registration papers or other identifying documents."

"What survived reinforces to me that it's Dad's Impala." Tal reached for the pitcher of iced tea and poured more into his glass. "A couple of condoms, some spare change, and this." He reached into his pocket and placed the Claddagh ring on the table.

Joyce gasped. She pushed back her chair and hurried outside to the deck. Clio could see her mother's shoulders shaking as Joyce cried.

"Geez, what did that?" Brigid asked. She looked at Tal and then at the ring on the table.

Clio joined her mother on the deck. "Mom? Do you recognize that ring?"

"It could be... Well, really millions of them are around." She sniffed and straightened her shoulders, as if bracing for a blow. "I gave Finn a Claddagh ring when we dated in high school. He always wore it on a chain around his neck." Tal and Brigid joined them on the deck. "Tal," Joyce said. "Do you remember Finn wearing that ring on a chain? I gave him one."

He thought for a moment. "He had a ring on a chain – I had thought it was his wedding ring. I can barely remember. I was ten when he left. Hold on." Tal headed back into the house and returned with the ring plus the photo of him and Finn sitting on the hood of the Impala. "There." He pointed at Finn in the photo, his father's arms crossed over his bare chest. "That looks like a chain, but I can't quite see what is on the end of it."

"I wonder how he explained it to Aunt Kay?" Brigid asked.

"One way to find out." Tal handed the photo and ring to Joyce. He pulled his phone out of his pocket and called his mother. "Hey, Mom. Quick question: did Dad wear a ring on a chain?" He listened for a moment. "Sure. Yeah, that sounds like something Grandmaw Roane would do with her boys." He looked at Joyce and winked. "Okay, I got to get back to Brigid. Love you." He clicked off the phone. "She says he told her that ring was from Grandmaw. Guess he didn't want to start a fight about hanging onto a former girlfriend's gift."

"It was one of those high school things you do," Joyce explained. She turned the ring over in the palm of her hand. "We weren't old enough to have our class rings, but I thought the Claddagh expressed us." She handed it back to Tal. "Friendship, love, and loyalty."

Clio saw a look in her mother's eyes she had never seen before: longing. Did she yearn for the simple times of her youth, for her time with Finn, for a way to go back and take a different route? No, she knew there was no regret or remorse in that look, but more a plea for understanding what had happened to her first love, maybe her only love. "Mom, do you know why Finn was here?"

She looked through Clio, as if not hearing her or hearing something beyond her. A jerk of her head brought her back to the present. "Tal," Joyce asked, "did they have anything in the report about the bodies?"

"Bodies?" Brigid asked. "Do you mean more than one?"

Clio put her hand on Joyce's shoulder. "Mom?"

Chapter Thirty

September 1708 – James Cittie Shire, Virginia Colony

On the banks of the Pamunkey River, in a small cove, Thistle watched the white people force Anna Mayfield to the water's edge. Women covered her with a cloth, while men strapped her to a long sycamore branch.

"Hoo, hoo, hoooo," Thistle called. In the crowd of bystanders, Stanton – Anna and Edward's son – jerked his head up and toward the woods. The son, still a boy at nine, but trying to be a man, glanced around. He began to walk toward the woods, but Tristan Hart, watching nearby, pulled him back.

Two young women from the tribe waited for Thistle's signal. They had covered themselves with silvery paint made from crushed shells and sand. The river water lapped at their feet. Knives tucked in doeskin sheaths on their hips.

Four young braves fanned out along the river bank, hidden in clumps of reeds, on each side of the crowd that had gathered for the witch ducking.

The magistrate stepped up on a rock among the crowd. He gestured to Anna, tied by ropes to the sturdy branch, loosely wrapped – for modesty – with a cotton cloth. "Anna Mayford having two independent witnesses of her conjuring and evidence of a familiar and Devil's marks on her body continues to, on oath, deny the charge of witchcraft. This morning, we pass the judgment to our

Lord. Anna Mayford will be ducked into the righteous waters of the river."

The opposite bank of the cove lay no more than fifty feet from the assemblage witnessing the spectacle. They had a clear view of the men leveraging the sycamore branch over a boulder to dangle Anna, only in her shift, cloaked in a sheet of fabric, over the calm waters. Clouds roused and coiled to hide the early September sun. A crisp breeze blew across the water churning up small whitecaps.

Hands in the air, turning to address the bystanders on each side of him, the magistrate drew in a deep breath. "As followers of Satan, witches renounce the Holy Baptism. Therefore, the waters shun the witch's body. Anna Mayford's guilt will be determined by the waters. Guilty and the waters reject her and she floats. Innocent and the waters embrace her."

"No!" young Stanton yelled, fists clinched. "She is a good woman and mother. She is not a witch."

Tristan Hart held him back from running toward the magistrate. "Be still," he urged. "She must prove them wrong."

"To prove this sorry lot mistaken, she may die." Stanton struggled again to loosen himself from Tristan Hart's grip. "I shall pummel the magistrate for the shame he has bestowed on my family."

The wind grew strong, sweeping hats from heads and whipping skirts.

An ancient woman near the boy, whispered to her husband, "A spirit tries to assist the Widow Mayford with mighty gusts."

Eyes closed, Stanton tried to calm himself.

The cold water rushed around her. Arms and legs bound to the tree limb, Anna struggled to free herself, but the binds were too tight. The branch jerked down then up, right then left. She could feel the men guiding it deeper into the water. The branch pushed her up out of the water in a splash and she gasped for air. Swoosh. She fell back into the depths of the murky water. Heart beats pounded in her ears. The bark of the limb rubbed her skin raw. The more she struggled, the deeper she sank. Panic seized her mind with a squeezing pressure.

A tug at the ropes from each side of her caused her to strain her eyes in the dark waters. Sea nymphs circled her, pearly like fish, but with the long flowing hair of maidens. With sharp claws, they severed the binds and pulled her from the sycamore branch. She fought the water's pull to surface. Her lungs burned as she gulped for air. Screams with musket and pistol shots bombarded her ears. To stay afloat, she kicked and pushed the cotton cloth from her body. Her eyes adjusted. Along the shore, people ran from Thistle and other braves. Battle cries rose above the shrieks and howls of the settlers. The Indians didn't attempt to hurt anyone, but the settlers – if they possessed a weapon – tried to shoot at the braves. Scattering like mice, the settlers ran toward the Williamsburg road. The braves shouted after them. Silence fell over the shore and the waters of the cove calmed. Anna pulled herself to the bank still catching her breath. A man lay bleeding on the ground from an errant shot. The magistrate peered at her from the edge of the road. Three other men cowered next to him.

Thistle pointed to them and then motioned to the bleeding man as if to signal for them to take him. He turned away from the men and walked to Anna at the water's edge.

"You well?"

She nodded her head, and managed to say, "Yes." An object in the water a few feet off shore caught her vision. She grabbed Thistle's arm to help rise up to see better. "Stanton!"

Her son floated in the cove, his face toward the sky, eyes open, and his ruddy skin, now pale under the clouds.

She and Thistle rushed into the water to pull Stanton to the sandy bank. The youth didn't breath. Anna tore open his shirt and listened for a heartbeat. Silence.

Anna left the settlement and the farm. She lived with the tribe as Thistle's wife. When the child arrived, they named him Edward

Onxe. Onxe, a Powhatan word, chosen by Thistle because he predicted the baby would be shrewd as a fox like his mother. Both Anna and Thistle wanted to honor the memory of Edward – her first husband and his friend.

As baby Onxe grew, he favored his mother with her Scots-Irish heritage and his father's mixed race. "Onxe," Thistle told the five year old boy, "you have much white blood in you. My ancestor came from the Roanoke people. That is why you look different than your tribe. As they loved and accepted me, they love and accept you."

Onxe grew and flourished with the tribe. Anna taught him English, beer making, and the European ways. Thistle ensured he could hunt, fish, and farm. They both advised him on respect for the land, elders, and those with different backgrounds. When he reached the age of twelve, Anna took him to the College of William and Mary's Grammar School. Her intent was the Indian School, but as they walked across the campus, she and Onxe realized he appeared more like the white students than the Indians.

"Sir," Anna addressed the Indian Master of the school, "My son is part English and part Indian, and actually he has more English than half because his father has English ancestors as well."

The three of them sat in the Master's office in the newly constructed Brafferton building. The structure held the Indian School, the Master's office, and lodging for the boys. Onxe stared at the glass windows and high ceilings of the room. Anna nudged him to pay attention to their conversation. She had cut his hair in the English tradition – over his ears with a short ponytail tied with an emerald ribbon. He wore a suit that she had sewn for him. He had grown into a handsome boy with the green eyes and dark hair of his father and the height and sturdiness of her. Onxe reminded her of Stanton, although he was now older than Stanton lived to be.

"I must say your son could pass for a white student." The Master, in his black robes, stood up and paced before them. "I feel we should have him in the Grammar School instead of the Indian School."

"We haven't the funds to pay his tuition. I understood that the Indian School and his board were covered by his future ambassadorship between the white colonists and the local tribes," Anna said. "He can read and speak English."

"Yes, sir, my mother taught me the English ways, the ways of her people," Onxe said.

"Do you identify as an Indian or an Englishman?" the Master asked. He sat back at his desk while Oxne stared at the plank floor.

"I... I am a citizen of both. I neither deny my mother's nor my father's ancestors. Can I not be me?"

The Master smiled. "The Indian School conducts a strong education for the boys, but you have accomplished much that is taught here. I recommend you enroll in the college's Grammar School." He looked to Anna. "I will set his admission to the Indian School with an immediate transfer to the Grammar School. You will have no financial obligation. This young man is the goal of what we try to achieve in the Indian School. He can and will assimilate into the general college."

As they left the College of William and Mary to prepare Onxe for moving to the campus, Anna avoided the Marketplace and the roads that led to the river and the eastern farming areas. The reach of her dead husband and son's memories were too strong and too tortuous for her to walk that way. Also, she knew that the legends of her ducking had grown over time in the region, but she hoped Onxe would not be associated with that event. She and Thistle decided on Onxe's English name to be Edward Fox Thistle and that was how he came to be known in the English-speaking world.

"Sometimes, you have to bend to keep from being snapped in two." She explained to Onxe when he complained about the English name as they walked back to the tribe. "I didn't learn that lesson and was labeled a witch."

"I would rather be a witch than a cottonwood seed floating with the wind."

"Yet, you must know when to stand firm and when to harmonize." She rested her hand on Onxe's shoulder. "Fighting is not a way of life. Explore what others have learned; inspect that knowledge and ways for your journey. Don't be afraid to resist, but understand to accommodate, to attune, to be part of the tribe."

Edward Fox Thistle, his sons and his grandsons had resisted the King's control of the Colonies. In the autumn of 1781, Cornwallis surrendered at Yorktown. Two of his grandsons died during the battle, found floating in the York River – the river his father and mother had known as the Pamunkey. He'd had enough of the conflict, the reminders of the past, the battlefields of death, and he rallied his sons and their families to cross the mountains to the west and settle near the north fork of the Holston River along the Wilderness Road. The community had been called Wolf Hills, then Black's Fort, then Abingdon.

Chapter Thirty-one

They gathered the deck's Adirondack chairs together in a circle, and Tal brought out wine and beer. Early afternoon shade from the house and the ocean breeze kept them cool. Joyce had thought about that night almost every day, feeling as if she had put it all into motion and wondering if she could have said or done anything differently.

"It was 1990, early April —" she started.

"April fifth," Tal added.

"Yes. I called Finn at home. I never called there because I knew Kay would be upset. She knew our history, as did most of our friends and family in Abingdon and Bristol." She looked at Clio. "I'm surprised you don't remember that night, but you were young and it was late… And early the next morning."

Clio stared at her wine glass, took a sip, and gently set it down on the arm of her chair. "Yes. I remember the fight. I huddled in my bedroom closet until things got quiet, and I fell asleep surrounded by stuffed toys and my shoes. I woke up and Dad was gone. After that, we never talked about him."

Many times, Joyce had wanted to talk to Clio about her father, but she couldn't bring herself to explain their relationship. She couldn't even explain it to herself now. "Your dad was at times the most loving man. Other times, he lost himself. That night, something had sparked his dark side."

What had set Dylan off this time? Joyce couldn't understand as she searched her memory for the trigger. She had said nothing to him. Clio had kept quiet in her room watching television. The neighbors didn't come around anymore. She had no friends in this town, no family, no co-workers, no contacts. He was all they knew.

The silent treatment would be the next stage. After Dylan had blown off the steam of his accusations, and by not finding her a willing participant in the process, he'd walked out the door, muttering to himself. Dylan would be sitting at the bar down the street, a local hangout of some of the shipyard workers. After an hour or two, he would walk back in the small house, calmed by beer and sleep it off until the next morning when he left for work. That's how it usually went. She hoped it would go that way this time, too.

Sure, she thought, she was at fault for allowing the shadow of her past to hang over their marriage. Well, if she was honest, it was just as much his past too.

The old scab of her relationship with Finn still irritated her husband. In his mind he picked at it. Her child was not fathered by Finn. She knew it. But Dylan had always kept some doubt in his mind, hunched in the dark corners, stroking the thought like a guard dog to sic on her at unexpected times.

This was no life, for her or for Clio. Dylan needed psychological help. They all did. He didn't trust her enough to talk openly about his thoughts. She certainly didn't trust him since his story of her had been set years before. No amount of talking or commitment or loving expressions could alleviate his morass of misguided perception about Clio not being his child.

The quiet of the house settled around her. She began to relax, then drifted off to sleep.

She woke to the slam of the car door outside the house. Dylan was back.

When he opened the front door, she was wide awake and sitting up on the couch.

"I can't take you anymore," he said. He walked toward the couch, but stopped, turned, and went to the kitchen to retrieve a beer. She heard the pop of the bottle cap. "You aren't satisfied with me."

"I never said that." She twisted around to look at him standing by the kitchen doorway.

"You don't have to say it. It's in everything you do. You have the look of a woman trapped."

"Me? You're the one who stalks around the house like a caged animal."

"A cage we're both in, cornered, baring our teeth." He started for the easy chair, but stopped, glanced around the room, and then leaned against the front door. "We never should have married. You don't love me. You don't love Clio. You only love him."

Her hands trembled and she tucked them between the couch cushion and her back. "That's not true. You and Clio are my family. All we have is each other."

"I can see it clearly now."

The smirk on his face infuriated her. "You can't see anything. You're drunk."

The beer bottle fell from his hand as he grabbed for her. She jumped from the couch, stepping on the wet, beer-soaked carpet. The bottle lay on its side, the brown liquid gurgling out. Dylan kicked it out of his way, smashing the bottle against the entertainment center. Compact discs from the bottom shelf scattered across the floor. "Get back here or I'll make you sorry for running."

She panicked. Down the hall and into their bedroom, she slammed the door closed and locked it.

Thwack, Dylan pounded. "Open this god-damned door."

She pushed the chest of drawers and wedged it behind the flimsy door. Her next thought was to climb out the window, but she knew she had no car keys and couldn't leave Clio. Clio – what was going through her mind? Dylan had never acted like this. Something was wrong with him. Calling the police occurred to her, but that would set him off more. She grabbed the phone and dialed Finn.

The phone rang and rang. She hoped Finn's wife wouldn't answer. Finally, she heard his voice. She whispered as to not alert Dylan she was on the bedroom extension. "He's in a rage," she said.

"What do you mean?"

"Drunk. Threatening. I need to get Clio and me out."

"Has he touched you or your daughter?"

"No. I think he's quieted down. I don't hear him outside the door." She checked out the bedroom window and his car sat in the driveway. "He's still here, but I don't hear him moving around."

"Stay put. I'm on my way." With that, he hung up the phone.

The drive from Bristol would take all night, at least six to seven hours. She sat on the carpet by the chest blocking the door and waited, listening for any movement from Dylan. Why? What had gotten into his mind to make him so angry? If she heard him going into Clio's room or her crying, Joyce knew she would have to charge at him, do whatever she had to do to stop him. She hoped he had passed out from drinking so much. With no sounds coming from the rest of the house, Joyce drifted off to sleep, huddled behind the door.

She woke when a car drove up and parked in their driveway. The digital clock by the bed read 5:51 a.m. She peeked through the curtains to see Finn getting out of his car and rushing to their door. She heaved the chest from the back of the bedroom door and went down the hallway to find Dylan asleep on the couch.

She opened the front door. "Shh, he's passed out," she said to Finn. His face tense and eyes weary.

"Are you okay? Did he hit you or Cliodhna?"

"No, no." She stepped outside the door and closed it so Dylan wouldn't wake. She wrapped her arms around Finn's neck. He smelled of cigarettes and coffee. His warmth felt like home. The April morning held a chill. She realized she still had her nightgown on. "I'm sorry I panicked and brought you all the way here."

"You didn't panic. He's lost it." Finn reached for the doorknob, and she let him go in.

"Dylan," he said and shook his brother's shoulder to rouse him. "Wake up, man."

Dylan struggled to open and focus his eyes. "Finn?" He straightened up on the couch. "What are you – wait." He looked to Joyce. "What's going on?"

"Just calm down," Finn said. "She called me because she was scared of how you were acting. She could have just as easily called Daddy or Brendan or Oscar, but she thought I could put your mind at ease. I thought a lot about this driving here."

Dylan turned to check the clock on the cable box. "You drove all night to get here?"

"Are you feeling better?" Finn asked and sat on the edge of the couch. "You sleep it off?"

"Hell, I didn't need to sleep anything off. I know she wants to be with you –"

"No, Dylan," Joyce protested. "Not at all." She stayed close to the hallway, in case she needed to get away from Dylan.

Finn looked down at the beer bottle smashed against the TV stand and the scattered CDs across the carpet. "There ain't been a thing between us since high school." He didn't look at Joyce or at Dylan. "I have my family, and you have yours."

"Shit, I don't believe you." Dylan pushed himself up from the couch. Joyce took a step back into the hall, but he moved past her and into the kitchen, popping open a beer. "Finn, you must want a beer after that long drive. Does Daddy know you're here?"

Finn walked into the kitchen, while Joyce stayed away. She wanted to make sure they could talk it out without her being in the middle. She listened, but couldn't see them.

"No one knows. I should call Brendan to let him know I won't be at the shop today, but I felt I needed to get here fast and make sure you are okay."

Dylan stayed quiet, and Joyce wondered if he believed Finn had come for him or for her. Finally, Dylan said, "Man, I feel lost. How the hell did I end up with a wife that can't stand me and a daughter who will eventually see me as the asshole I am?"

"Oh, Dyll," Finn said, "it's just as much my fault. A woman can't come between brothers, but I let that happen."

She almost spoke up, but caught herself. She hadn't torn them apart. They did that on their own. Male pride. The warrior trying to claim a prize. Those boys think they run the world, she thought, but I made my own decisions. I'm not immature or beholden to any man. She let out a deep breath and glanced back toward Clio's bedroom door.

"Are you honest in telling me you and her ain't sneaking

around?" Dylan asked.

"Hell, I live 350 miles away."

"That doesn't answer my question. There's more to cheating than a physical affair. She still loves you. You love her?"

Joyce braced herself against the wall and waited for Finn's answer.

Nothing came from Finn.

The sound of a beer bottle slammed down on the kitchen counter made Joyce jump. "I knew it," Dylan yelled. "You and her have been plotting for over ten years. Just answer me this: Is Clio your daughter or mine?"

"Come on, Dyll. You know better than that. Okay, there might be some emotion left between us, but I hadn't touched her."

"Since when? When was the last time you had my wife?"

"We're not going down that road. We've all made some mistakes, but it's all behind us."

Joyce stood still as Dylan stomped past her and back into the living room. He glanced her way then to Finn who had followed him out of the kitchen. "I got to get out of this house," Dylan said. "She's against me. You, my own brother, and her have been sleeping around for years."

"Now, you know better than that," Finn said. He stood between Joyce and Dylan as he talked. "All these years y'all have been here, this is the first time I ever set foot in Newport News." He gestured toward the window. "Ain't very pretty." He smiled at Dylan. "Come on, let's go and you can show me your favorite spot in this town. Where's the scenic view? What would Maw and Daddy love to see if they came for a visit?"

Reminding him of his family and their closeness, Joyce thought, good move Finn.

Dylan staggered a bit, but steadied himself with a hand to the back of the couch. "Yeah, we need to clear the air." He dug in his pants pocket, jingling his keys.

"Hold on, I'll drive." Finn headed for the door, but stopped. "Why don't you hit the John before we go?"

When Dylan had gone into the small bathroom at the end of

the hall, Joyce walked up to Finn and whispered, "Where are you taking him?"

"Nowhere in particular. He needs to get in a different environment, away from you and me together. We'll ride around for awhile for him to sober up and cool down."

Just a few minutes after six, the morning sun had not come up, but its glow had started to bleach the eastern horizon to a jaundiced yellow. Joyce adjusted the blinds a bit to let the emerging light into the room. "Be careful driving with him. I'll call his work and tell them he's sick today." She heard the toilet flush and moved across the room away from Finn.

Dylan had brushed his hair and tucked in his shirt. "I'm ready." He didn't look at Joyce, but walked straight out the door.

Dylan directed and Finn drove them by the Newport News Shipbuilding gates. Dylan explained what he did on the current refurbishing of an aircraft carrier. Traffic had thickened, so Finn looped off the highways and drove toward the James River. The James River Bridge loomed in the distance, so Finn steered for it.

"That bridge takes us over to Smithfield or we could go see the Great Dismal Swamp," Dylan said. Finn could tell by Dylan's mood change from pissed off brother to tour guide that he was sobering up and relaxing.

"I'm glad to see more trees and water," Finn said. "How do you live in all that commotion in the city?"

"It's where the jobs are." He stretched out his legs as they drove over the bridge.

The view entranced Finn. Up and down the historic James River, the water seemed to stretch for miles. "Where's Jamestown?"

Dylan pointed out the passenger side window to the west. "Up a few miles, there's a bend, and around that bend is Jamestown."

"Daddy says we had people here around that time."

"How are they?" Dylan asked. "Maw and Daddy? I haven't talked to them in a while. I guess I left them with hard feelings."

"We all grow up and drift away, in one way or another," Finn said. "They're both in fine health." He thought about mentioning how much they would like a picture or even to see Dylan and Joyce's daughter, but he knew that would bring up Dylan's questions again. "My boy, Taliesin, is growing like a weed. He takes after us more so than Kay's family."

"Why'd you name him Taliesin? Do the kids at school make fun of that name?"

"I can ask you the same about Cliodhna. Talie is a bard. He sings all the time, makes up lyrics. So it fits him. Of course I didn't know that when he was born. I liked the Frank Lloyd Wright house design and name. Talie doesn't take shit from any kid. Not that he's a fighter, but he's a charmer. He can disarm a situation, even at his age."

"Like his dad, Finn MacCool," Dylan said. They travelled through pine forests. Logging trucks sped by them. "Cliodhna is the Queen of the Banshees. Also, she was taken far from home in the legends. I guess when she was born, I knew we'd leave."

Not wanting to follow that particular thought at the moment, Finn asked, "Where are we headed on this road?"

"Stay on Route 17, and it will skirt the Dismal Swamp."

The sun peaked over the pine trees. Finn put on his sunglasses. "How far are we from the fishing cottage?"

"Probably an hour," Dylan said. "I didn't hurt Maw, did I?"

"Of course she wants her boys together. But nowadays people move around. Tristan moved to Atlanta. You're in Newport News. I think she understands."

"I rarely talk to them. I don't think I ever sent Maw a school photo of Clio. We don't talk about the family. All Clio knows is Joyce's mother."

"Marian? How is old Marian? She couldn't stand me," Finn said with a laugh.

"Marian claims I'm the only good son of the MacGuires." Dylan leaned his head against the Impala's headrest and smiled.

Finn chuckled. "I miss this," he said. "I miss you."

Dylan didn't look over at him, but Finn could see that his eyes watered a little. Dylan reached up and rubbed his face and eyes as if he were tired and forced a yawn.

"Let's go to the fishing cottage. Daddy gave it to me and Joyce a few years ago – my early inheritance."

"Yeah, he let us all know. He didn't say where you were living, but said you could use it more often and keep it up."

"Joyce tell you where we were?"

"Yeah," Finn didn't want to get more into it, especially while they were driving. "She wanted to know if anything ever happened to Maw or Daddy. Your phone number and address is in a file folder at the shop."

"For emergencies? Like last night?"

"Yes. Last night scared her."

"Sometimes I get low," Dylan said. "I never thought this would be my life. Not that I had anything planned, but this ain't what I pictured."

They drove on in silence. Dylan directed Finn off Route 17 and over to the highway that led to the Outer Banks of North Carolina. "Maybe we can do some fishing," Finn said. He looked over to Dylan, who only nodded.

"What made you think they had come here?" Clio asked Joyce. The summer breeze lifted Clio's hair and dropped it back, tickling her neck. She reached up and twisted it into a short knot.

"Old man Jerry, who used to live over there," Joyce said and motioned toward the house across the road. "When Dylan didn't return, I thought he and Finn had come here or gone back to Abingdon to see their parents. There was no phone here at the cottage, so I couldn't call, but I knew that Jerry lived in the village full-time and had a phone. I called him to look across the road to see if a car was here. Jerry told me he'd seen Dylan and another man one night. But they were gone. That's really all I had to go on."

"Is Jerry still living next door?" Tal asked.

"No, Jerry died years ago. His son runs a charter fishing boat, though I think he might be ready to retire." She got out of the chair and walked to the railing, facing the large house across the road. "They sold their place about twenty years ago and it was bulldozed so that house could be built." She turned back to Clio and said, "Honestly, the relief I felt by not having Dylan there kept me from looking for him. I convinced myself that he had abandoned us. Mom said I should go on with my life. She stepped in to help us get by."

"Grandmother," Clio said, but stopped and just shook her head at the memory of the overbearing woman who had shaped both Joyce and her.

"Jerry's son," Tal said. "Do you think we can we find him?"

"Their bait and tackle shop is just over at the Sound side. We can walk over there now," Joyce said and gathered up their glasses and bottles from the deck to take them inside.

Jerry's Bait & Tackle consisted of a small wood building behind a t-shirt shop along the Sound side's boardwalk. Rods and reels of all sorts sat outside the door; inside the odor of fresh bait permeated the entire structure. Mounted large mahi, tuna, and marlin with black glass eyes stared down at visitors from the walls. Tal and Joyce walked up to the counter and asked for Jerry's son.

"That would be my dad," a tanned, sinewy man in his mid-forties said. "He's not here. We moved him to Kill Devil Hills last year, an assisted living place there. He's got some early dementia and needed looking after." He stuck out his hand to Tal. "I'm Trey. Really, Jerry the third. What can I help you with?"

The place didn't have other customers at that hour of the afternoon, so Clio felt Trey was glad to have some visitors. She reached out her hand after Trey shook Tal's. "I'm Clio Fitz-Adams. This is my mom, Joyce, and my cousins, Tal and Brigid. We're trying to find out some information about my dad. Your grandfather told my mom he remembered seeing him the day he went missing – that was about thirty years ago."

"Well, Granddad is gone and Dad is hazy."

Brigid fiddled with a bright amber artificial lure, shaped like a small squid, a tassel of gold and crimson plastic strips concealed the double hook. She smiled at Trey. "You must have been about thirteen or fourteen then – like me. Did you hang out at your grandfather's house across the highway? That's where our family's fishing cottage was. It's where Joyce lives now."

"Yeah I seen Joyce at the town's chamber of commerce events." He nodded to her. "The MacGuires? That your family? I think I remember you," he said to Brigid. "Pretty redheaded girl, wore a lime green bikini."

She laughed and grinned at Trey. "You sure have some memory."

Tal looked at Clio and rolled his eyes.

"Did you ever see two men at the cottage across the street with a blue Impala?" Clio asked.

"Two of the brothers?" Trey said slowly as if searching his memory. "There was a bunch of those boys in that family. Yeah, I remember that Impala. What a cool car, especially when I was thirteen and had cars and girls on my mind. An azure Impala and a lime green bikini." He winked at Brigid.

"Was this a few years later – after the bikini, around early April of 1990?" Tal asked.

"Can't say I remember, but Dad might have. Who knows what he can remember now."

Brigid nodded and smiled. "Do you think Clio and I could go talk to your father? Most dementia patients have remarkable long-term memories."

"We could ride down there after I close up shop," he said. He walked around the counter to arrange a few lures on the wall near Brigid. "Maybe me and you could get dinner later."

"She'd love that," Tal said. "The rest of us have plans, but Brigid is free tonight."

She raised an eyebrow at Tal, but didn't contradict him. "Yes," she said. "It's a date after we talk to your father."

"I can't believe you pimped me out in order to get to the old man," Brigid said to Tal as they walked back to Joyce's house.

"Shit, Brigid. You haven't had a man in a while. He's handsome in his own rough way. Go have fun. Obviously he's had that bikini-wearing redhead on his mind for years; make his teenage fantasy come alive."

"Thirty years later," Clio added.

Joyce unlocked the door, and they climbed the stairs to the upper level of the beach house. "Maybe I should go to the assisted living home as well. He might remember me. JR was several years older than me and Dylan, but I remember him helping his father around the house." She looked at Clio. "He might remember me."

"Sure, but we don't want to overwhelm the guy," Clio said. "We can decide who goes in and who stays in the lobby once we get there."

When five o'clock came, they drove over to Jerry's Bait and Tackle. Trey had just locked up the shop. Brigid rode with him in his truck, while Joyce, Tal, and Clio followed in Tal's SUV. Down route 158, they drove through Kitty Hawk to Kill Devil Hills, turning at the Wright Brothers National Memorial. The assisted living facility had a front porch with rocking chairs where many residents relaxed after dinner. Tal and Clio decided they would wait on the porch while Trey, Brigid, and Joyce went into JR's apartment.

The cottage where JR grew up was similar to the MacGuire's fishing cottage. When his mother died and a few years later his father, Jerry, died, JR decided to sell the cottage and land to a developer. She hadn't seen JR since. Joyce wasn't a customer of the bait and tackle shop, so she'd lost touch with that family. Now, as they walked into JR's small studio apartment at the senior facility, she found reconciling the man she remembered with the man in front of her, an almost impossible task. JR had been a burly man, boisterous and swarthy. Before her now, JR sat slumped in a wheelchair, pale and vacant. His clothes seemed three sizes too large for him.

"Dad, how are you today?" Trey asked.

The old man reached up and held his son's hand. "Good." He looked at Brigid and Joyce. "Who are these pretty girls?"

"Hi, JR." Joyce kneeled down to be on eye level with him. "I used to live across the street from your dad and mother… In Duck, not far from the bait and tackle shop. This," she said and took Brigid's hand, "is little Brigid MacGuire – all grown up. She and Trey are about the same age."

"Pretty," he said.

"We don't want to bother you, but were wondering if you remember when my husband Dylan and his brother came to our cottage together many years ago. We hoped that you or your father or mother might have seen them or talked to them during that visit. It was the last time anyone heard from those two. Their children are trying to find out what happened."

"Joyce," Brigid whispered, "for dementia patients, a condition we call 'Sundown Syndrome' is when they may have more confusion in the evenings. We probably don't want to push too much information at him."

"Dad, you remember all those MacGuire boys? Some of them were your age and some younger. The MacGuires had the place across the street from Granddad and Grandma."

"Joe and Roane MacGuire are their names," JR said. "They had good kids, polite boys, more so than me." He chuckled a little. "Dad and Mom liked them. Are they gone?"

"Yes, Dad. Granddad and Grandma are dead."

"Hmm."

Brigid patted Trey's shoulder. "JR, when you visited your mother and father, do you ever remember an argument over there between two of the brothers?" she asked.

"Oh, like cats and dogs. They fought."

Brigid turned to Joyce with an expression of disbelief. Joyce knew that the boys would argue, but never knew them to do so in front of other people – especially neighbors.

"What happened that time?" Joyce prompted JR.

"Oh, they were grown men. Drinking too much." He leaned in and added, "You know they're Irish."

"Irishmen can be fighters," Joyce said. "Can you remember when this was? Or how old Trey might have been then?"

"Trey was a boy. Not driving yet."

Trey spoke up, "Yeah, I can kind of remember. Can't pinpoint that specific time. Must have been spring because we had the windows open and I remember some arguing going on over there. Not like the MacGuires to cause a ruckus. Me and Dad were staying with Granddad to help with a charter."

"Arguing?" Joyce asked. "Can you remember anything more?"

"I only remember that because no one came back to that cottage for several years after that. Figured you had moved on," Trey said. "But, that night sounded like drinking and arguing – usual for guys on fishing trips, but odd for that family."

"Brothers take things too personal," JR said, looking out the window. "One started to take off in that blue car and the other ran after, jumped in at the last moment. Just like a stunt car driver. Drinking too much. Brothers take things wrong." He sighed and stared out his window at the deepening shadows. "Dad said they'd settle down and come back. Too much drink. I locked up the house for them. Are they back?"

"In a way," Brigid said to him. "Thank you for talking to us." She told Trey that they'd wait for him outside while he said goodnight to his father.

Chapter Thirty-two

April 1990 – Duck, North Carolina

Dylan grabbed Finn's key chain from the kitchen counter and stormed out the cottage's front door. He headed straight for the Impala.

"Damn it, Dylan," Finn yelled. "You can't drive. You're too drunk." He'd had little sleep from driving all night to get to Newport News and then to the cottage on the Outer Banks. After they'd arrived in Duck, he and Dylan had hit Wee Wink's grocery store for beer. The rest of the day alternated between drinks, sermons, confessions, promises, vows, cigarettes, toasts, admissions. The sunset provided shadows to their suspicions. Dylan churned up every insult to hurl at Finn. Finn took all he could, but finally fell into the mire, which ended with a brawl as midnight approached.

Finn stumbled out the door after Dylan. The car's engine started. Dylan slammed it into reverse, hitting a pine, breaking a taillight and knocking off the back license plate. Then, wheels spun forward in the sand, pelting Finn as he ran to grab the passenger door handle. He jerked it open and dove in, head first. The car weaved. Finn's legs dragged the road until he pulled himself into the seat and slammed the door.

"Pull over," Finn said to Dylan. The Impala's tires ran onto the sandy shoulder of the highway several times before Dylan steered it back onto the road and kept it steady. No other cars came in their direction – little traffic headed to the northern beach towns on a weeknight, just their blue Impala racing up the highway.

The night blurred and Finn's head ached. "Dyll, stop! You are going to kill us both."

"Shut up," Dylan yelled. "I've had all I can take of you and your shame."

"My shame?" Finn replied. "My shame? You have done far worse than I could ever do. Pull this damn car over."

The car lurched and veered toward a sand dune.

Finn grabbed the steering wheel and struggled against Dylan to bring them back on the road. White hot pain stabbed his head as Dylan's elbow cracked into the side of Finn's skull. He couldn't focus, his eyes blurred, but he heard the screech of tires.

The windshield didn't hurt as much as he would have thought. Finn's shoulder saved his face. The windshield shattered, but held as one piece and kept him from flying out the front of the Impala. His door opened with the impact, and he rolled out onto the cool sandy soil.

He wanted to sleep.

Finn opened his eyes, not sure how much time had passed. He blinked and reached up to clear his vision. Warm blood covered his fingers. A cut on his head, he reasoned. Maybe he should sleep a little more. The bottom of the car door pressed against his leg. He pulled himself the rest of the way out of the car.

"Dylan," he called. "Dylan, where are you? You asshole. I knew you'd fuck up my car." Pain stabbed his side as he pushed himself up to a sitting position. "Dyll?" From his seat on the sand, he could barely see back into the car. He recalled television series where a car wreck usually ignited then exploded into a fireball. He needed to get Dylan out. He shifted his position, to grab the side of the door and use it to pull himself up.

Dylan slumped over the steering wheel.

"Come on, man. Get out of there. Dylan?" Finn pushed the passenger seatback out of his way. "Dylan? You awake?" The touch to Dylan's arm caused Finn to recoil. He steadied himself and placed his hand on the side of Dylan's neck – cold.

"Oh, God, Dylan. Say something. Dylan." He pulled Dylan off

the steering wheel. Blood covered his face. His eyes were open, a flat stare. The skin of his face, where not covered with blood, appeared gray in the light of the dashboard. The headlights of the car were not on, but the dashboard still cast a silvery light. Finn reached over and turned the ignition off and took the keys. "My fault. I shouldn't have come. I'm sorry, Dylan. You and Joyce didn't need me in the middle of things." Tears began to flow. He put his arm under Dylan's and pulled him across the seats, out the passenger door, and away from the car.

Finn realized that the car had travelled across the road and crashed into a thick, squat wax myrtle, just far enough to be out of sight from the highway. The water from the Sound splashed against the bank just feet from the driver's side of the car. Without a thought, just anger at the car and at Dylan and at God, Finn reached in and shifted the Impala into neutral. He shoved and pushed as best he could until it was loose from the tree, the front license plate stayed embedded in the tree's trunk. With a quick turn of the steering wheel, Finn pointed the crumpled Impala toward the water. A slight slope helped him roll the car into the Currituck Sound. The water rushed around it, flowing in the open door and windows until the roof submerged and dark water swallowed the car.

Finn stumbled over to Dylan, lay down next to the lifeless body of his brother, and cried.

The haze of his mind and body devoured his concept of time. The sky was still dark as if in mourning. Finn resolved to honor Dylan in his death, a death that Finn convinced himself had been a result of the entire path of his life.

The seventh son of a seventh son, Finn said in his mind, will cause havoc to all those around him.

He crawled to his feet and searched the highway for signs of life. The stars splayed across the sky; the moon hid from him, as if she had deserted Finn in his time of need. Looking north and east, he could see the black outline of a small lone house in the scrub brush of the sand. He walked in that direction.

As he approached the solitary cottage, Finn saw a Honda ATV under the carport. The vehicle looked like a riding lawn mower with huge all-terrain tires; the key left in the ignition. He rolled it back and pushed the ATV silently to where he'd left Dylan.

With a struggle and stabbing pain, Finn placed Dylan on the seat of the ATV, then slipped behind him, as Dylan had done with him when they were kids riding their own ATV across the farm. Dylan's head leaned back against Finn's cheek. The coolness of the touch didn't alarm him any longer, but helped calm his resolve. He turned the ignition key to On, moved the choke to the half position, and pressed the Starter button. The ATV coughed a couple of times and then caught on with a low roar. He steered them up to the road and away from the ATV owner's cottage. The quiet night seemed to amplify the sputtering of the engine. Finn drove slowly, as if in a procession, a slow funeral for his brother. He turned off the highway as soon as possible and followed a road to the Atlantic.

Finn sat on the beach at the surf's edge with his arms around Dylan. He couldn't cry any more. He straightened Dylan's shirt and tried to rake his hair into place. The shriek of banshees rolled over the surf, beckoning him. Finn was able to hoist Dylan onto his shoulder. He refused to drag his brother across the sand. Step by shaky step, Finn carried his brother into the waves. The water cold, numbing. Once past the breakers, he allowed Dylan to float and he swam with his arm encircling Dylan's head, hauling his brother out to sea.

The swells of the ocean lifted them up and back down. His feet couldn't touch the bottom anymore on the troughs of the waves. The peak of a wave hit him in the face, and he swallowed the salty water, coughing. Dylan slipped free. Finn swam after him and hooked one arm around him. He tried to tread water, but the

ocean pulled at him. His legs ached.
   No sound. The banshees silent.
   He stopped moving.
   Water overflowed his face, his head.
   Finn and Dylan drifted down into the dark, cold Atlantic.

Chapter Thirty-three

The night sky had filled with stars. Brigid hadn't returned yet from her dinner with Trey. Joyce and Clio sat at the table on the deck. Tal paced back and forth across the deck. "I tried to call Finn. I knew better than to phone your house," Joyce said to Tal. "Your mother would have had a fit. A woman I worked with called and asked for Finn at the machine shop. When she did, whoever answered, said he didn't work there anymore."

Tal leaned over the railing of the deck and stared at the distant ocean, black against the horizon. "The uncles felt like he'd run off with a girlfriend. That's always been the story," Tal said.

"I had that same co-worker phone your house after I heard that from the shop. But Kay yelled at her when she asked for Finn. Called the poor woman all kinds of names. After that, I assumed he'd gone home and had a fight with Kay. I thought I'd hear from him again. A few years ago, I searched the Internet for any reference to Finn – and Dylan – but nothing came up. That's so hard to believe these days that there would be no reference to a person."

"They died before they could be documented in cyberspace," Clio said.

Tal stopped his pacing at the table, reluctantly taking a seat.

"Can we say with confidence to Grandmaw Roane that Finn is dead? That Dylan is dead?" Clio asked.

Tal closed his eyes. An image swept across his mind. "I need to go to the beach." Before anyone had a chance to respond, he headed for the stairs.

Clio and Joyce followed him along the road, neither questioning what he was doing.

The beach access boardwalk took them past the community pool and to the rough wooden stairs down to the sand. The tide had rolled in and left little space between the dunes and the water, but Tal walked to the water's edge and sat down. The surf crept up the shore to touch his shoes and then retreated as if enticing him into the water. Clio sat a few feet away, and Joyce settled on the other side of Tal.

With eyes closed, Tal listened to the roar of the surf, felt the jagged shells and gritty sand beneath him, smelled the briny air, tasted the grainy wind on his lips.

He waited.

Dad, he ran the prayer through his mind, we're here: your son, Dylan's daughter, and the woman you both loved. Tell us what happened.

He waited.

He felt the presence of Clio and Joyce without opening his eyes.

A tune haunted his mind. A slow melody in rhythm to the crash of the waves rose and fell, a cadence of harmony and balance, a low frequency hummed in his ear. The sounds blended and mixed to become a single chant with the texture of a lullaby – a requiem for the dead.

He knew then.

He heard a sob at his left. He opened his eyes to see Joyce crying. He looked to his right and Clio, sitting crossed legged in the sand, cried as well.

They must have heard it, too.

Chapter Thirty-four

Grandmaw Roane rocked in her chair on the front porch of her river rock house overlooking Lee Highway. Cars moved up and down the road going from Abingdon to Bristol. Tal and Brigid sat in the glider next to her, and Clio perched on the low stone wall that served as the banister for the porch.

Grandmaw had recovered from her stroke with the help of Brigid's alternative treatments, but also with Brigid's willingness to work within the established hospital and therapy regimens to bring her grandmother the best of all methods.

When Tal had introduced Clio to Grandmaw Roane and told her that Clio was Dylan and Joyce's daughter, tears flowed from Grandmaw and from Tal and Clio. Spending time together with her newly discovered family had taken priority for Cliodhna. She took a temporary leave of absence from her job and perhaps a permanent one from Devin. Transformation and resurrection replaced productivity and technology in her life. She and Joyce spent more time together and mended connections that had been broken over the years.

On the porch of the stone house, Tal whistled to himself, thoughts of his father drifting through his mind. The realization that Finn had not abandoned him and his mother gave him a feeling of soft, cool calm. "I understand Dad better," Taliesin said. "I know he had wolf in him, chasing women, seeing a conquest to be made, but now I feel I know why. He tried to recapture that love he'd had early in life. He wanted to feel, again, the way he did with Joyce."

Grandmaw nodded her gray head. "I don't think he knew that himself. Joe thought Finn was the spoiled baby of the family, but I kept telling him that his youngest son was different. He felt things deeper than the other boys, took things more personally." She looked to Cliodhna. "I'm comforted with the fact that our baby girl has come back to the family. Your father took things almost as hard as Finn. Dylan needed more attention than I gave him. He wanted what Finn had. Once he got it, he still resented Finn."

Clio sighed. "Mom and Dad thought I should be raised away from that history. But then I grew up with no background, no roots."

"Messy entanglements," Brigid said. "At least now you realize where you come from and why you might be the way you are. Not that you can put every trait or psychological issue on family, but the knowledge gives perspective."

"Brigid," Tal said and nudged his cousin with his elbow. "What do you hear from the Bait & Tackle man?"

She smiled. "I might be going to stay with Aunt Joyce for a few days soon. I hear September is a beautiful time of year on the Outer Banks."

"We had some good times there when the boys were growing up," Grandmaw said. She rocked the chair a few times. "All seven of those boys would pile into one bedroom. Joe and I would look in on them before we went to bed. They'd be tangled together like puppies as they slept. Lord knows, once they woke up, they'd bump heads and scrap over anything that came to mind."

Taliesin had explained to his grandmother about the Outer Banks neighbors seeing Dylan and Finn together leaving in the car and the later discovery of the Impala in the Currituck Sound. Knowing his grandmother's openness to her family's intuition, he confided to her the message he'd received at the beach. She had nodded and smiled. Peaceful relaxation calmed her facial features. She looked twenty years younger after their conversation.

For his own peace of mind, Tal felt he knew himself better. The actions of his father had an impact on him, if he'd ever acknowledged it or not. Finn had loved deeply. He had treasured his parents, Joyce, his brothers, in his way – his wife, Kay – and definitely Taliesin. The concept of abandonment no longer lingered in Tal's thoughts. His father had too many commitments, too many attachments. He couldn't manage them all. He was a pack wolf, overwhelmed by his emotions and pulled in many directions. The lure of sexual conquests stoked Finn's poor self-esteem. A quick fix didn't lead to long term satisfaction. Tal realized this as well.

Now, Grandmaw rocked in silence for a few moments. "You seem more settled," she said to Tal. "You know that he didn't discard you."

"That's hard to accept when my adult life used abandonment as its foundation," he said. Clio knitted her brows, but then nodded. Brigid reached for his hand and held it tight. He continued, "I had thought I needed to flee this area, start new somewhere that no one knew me or my history."

"But now?" Brigid asked.

"I don't think I could survive without being smothered by family and life-long friends. This old highway," he said and lifted his chin toward the road in front of his grandmother's house, "is like blood running through my veins."

"Uncle Finn and Uncle Dylan feel like they are here in you and Clio," Brigid added. She stood and walked over to her grandmother and kissed the top of Grandmaw Roane's head.

"This old heart can go in peace now," Grandmaw said. "My boys weren't alone when they passed, they had each other." She began to hum a slow melody that rose and fell filled with the balance of two souls, a requiem for her youngest sons.

Greg Lilly

Growing up in Bristol, Virginia and then living in Charlotte, North Carolina, Greg Lilly experienced the rich storytelling tradition of the South.

He first turned to writing short stories after plot lines and characters emerged from the technical manuals he wrote for a large family-owned corporation.

To escape the city and find a slower pace, he relocated to Sedona, Arizona for several years. During that time, he chronicled adventures of the high desert—present and past—in his novels.

After many years in the colonial atmosphere of Williamsburg, Virginia, Greg returned to his native Southwest Virginia. The history and mystery of the area, including the lore of the Lilly family, inspired him to write *STRAY*.

Other books by Greg Lilly

Derek Mason Mysteries
- *Fingering the Family Jewels* (book 1)
- *Scalping the Red Rocks* (book 2)

Novels
- *Devil's Bridge*
- *Under a Copper Moon*

Novellas
- *The Wolf Crystal* (Tales of the Abingdon Wolves – Book 1)
- *The Shadow Wolf* (Tales of the Abingdon Wolves – Book 2)

Non-Fiction
- *Sunsets & Semicolons* - *a Frank and Revealing Field Guide to the Writer's Life.*

Available in fine bookstores everywhere.
Also available eBook formats for Kindle and Nook.

www.GregLilly.com